JERK

A Taggart McGill Mystery

TAGGART MCGILL MYSTERIES:

Prick
Jerk

ALSO BY DL HAMMONS

Knight Rise
Fallen Knight

Trigger Warning:

Self-harm, suicide, or suicidal thoughts
Sexual abuse

While this book touches on the topic of suicide in a fictional setting, the problem is very real and should never be minimized. Suicide prevention is a critical need. Individuals in crisis who need help today can find it by calling or texting 988. The easy-to-remember 988 makes it easier for people in crisis to access the help they need and decrease the stigma surrounding suicide and mental health issues. Please spread the word.

National Suicide Prevention Hotline: 800-273-8255

My parents only wanted one thing for me.

Mom... Dad... wherever you are.

I'm HAPPY!

This one's for you.

Prologue
October 4th, 1997

At one in the morning Trina had only two fast-food choices, and neither seemed appealing. Cullman didn't have that many restaurants during the daylight hours, and the pickens dried up considerably when the moon was high in the night sky. The Pancake Stack on Washington Avenue was the first option, but Trina thought she remembered hearing that it had been shut down twice in the last year for health violations. The other possibility was the McDonald's up on the causeway, but they only offered drive-thru service at this time of night. Being on foot could make that awkward.

Trina stood swaying back and forth at the curb, staring straight-ahead through blurry vision. Her two alternatives bounced around inside her head. It was early fall and chilly, but the jean jacket and skin-tight faux leather pants she'd chosen that night provided enough insulation. At thirty-eight years old, she wasn't a spring chicken anymore, far from it, which was another factor in her decision. The Pancake Stack would provide her a place to rest her sore feet while she ate, but the chances of devouring something toxic were much greater. Still, laying back in a stall, relaxing, and not having to eat food out of a bag was appealing. Besides, she wagered, there was enough alcohol in her system to kill off anything that might cause food poisoning.

"The Pancake Stack it is," Trina said out loud to an empty street, turning left and stumbling off towards her chosen destination. McDonald's might be closer, but she'd be damned if she'd have some pimply-faced teenager working for minimum wage look down their nose at her while she waited for her McNuggets. She might be a middle-aged woman with a drinking problem and questionable decision-making skills, but dammit—she still had her pride.

Making her way down the block, she noticed how the streets at this time of night were dark, deserted, and gloomy. The neighborhood had fallen on bad times as of late, with several shops closing their doors, but her watering hole of choice—the White Horse—was still doing decent business. Somebody once told her that bars were recession-proof, that they saw an increase in business during hard times. Trina could attest to that fact.

As she continued walking, a sense of melancholy crept over her, thinking about how the night had gone. Once again it ended with her alone, and drunk, like so many of her nights in the past. It should have been different because of Jim, a lead mechanic at the shop where she handled customers at the cash register. Despite being at least ten years younger and married, he flirted with her at every opportunity. She didn't care. At this point she'd accept interest from anyone, married or not. It also didn't matter that he always looked like he had just crawled out from under a car, never seeming to be able to wash off the shop's dirt and grime. He had a million-dollar smile and made her laugh. Tonight's no show confused her.

Had he suddenly grown a conscience about betraying his wife? It didn't really matter because the end result was the same… Trina settling a hefty bar tab by herself.

She did her best to push those depressing thoughts away by consoling herself with the knowledge that if it was over between her and Jim, at least she wouldn't be a home-wrecker anymore. She purposefully ignored the fact that it wasn't by her choice. She was getting good at that.

The trek to the Pancake Stack helped Trina's head to clear, but it also raised her appetite to the voracious level. Walking through the door, she was hit by the unpleasant smell of stale bacon grease and maple syrup. Undeterred, she glanced right to the booths lining the windows. A group of four teenagers occupied the closest one on that side, so she looked left, where two similar cubicles remained unoccupied. She slipped into the farthest one, facing the front door, and the pack of noisy teenagers.

An elderly waiter meandered his way to her booth. Without waiting for him to ask what she wanted or looking at the menu, she ordered a full-stack of banana pancakes, a bowl of grits, and a couple of links of sausage with a glass of water to drink. Without saying a word, he turned and limped away.

Trina pulled her phone from her back pocket and checked for a text from Jim. Nothing. It wasn't like him, to not show up without some kind of word. Maybe he was working on his Mustang and lost track of time again, but he'd always called before when he realized he was going to be late. Could there be another reason for his no-show? They had only been seeing each other for a couple of months, and she thought things between them were going fine. The way he talked trash about his wife, Trina doubted he was having second thoughts about stepping out on her. What was more likely was he'd grown tired of getting drunk together and decided to move on to someone more exciting. Men like him always did. It saddened Trina to think that her dreams of finding a meaningful relationship had eroded to the point where she'd gladly accept a few months of distracted attention from a married man.

Trina glanced down the row of booths to the teenagers. All four of them wore hoodies with the hoods down, and none of them appeared older than sixteen or seventeen. What were they doing at Pancake Stack at 1:30 in the morning… on a school night? Wasn't there some sort of city-wide curfew at midnight or something? And where were their parents?

"Like I should talk," Trina whispered to herself, shaking her head. Her own son, Vern, had gone through a rough patch when he was sixteen, rebelling against anything she said. If something was white, to him it was black. If she wanted to turn left, he'd go right. It was a difficult time, made worse because she was a struggling single-parent and her son had no positive role-models around. But they got through it, together. Vern had graduated with the rest of his class and joined the Marine Corps straight out of school. He'd rapidly rose through the ranks and distinguished himself amongst his peers.

She had been so proud of him, still was, even after the IED he stepped on in Afghanistan stole him away from her.

The depressing feeling returned, and this time it clung to Trina like a frightened kitten. She wished she hadn't left the White Horse so early, relinquishing easy access to more alcohol. She desperately needed something to numb her mind again and block out the negative thoughts creeping in. Every time she thought about her son it eventually led to assessing her own life. That never turned out well. Since that day when she received notification of her son's death, she'd been in a slow downward spiral, one from which she felt helpless to stop. She knew something had to change, but she didn't have the self-motivation or grit to do it.

She wiped the tears from her eyes and started rummaging through her purse, looking for a stick of gum, a mint, or something to mask the foul taste that had seeped into her mouth. The front door swung open, causing Trina to look up from her purse. In stepped a young woman carrying a bulky object that Trina couldn't make out. The woman looked to be in her mid-twenties, blonde hair, well-dressed in a single-breasted cashmere coat with slim lapels that had to run about two-thousand dollars, if Trina remembered that Neiman Marcus Facebook Ad correctly. The woman certainly seemed out-of-place considering where they were, and the time, but the way she acted was anything but. She casually glanced to her right, just as Trina had when she arrived, then looked back to her left and spotted Trina. The new arrival flashed Trina a toothy smile, which Trina returned with something that felt more like a grimace, then the woman turned her body in Trina's direction. That's when Trina could finally see what the woman was carrying on her arm.

A baby carrier with a tiny infant snuggled inside.

The woman took a seat in the first booth, her back to the door and facing Trina, sliding the baby carrier between herself and the wall.

Okay, a bunch of sixteen-year-olds out on a school night was one thing, Trina thought to herself, but a baby, at this hour, here? She looked past the woman to the teenagers on the other side of the restaurant. They had taken notice of the unusual arrival as well.

The elderly waiter appeared from the back and made his way to the woman's booth, his head down the entire way. He registered no surprise at his new customers.

"I'll have a cup of coffee and some dry toast," the woman ordered with a deep southern accent. "Oh, and a glass of water as well."

Trina watched the woman unbuttoning her coat, knowing that it was impolite to stare, but she couldn't help herself. When the woman looked up and caught Trina's eyes, bringing out that toothy-smile again, Trina felt compelled to say something as penance for her bad manners.

"How old is your baby?"

"She's eleven months," the woman answered, holding the same smile. The woman was quite attractive, but the longer Trina looked at her, the less friendly her smile seemed.

Trina nodded her head. And that was it, the extent of her small talk ability. She had a follow-up question planned, but the woman ruined it by revealing the baby's gender in her first answer.

"Are you a mother?" The woman surprised Trina with a question of her own.

"I was," Trina answered, feeling her throat constrict. "I lost my son in Afghanistan."

"How terrible."

Trina didn't bother to respond. There was nothing to say.

"I wonder if I might ask a huge favor of you," the woman continued.

"Sure," Trina answered without thinking.

"I really have to use the restroom, and I know the one they have here is quite small. Would you mind keeping an eye on my little girl until I get back? She's just been fed and is sleeping, so she won't be any trouble."

"I don't mind," Trina answered positively, although all her thoughts were negative. *How could this woman leave her precious child with a total stranger? I'm just this random person in the booth next to hers. Doesn't she realize all the things that could go wrong?*

"Thank you so much. Let me move her over there next to you, if you don't mind."

Trina watched the woman reach over to pick up the carrier, but before she did, she removed something from her pocket and placed it inside the carrier. Then she cautiously lifted the carrier and stepped around to Trina's booth. Trina slid closer to the wall, so the woman had room to set the carrier and the baby on the bench seat, with the baby's head facing Trina.

"She's beautiful," Trina said.

"Thank you."

"What's her name?"

"Bella," the woman said flatly, smiling again. She proceeded to stroll down the corridor, past the teenage boys who eyed her with suspicion, then turned left and disappeared.

Trina looked down at the baby, wrapped tightly in a plain white blanket with a matching white cap. Her mind drifted to memories of her son at the same age. They were much simpler times back then. So full of promise. Vern slept through the night early on and took to the bottle like a fish to water. If she could only return to those times.

The arrival of the waiter with her food startled her. As he began placing plates on the table, Trina wondered how long the woman had been gone. How long had she been reminiscing? She was getting worried, which led her to question why the woman wore her expensive coat to the bathroom and didn't leave it in the booth. You trust someone with your baby, but not your jacket? Should she walk back there and check on her? Then what would she do with the baby?

Panic rose in Trina. When the waiter finished delivering the food, she started making her way out of the booth, pushing the carrier ahead of her on the bench seat. That's when she noticed a folded piece of paper nestled in with the baby. A sickening feeling came over her. She twisted around in her seat to look towards the rear of the restaurant where the restroom was. Trina gasped as her eyes landed on a back exit door opposite the bathrooms.

Although her mind was screaming not to, she grabbed up the folded paper. Unfurling it with shaky hands, she read the note.

Any lingering effects of the alcohol disappeared. She became stone-cold sober. Looking past the note to the baby, she spotted an envelope tucked inside the sleeping infant's blanket. She gently pulled out the envelope until she could read what was written across its face.

DO NOT OPEN UNTIL MARCH 3rd, 2021 (18TH BIRTHDAY).

Trina opened her mouth to cry out in alarm, then stopped. Looking down at the sleeping child an idea began to form. Not so much of an idea—more of a need. A yearning. A belief that quickly became a certainty.

She read the note once more.

This is Bella. Please see that she finds her way to the proper authorities and is given this envelope on her 18th birthday.

Trina then did something that would change lives forever.

She crumbled up the note.

One
Thursday, June 27th, 2024 – 4:51PM

"Cassie!"

I turned in the direction of the voice calling my name and spotted a girl waving at me. It was someone I had struck up a casual acquaintance with in my Social Economics course.

"Come sit with us," she beckoned.

"Thanks, but I'm meeting somebody," I replied, offering her a weak smile.

I set my tray down at an unoccupied table close to the university food court's exit, allowing my backpack to slide off my shoulders and drop to the floor. Then, I plopped down into a chair and let out a sigh I'd been holding in for weeks.

The thing nobody tells you about going to college is that it basically consists of three things—studying, partying, and sleep. Okay, maybe you are aware of that going in, but what they don't say is that it's more like a game of reverse whack-a-mole—pick one and all other choices disappears. I'm the sucker who picked studying.

Staring at the food on my tray, I wondered why I bothered. I was so exhausted from the late nights and lack of sleep that my appetite was non-existent, and I was just going through the motions. Of course I didn't have to worry the food would be wasted because Delta and her boyfriend, Jon, would be here soon. Jon had a habit of stealing food off everyone's tray, invited or not. He was in for a treat today.

Over my shoulder, in the bustling food court, I caught glimpses of smiles, lively conversations, and playful antics. How was it that my fellow students looked like they were on vacation instead of enduring a grueling mid-term test schedule? Surely I wasn't the only student who took their studies seriously. What was I doing wrong?

Another lesser-known tidbit about college I'd discovered was just how impersonal it could be. The educational part, that is. I remembered in high school being close to all of my teachers, especially during my senior year. Those relationships helped me overcome my struggles from time to time, grasping the material in their subjects—or life in general. God knows I experienced plenty of problematic patches during my final year at New Haven High. I started that year off at the top of the social ladder, even being elected homecoming queen, before deciding to break up with my longtime boyfriend and altering the course of my life. My so-called plan was to focus less on who—or—what was popular and concentrate on my future instead. Then came the loss of my younger sister in a terrible accident. My teachers did their part to help me through that devastation. On top of all that was the whole thing with Taggart's murderous mother and almost getting killed by her myself, and the media firestorm that followed it all. I leaned hard on my teachers through it all.

Then there was Taggart himself.

Like I said, difficult patches.

Taggart was an orphan who'd grown up in a less than ideal foster care system. He'd bounced from home to home for years and became a virtual outcast in our small town. I'm ashamed to admit that I shunned him right along with everyone else. In everyone's defense, he never tried to get to know any of us, walking away without saying a word when anyone approached him. People continuously blamed him for all the anonymous, mean-spirited pranks around the school, which he never denied. He earned a terrible reputation because he never refuted any of the rumors. What none of us knew was that he possessed a near-genius IQ but suffered from crippling social anxiety, and because of that, he kept to himself. He did have one friend, however, and ironically it was my younger sister Becca. Their friendship was a major source of friction between me and her because of Taggart's image. What I found out later was that befriending Becca was Taggart's way of getting closer to me, because it was me he was really attracted to. My sister didn't seem to mind. She fiercely looked out for Taggart, right up until the day she died. The death of my sister and everything that followed thrust Taggart and me together, and that's when I finally got a peek of the gentle soul hiding beneath the layers of abrasiveness. After he eventually revealed his true feelings to me, I slowly developed my own feelings for him. Even though things between us were awkward at times, or downright embarrassing, finding a way for us to be together was never hard.

Reminiscing about our hometown of New Haven made me remember something else that was different at Truman…the instructors. Despite being only five weeks into my first quarter, I already realized that the instructors were nothing like those in high school. In fact the whole collegiate experience, at least during this freshman year, seemed to embrace the assembly-line approach. I'd selected Truman for several reasons. To begin with, it resided to the west of Atlanta and was only a few hours' drive from New Haven, striking the perfect balance where my parents wouldn't constantly bother me to come home, yet the trip wouldn't be a hassle. Second, it had a respected Social Sciences department–my intended field of study. Lastly, the smaller school size would foster a more intimate class environment, or so I thought. What wasn't in the brochures was that the size of the freshman classes was still massive and one-on-one time with the instructors was a pipe dream. I'd tried multiple times to sign-up for office hours, but every time I went online, all of the spots had been booked. If I knew back then what I do now, I would have taken more advance placement classes in high school to allow me to skip some of the freshman level courses and avoid getting caught up in the crowd. It was deep in the middle of mid-terms, and I was missing the student-teacher relationships I took for granted less than six months ago. My dad wasn't joking when he said one thing I'd learn in college was how to become more self-sufficient.

"Whatcha thinking about?" Delta's voice breached my thoughts. She plunked her overflowing tray, sending a piece of broccoli tumbling onto the table, next to mine, then slid into the chair to my left. Her current boyfriend—number three this term I think—took the next seat over.

"Hey Cass," Jon greeted me as he reached over and grabbed a banana from Delta's tray and began peeling it.

Delta and I had been best friends since—well, forever—and during that time I've accepted that she has the worst taste in boys, which was befuddling to me. She was cute (when she didn't overdo the makeup), smart, funny, and above all else, loyal. She never let her eyes wander when she was in a relationship. The problem was, the boys she had her eyes on usually came with a long list of character flaws. Jon, for example, was an unapologetic moocher. His parents lived ten minutes from campus, so he wasn't staying in a dorm, and he wasn't on a dining plan. Yet the guy sat with Delta for every meal and usually polished off half of what she put on her tray, which was why she constantly overloaded it with food she'd never be able to eat by herself. At least he was a step up from her last boyfriend, who I swear must have undergone a funectomy—the procedure to remove all traces of fun from his personality.

"I'm so fried," I said in answer to Delta's question. "Two of my mid-terms are tomorrow, and I don't feel ready. When I'm not in class, I'm studying round the clock. I'm not a fan of Truman's quarter system instead of semesters either. Who wants to take tests right in the middle of summer? I feel like something out of The Walking Dead. You would know all that if you'd drop by our room now and then."

Delta and I were roommates, at least on paper, but she had been spending so much time socializing that it felt more like I had the room to myself.

"You do look like shit," Delta said, taking a bite off a french fry she picked from her tray.

"Thanks," I replied tiredly. One of my favorite, and least favorite, of Delta's traits was her 'call it like I see it' attitude. While it had gotten us out of our share of jams over the years, it could also sting.

"I'm finished with all my mid-terms."

"I would be too if I was taking the minimum number of hours allowed, with one of them being online. And you wouldn't even be taking the easy classes you are if you'd bothered to take the proper pre-enrollment tests," I replied, half laughing.

Delta shrugged and popped a fry into her mouth. The girl was intelligent, but in no hurry to get a degree, or concerned with how much money her parents would fork out for her to do so, evidenced by the fact I rarely saw her with her head in a textbook or even carrying one. I discovered early on that our college experiences were going to be distinctly different.

"What about you, Jon?" I asked, attempting to be friendly.

Delta's boyfriend was about to take a bite out of her tuna-sandwich, freezing when he heard his name. He had a sizeable gap between his two front teeth, made even more noticeable by the pitiful excuse for a mustache he was trying to cultivate on his upper lip.

"Huh?"

"How are your mid-terms going?"

Jon indifferently shrugged and bit into the sandwich.

I leveled my best **what the hell are you doing with this guy** expression at Delta, which only yielded me an embarrassed smile in return. A smile I knew meant, "It's college. I'm supposed to make bad choices."

"Where's Taggart?" Delta asked, no doubt eager to change the subject.

I thought I couldn't feel any worse, but the mention of Taggart's name brought an ache to my heart.

"I'm not sure."

"What?" Delta's eyebrows raised in astonishment. "Before school began, you two were joined at the hip. Now you don't even know where he's at?"

Having Delta point out the obvious was like soaking your nails in polish remover with ten million paper cuts. I did my best to not let my hurt show. It was true, Taggart and I had spent almost every waking hour together before coming to Truman. Our relationship was still relatively new, a mere six months old, but it was so unlike what I had experienced with my previous boyfriend.

Taggart could have gone to any college he wanted after earning a perfect score on the ACT exam, but early in our relationship Taggart told me he had no interest in attending college. It didn't appeal to him. Because of that, I had been dreading our eventual separation. When the time came for me to leave, Taggart surprised me by announcing he indeed would attend college, at Truman no less. He had used his perfect ACT score to not only secure a full-ride scholarship at Truman, but also finagle room and board at the college's associated apartments right off-campus. Freshman were normally required to live on-campus their first year, but that would never work for Taggart so he made the special housing arrangements conditional upon his acceptance.

I know it was immature of me to assume that after we arrived at Truman things between us would continue exactly like they had been back home. Maybe assume was the wrong word. Hoped would be more accurate.

"Why do you look like someone just stole your puppy?" Delta asked, leaning forward and giving me her full attention. "Is there something wrong between you and Taggart?"

I shook my head. "No, not really. It's just so different here. He's different."

"What do you mean?"

"I don't know. Back home, it was only the two of us. I mean, he was fine hanging out with our little group—you, Chewy, and Tunes—but he wasn't interested in anyone else. I guess I got used to having him all to myself, and I kinda enjoyed having him depend on me."

"But you knew that wouldn't last forever," Delta said. "You were slowly teaching him how to be more social."

"I know. But here at Truman, he has—I don't know—what's the word? Blossomed, I guess. He's been given the star treatment here and spends a lot of time with professors and some of the other faculty, which is great. But I miss having his sole focus be on me. I know that's selfish, but I can't help it. And if I'm really truthful, I'm worried that he'll drift away altogether."

Delta didn't reply right away, and when I looked up, I could tell from her expression she was trying to think of the right thing to say.

"Listen, school is an adjustment for everyone, Taggart more than anyone. Give him time. I've seen the way he looks at you. That boy isn't going anywhere. Besides, at least he isn't obsessing over locating his sister now."

Delta made a good point. If I wasn't run down to the point of exhaustion, I would have realized that myself. Still, I'd needed any piece of encouragement I could get, especially from Delta.

"You're probably right."

"Damn right, I am. Listen, he killed his mother for you. What more proof do you need?"

"What?" Jon blurted out, a piece of a chip falling out of his mouth. "Who killed whose mother?"

"Cassie's boyfriend, Taggart," Delta replied nonchalantly while grabbing one of the remaining french fries. "I know it's kinda been on the back-burner, but what's the latest on the search for his sister, anyway?"

It was one thing to find out that the woman who brought Taggart to New Haven, who he believed was his mother, was actually his aunt. Then add to that the fact his birth mother had been covertly living in New Haven, observing her son from afar, killing anyone she felt had wronged him, was quite a revelation. On top of all of that, he discovered he had a sister he never knew about.

"Still a dead-end. We know she's three years older than Taggart. That's about it," I said.

"That's not much. It's good that he's distracted here. It was tearing Taggart up knowing she's out there and not being able to find her."

"I guess. Taggart still won't talk about it."

"Talk about what?" came Taggart's voice from behind me.

I half-turned in my seat and watched Taggart, dressed in his trademark disheveled cargo pants and solid black hoodie, step up between Delta and me. It still amazed me how much he resembled a scruffy Ian Somerhalder of The Vampire Diaries, giving off that rough around the edges vibe. Although I had made some progress in improving his appearance, his shoulder-length brown hair was still largely a stranger to a brush. A white cord attached to earbuds in his ears dangled down the front of his chest and disappeared into the front pouch.

"Delta wanted to know if we'd heard anything more about your sister," I replied, fully aware that Taggart distinctly hated it when people talked about him when he wasn't present.

My remark drew only a grunt from Taggart.

"Dude, you killed your mom?" Jon asked, momentarily distracted from eating.

Taggart ignored the question and looked at me. "Did you want to follow me to my apartment? I can give you the book on social economy?"

"Hey man, I was talking to you," Jon stated forcefully.

"Jon, don't," Delta said.

For the first time, Taggart looked in Jon's direction.

This is where I would typically step in and steer Taggart away from one of several predictable outcomes when he interacted with people he deemed—in his words—superfluous. Some of the typical reactions were hurt feelings, shock, and outrage. Today, however, I was too tired and too upset to care.

"I believe what you meant to say—" Taggart said to Jon in a tone our instructors typically used, "—was 'I was talking **AT** you'. 'Talking **TO** you' would assume we were having a conversation, which wasn't the case."

Jon's face went blank for a few seconds before understanding hit him, and he rose from his chair. "What the hell?"

If Taggart felt threatened, he didn't show it. "Interesting, that same question popped into my head, except my question was directed at Delta regarding her relationship with you."

Delta, now standing, put her hand on Jon's chest, and then looked at Taggart. "Taggart, play nice. He's my boyfriend."

"This week," Taggart pointed out.

"That's our cue to go," I said as I grabbed my backpack and stood up. Things were getting out of hand and, try as I might, I couldn't allow myself not to be bothered by it. I focused my attention first on Jon. "You were out of bounds," then to Delta I said, "I'll see you back at the room."

"You haven't touched your food," Delta pointed out.

I slid the tray in Jon's direction. "Go nuts, Jon."

I shoved Taggart towards the exit and followed him out into the hallway.

"That was rude," I said as I positioned my pack on my back, then started walking.

Taggart appeared confused. "Was I inaccurate?"

"Not the point. Let's just go."

The two of us walked in silence down a short set of stairs that led us out the main doors of the student center. A wave of mid-summer heat hit me, forcing me to take a deep breath. It wasn't until we had crossed the street and were making our way across the commons area that Taggart finally spoke.

"He eats all her food."

"Yeah, I know, but she likes him."

"I repeat my earlier statement about him being this week's dalliance. Why does Delta go through so many male companions? I liked it better when she was with Tunes."

Taggart bringing up one of our friends from New Haven made me smile. Tunes had a thing for Delta for a brief time, but it ended when Delta moved on campus. Long distance wasn't going to work when neither had a car.

"Not sure I have the answer to that. Tunes is a unique person, so I think, maybe, that she's looking for someone as special as him, and she's quicker at cutting boys loose if they don't make the grade when compared to him. She's not willing to stick it out longer in mediocre relationships."

"I guess I can respect efficiency."

We walked a bit more in silence, reaching the other side of the commons and passing between the library and Stepford Hall.

"You must have been busy today. I haven't seen you for a while," I said.

"I devoted a good portion of my time talking with Professor Ring regarding the recently published paper about time convergence. His theories differ dramatically from the findings in the paper."

"Oh," was all I could think to say.

"But I also knew you would be studying, and I didn't want to distract you."

That made me smile. I took hold of his hand and kissed the back of it.

"This walk is nice, and a most needed distraction," I commented.

"I'm glad."

As we crossed Union Street, the main thoroughfare that separated the west side of Truman College from off-campus, I could see part of Taggart's apartments over the top of the businesses that ran up and down Union. Originally built in the 1920s, the flats had fallen into poor shape, to the point that the city debated tearing them down. However, because of their proximity to campus, Truman College purchased the land and all the buildings, spent millions of dollars renovating them, and now rents the units to faculty and select students. The department Taggart was currently majoring in claimed one of the buildings for its graduate students, and the administrator dangled being able to live there as a freshman as a carrot to get Taggart to come to Truman as opposed to an ivy league school.

Taggart's one-bedroom split-level loft was a corner unit. I had been there a couple of times before but didn't really like hanging there. I didn't have much in common with anyone else living in the building and didn't know what to say to anyone we came across. While it often felt like Taggart was speaking another language, being around a bunch of Taggarts was too much. Besides that… well… there just wasn't much there. Taggart wasn't big into personal possessions—or comfort. The only thing he had on the first floor was a simple table for his laptop and two old chairs. In fact, before I'd said something about needing a place to sit, he'd only had a single chair. Up the spiral staircase to the bedroom, which looked out over part of the living room, was a mattress.

When we walked up to the front door, Taggart pulled a single key from his front pocket and slid it into the door handle.

"Why don't you use the deadbolt?"

"You've seen my apartment. That level of security is unwarranted, wouldn't you agree?"

"You have a point."

When the door swung open, the two of us stepped into the middle of his baren apartment. Taggart immediately turned to the left, heading towards a small kitchen with an adjacent bathroom.

"I'm going to make a cup of tea; would you care for some?"

"Sure," I replied, stepping straight ahead towards Taggart's table and chairs to look for the book he had promised me.

The afternoon was slipping away, and from my previous visits I remembered that sunlight would stream through the windows next to the spiral staircase at this time of day, making the room glow. The windows were at the opposite end of the room from the kitchen. It was a cloudless day but for some reason the lighting today seemed muted. Surely Taggart wouldn't have put up curtains to spoil one of the apartment's best features. I turned to see what was blocking the light, then froze.

The high-pitched scream that came out of me was involuntary. "Taggart!"

My mind managed to register several impressions before shutting down.

A thick rope tied to the second-floor railing.

The head on the other end of the rope, and the odd angle of the person's neck.

The way the body twisted back and forth sleepily.

The arms dangling loosely at his sides.

One shoe missing, revealing a solid black sock.

All these pieces made up a terrible image—one that I was having trouble processing.

The image of a man hanging from a rope in the middle of Taggart's living room.

Two
Thursday, July 11ᵗʰ 6:05 PM

Standing outside of Taggart's apartment, taking in the frenetic activity going on around us, I felt numb, chilled, probably from the adrenaline hangover. Everything seemed so surreal. This was the second time since becoming involved with Taggart that I'd found myself surrounded by flashing blue lights and in close proximity to yellow crime scene tape. It wasn't a comfortable feeling. Certainly not one you could ever get used to. At least I couldn't. Anxiety riddled my body. Taggart, on the other hand, appeared bored. Like he could nod off standing there next to me.

"You recognized who that was, right?" I asked, even though I knew his answer.

"I did."

I waited for Taggart to say something else, and when he didn't, I took hold of his shoulders and turned him to face me directly.

"I know that on your best days you're not much of a conversationalist, and normally I'm okay with that, but right now I need you to talk to me so I can get the picture of the dangling body out of my head."

Taggart frowned before responding. I knew he was bewildered about why the dangling body would bother me. "Okay. What should we talk about?"

"Why was Jim hanging from a noose in your apartment?"

"Doesn't discussing the person whose image you're attempting to erase from your mind negate the conversational exercise?"

"No, because when I'm doing that I'm thinking about the alive Jim, not the dead one."

Taggart's expression changed from concern to confusion.

"Just answer the question, please."

Before he could answer, an ambulance rounded the corner and came to a stop alongside the police vehicles. A fair size crowd of apartment residents and other curious onlookers had gathered and were watching as the two EMT technicians pulled a stretcher from the back. With one at the head and the other at the foot, the men carried the stretcher and made their way to the open doorway into Taggart's loft. Just before they entered, a man dressed in a white button-down dress shirt with a black tie stepped out.

The man said a few words to one of the techs, then stepped aside to allow them to pass. He was in his mid-thirties, slimly built, sporting a goatee, and a close-cropped haircut. To me the goatee contrasted with the military-style haircut, giving him a vibe that was too stylish for a detective. I assumed by the way he carried himself that he was one of the people in charge. His eyes zeroed in on Taggart and me and headed in our direction.

"I'm Detective Moss," the man stated when he reached us. "This your apartment?"

"I am the sole occupant," Taggart stated.

The detective pulled a notepad from his pockets and removed a pen from his shirt. "Your name is?"

"Taggart McGill."

The detective looked in my direction. "And you are?"

I opened my mouth to answer, but Taggart cut me off. "An acquaintance."

Hearing myself described that way sent a wave of irritable heat through my body. It took everything I had not to look at Taggart.

Detective Moss glanced at Taggart, then returned his gaze to me. "Your name?"

"Cassie Underwood."

Addressing Taggart again, the detective said, "I need you to tell me everything you did and whatever you touched inside when you found the body."

"Understood. We entered the apartment at 4:13 PM and—"

"How do you know it was exactly 4:13?"

Taggart appeared annoyed with the interruption. "I noticed the time on the microwave clock when we stepped inside. May I continue?"

"Was the door locked?"

"It was, but the bolt lock was not engaged."

"Was that a surprise?"

"No. I don't usually make use of it."

"Okay, continue."

"Once inside, I proceeded to make some tea. I touched the handle of the teapot, the cabinet door where I keep the tea, and the knob to turn on the water. At that point, Cassie alerted me to the body's presence. I then touched the wrist of the corpse to check for a pulse; there was none, then the two of us immediately exited the apartment, and Cassie called 911."

"Why didn't you call?"

"I don't own a cellular device."

The detective looked up from his notepad, his eyebrows knitted together. "You don't own a cell phone?"

"That is correct."

"Do you have a landline?"

"I do, but that would have meant touching something else inside the apartment, so we used Cassie's phone once we were outside. I should also point out that the body was still swaying slightly when we arrived, so he couldn't have been dead long."

Detective Moss pursed his lips. "Where were you before coming back to your apartment?"

"I met Cassie in the Truman food court, and before that, I was having a discussion with one of the professors."

"Which professor was that?"

"Professor Ring."

"What class was he teaching?"

"He wasn't teaching at the time. Our conversation wasn't school related."

The detective turned his attention back to me. "And how about you?"

"Me? I actually didn't touch anything inside. I followed Taggart into the apartment, walked to his table, and then immediately spotted the body. We left right after Taggart checked to see if he was still alive."

"What was your reason for being there?"

"Taggart was loaning me a book to help me with my studies. I was here to pick it up."

"What book would that be?"

"Social Economics."

"Do either of you know the victim?"

"We both do," I spoke up before Taggart could cut me off. "His name is Jim Book. He's one of the RA's in my dorm. He also heads an orientation group for freshmen that I'm part of. I believe he's a 3rd year student."

"And you, Mr. McGill? How do you know him?"

"Only in an ancillary fashion. I attend the same support group that Cassie mentioned."

"The two of you are in the same support group?"

"Well, technically, I'm the only one assigned to the group," I answered. "Taggart comes with me sometimes."

Again the detective stopped writing in his notebook and looked up.

"And the two of you are just acquaintances?"

I refused to answer the question, and Taggart allowed it to go unanswered as well.

"Okay, so let me ask the one-hundred-thousand-dollar question. Why would Jim Book commit suicide in your apartment, Mr. McGill?"

"I have serious doubts that this was a suicide," Taggart said evenly, which made my head snap in his direction and my mouth drop open.

The police detective's posture stiffened.

"And what makes you think this wasn't a suicide?"

"We spoke to Jim Monday. He wasn't suicidal."

"He did seem perfectly normal to me as well," I added.

The detective dropped his head. "You know how many times people have said that exact thing after finding out someone close to them took their own lives?"

"Jim Book and I were not close. Secondly, this is different," Taggart said.

"Yeah, how so?"

"I listened."

I knew what was coming and thought about putting a stop to it before Taggart lost all credibility, but deep down, I knew he believed what he was about to say.

"You listened?" The detective cocked his head to the side as if perplexed by Taggarts response.

"Yes."

"And what makes you such a special listener?"

"I'm not sure you would understand."

"Try me, sport."

"Most of the world's population, including you, over-communicate. You use anywhere between 50-65% more vocabulary than is essential to deliver your core message. I have trained myself to filter out 50-65% of what people say and focus on the acoustics – vocal tones, intonation, fundamental frequency, speed of delivery. How a person communicates rather than what they communicate. A person who is in so much agony that they feel they're only option is to take their own life, that pain is ever-present. It's deep down, and you can hear it if you listen carefully. I would have heard that in his voice. He was guarded, and I did detect tension, but nothing rising to the self-harm level."

"You're right. I guess I don't get it."

"You just illustrated my point. You used eight words to communicate one thought. You should have said – I'm confused."

"Unbelievable."

"That's better," Taggart replied with a straight face.

The detective looked at me. "Is he pulling my leg or just being a jerk?"

"Neither, I'm afraid."

The detective yanked his thumb over his shoulder back towards Taggart's apartment.

"Everything I saw in there points to a by-the-numbers suicide, with the only exception being that Mr. Book chose to end his life in the apartment of somebody, according to you, he barely knew. Now you're trying to convince me this is something other than suicide. I don't know what game you're playing, Mr. McGill, but I don't like having my time wasted."

"I don't play games… unless you consider chess a game. I do enjoy a good match, but I don't classify chess as a game."

"I don't play games either. Now, is there anything else about our victim that ties him to either of you?"

"Actually, there is something else. All three of us went to the same high school. New Haven High. We didn't hang out or anything, he was a couple of years ahead of the two of us," I said.

Detective Moss jotted down this last piece of information, slid the notepad back into his pocket, then leveled an intense stare at Taggart.

"There's more to this story; I can smell it. There's a reason this boy hung himself in your apartment, Mr. McGill, and I'm going to find out what it is."

"I've provided you with my opinion. What you choose to do with it is up to you."

The detective looked skyward, and following his gaze I noticed dark clouds had begun moving in and the air felt heavy. "The apartment won't be released to you for another hour, maybe more. You might want to find someplace else to wait in case it rains."

The detective headed off towards a black sedan and climbed inside, then drove away.

The two of us stood there watching the policeman depart, and when his car was out of sight, I jumped in front of Taggart.

"You really believe someone murdered Jim?"

"There are only three possibilities. Suicide, which I've already made a case against. However, I will concede there could have been an event that took place in the timeline between Monday and now to alter Jim's paradigm, thus causing him to become suicidal. The second possibility is an accident, which isn't plausible here. Lastly, foul play."

"But why here? If it was murder and somebody was trying to frame you by leaving the body in your loft, why make it look like a suicide? It doesn't make sense."

"I agree."

"So, what are we going to do?"

"Nothing. We'll let the police do their job, and they'll sort it out."

That shocked me, and I'm sure the look on my face communicated that much to Taggart. "What? Aren't you curious?"

"I'll admit to a certain degree of fascination about why anyone would choose to implicate me in Tim's death, but beyond that it holds no interest for me."

If he wanted to, Taggart could make a fortune playing cards because he has the best poker face I'd ever seen. Most of the time it was impossible to tell how he was feeling, so I had no idea if he was being truthful with me or not.

"That's not the Taggart I know," I responded. "That's also not the Taggart who rooted out what his mother was up to in New Haven."

Taggart looked uncomfortable. "That was infinitely more personal. The matters of Jim Book do not compare. Now, we should go."

"Where are you going to stay? Do you think the school could move you to another apartment?"

"There is no need. I'll remain where I am."

I pointed towards his apartment. "But a dead body was found there."

Taggart looked confused. "Your point?"

Shivers ran up and down my spine when I thought about trying to sleep, knowing what had taken place there. "Never mind. Do you want to come back to my dorm until they allow you back in?"

"That would be nice."

We were halfway to my dorm before either of us spoke again. Finally, I couldn't hold it in any longer, and I had to let my feelings be known, or else I was going to explode.

"Is that really how you see me—as an acquaintance?"

"No."

"Then, how do you see me?"

We were several yards down the sidewalk before he answered.

"You are the most important person in my life. Without you, there is no me."

My vision blurred as tears flooded my eyes, but I kept my head facing forward so he couldn't see my reaction.

"Then why did you tell that detective we were only acquaintances?"

"It has been my observation that when a male introduces a female acquaintance to another male as his girlfriend, the female is then treated as subsidiary to the male, and her thoughts and opinions are given less weight. An unfair practice for sure, but unfortunately a real possibility. An acquaintance, on the other hand, is much less likely to suffer such a slight. My categorization of our relationship was to ensure that the detective wasn't prejudiced in his interview."

"Oh. Thank you, I guess."

"You're welcome."

We reached the street leading up to my dorm, and I stopped.

"You know, Taggart; the truth is that detective probably thinks less of you, than he does me."

The corner of Taggart's lip pulled up into a sly smile.

"I guess that makes me the boyfriend."

Three
Thursday, July 11th 7:20 PM

As the two of us strolled back to my dorm, I began to think about how I was going to break the news of Jim's death to Delta and the others. While Delta and I had been researching where to apply to college, I'd stumbled across Truman almost by accident. I'd made a list of all the factors I'd wanted to consider, thirty-three of them. A good many of the schools I'd looked at had high marks in most of the categories—a favorable graduation rate, a positive freshman retention rate, a faculty-to-student ratio that favored the student, the curriculum I was seeking, and so on and so forth. But what had sold me on Truman happened after I'd done an image search of the schools.

Truman College, founded by Mary Truman in 1912 as a Girls Economical School, was nestled in the rolling hills to the west of Atlanta, spanning more than 21,000 acres of woodlands, meadows, and streams. Going through the school's photographs, I was inspired by the tremendous physical beauty, and could imagine myself taking long walks and studying outside. The thirty-five primary buildings on campus, including fourteen classroom facilities and ten residence halls, were all clustered at the southern tip of the acreage and boasted historic architectural styles that seem to expand in every direction. I was breathless as I took in the intricate details of the buildings, topped off by an impressive chapel that I read was very popular for weddings. Everything looked like it came straight out of the pages of a fairy tale.

The small community of Wolfs Head surrounding Truman offered the conveniences that the school didn't - like decent pizza. It sure helped provide the close-knit feeling I had grown accustomed to in New Haven.

I decided right then Truman was the place I wanted to spend my next four years.

Making that decision was a lot easier and harder at the same time because I didn't have to worry about how Delta felt. We both knew early on that college was in our futures and assumed we would attend the same one, even sending in early applications to Georgia Tech together. But as application deadlines grew closer, it became apparent that what Delta wanted out of school was dramatically different than what I did. Even though she applied to Truman at the same time I did, it was only as a backup. She had her heart set on big-name schools like Georgia Tech, University of Georgia, Florida, Florida State—and I was starting to lean towards the exact opposite. It broke both of our hearts when we finally decided to go our separate ways, though, in the end, that's not what happened. Delta changed her mind at the last minute and enrolled at Truman with me. She chose friendship over partying, telling me that she would make her own party. So far, she's lived up to that promise.

As Taggart and I got closer to Barksdale Hall, I thought back to how Delta and I instantly knew this was the dorm for us. It was the oldest of all the residence halls, but it was in the center of the campus and no more than a fifteen-minute walk to anywhere we needed to go. It housed both male and females with a capacity of just over 120 students, but my understanding was the actual number of students living there was slightly less than that. Though the building was kept immaculately clean, the wear and tear from the flow of countless students throughout the years was inescapable, like bed linen that had seen one too many wash cycles. The floor layouts were mostly four-person suites, which is what Delta and I were in, but there were some two-person and single-occupant rooms as well.

Our suite was made up of two bedrooms, each bedroom containing two single beds and one desk. For our bedroom Delta initially wanted loads of florals, which of course turned my stomach. We eventually agreed on a color scheme so our bedding wasn't identical, but coordinated. It was a win/win solution. Delta and I had grown up together, spending hours and hours at each other's houses. Our sleepovers were frequent. But strangely there were still a few things we clashed over. Delta has a habit of leaving the lids off her bath products, and I had to get her to understand that with us sharing a bathroom she was going to do a better job of keeping things organized. I was used to sharing space with my sister before she died, but Delta was an only child. It showed at times. She adjusted without too much fuss, but there were relapses from time to time.

The bedrooms in the suite were linked by a common area made up of a half-kitchen, a couch, and two desks. Delta and I were both nervous to meet our suitemates. We hoped one of them could cook because both of us could burn water. The university's food plan provided three meals during the week, but we were on our own for the weekends and being able to prepare something simple would help cut down on expenses. In the end, we lucked out all around. Eve and JJ were perfect.

"That can't be right," Eve said when I finished explaining what we discovered in Taggarts apartment. "Jim wasn't suicidal."

Eve was dressed in her usual nightly outfit of sweatpants and a bright pink Truman School of Nursing t-shirt. She had taken a seat on my bed, directly across from where I was leaning against the desk.

"Everyone knows you can't really tell what's inside someone's head, Eve," Delta commented. She was lying on her side, looking down on me from the top bunk above Eve.

"But he was an RA, and he was in charge of our orientation group," JJ added from her spot next to Eve. JJ was short for Jennifer Jenkins, and she was from right here in Atlanta. "Surely, the school wouldn't put somebody in charge who was that mental."

Eve, JJ, and I were all part of the same freshman orientation group. Delta was in a different group because she'd enrolled so late. So last-minute that we had to fight tooth and nail to get her assigned to the same dorm room as me. All freshmen at Truman were assigned to an eight-member orientation group that met every week to assess our social life satisfaction, social anxiety, self-esteem, grades, stress levels, etc. Basically, a glorified discussion group that's goal was to help new students adjust and combat the high dropout level from first-year students to sophomore year. Our group met on Mondays at a local coffee house in Wolfs Head.

When Taggart and I arrived at Barksdale after walking back from his apartment, we were bombarded with questions from our classmates. Truman's pursuit of personifying a small town atmosphere had gotten at least one thing right -

news, especially the bad kind, traveled fast. When it became clear that my room was going to become ground zero for anyone after juicy gossip, Taggart bailed. He couldn't handle the crowd, and he was now downstairs hiding out in one of the study rooms, waiting to return to his apartment.

After a while, most of the curiosity seekers had returned to their rooms. That left only me, Delta, Eve, JJ, Tony, and Brent.

"I agree, Jim didn't come off as mental, but I did detect some sketch there," Brent said.

Brent reminded me a lot of my old boyfriend, Jason, from back in New Haven; athletic, good looking, and acutely aware he was both. I couldn't help but notice that he spent a lot of time looking in my direction when we were at group. He might have been interested in me, but I was pretty sure it was JJ who was interested in him.

"What do you mean by sketch?" Eve asked.

"Sketchiness. Not one-hundred percent on the up and up, if you know what I mean," Brent replied, smiling afterward.

My skin prickled. "What makes you say that, Brent?"

"Nothing in particular. Just a feeling I got from him."

My experiences with Taggart's own ragged reputation came to mind. "I think maybe you should keep comments like that to yourself before you trash a dead man's reputation based on a feeling."

I could tell what I said made an impact. Brent's face went slack.

"I'm sorry. You're right, that was stupid. Forget I said anything."

We sat in uncomfortable silence for a moment until Tony cleared his throat.

"You said Taggart didn't know Jim," Tony said. Tony heralded from somewhere on the west coast, with the "to die for", well-tanned complexion to go with it. I figured he was either rich, connected, or both because he had one of the few single occupancy rooms at Barksdale.

"The only time they've ever had contact was at our group, and all of you know how limited that was," I answered.

"Then it makes no sense that he would kill himself in Taggart's apartment. How would he even know where Taggart lived?" Tony asked.

I hadn't bothered relaying Taggart's theory about Jim's death not being a suicide to anyone. I couldn't see any benefit, and it would just end up casting my boyfriend in a bad light. And, as I'd learned in high school, Taggart wouldn't do a thing to dispel any rumors that might start flying around.

"Wait a minute. You said Jim is from New Haven and he went to your same high school. He was only two years ahead of you, so they might have known each other there," JJ pointed out.

I smiled at JJ and chuckled internally. "You don't understand what Taggart was like back then. The only time he talked was when the teachers made him. Trust me, Jim and Taggart didn't know each other in any meaningful way back then."

"About Taggart, Cassie," Eve said, lowering her voice. "I've been meaning to tell you that I heard some girls down the hall talking about him."

"What were they saying?" I asked, but I was pretty sure I already knew the answer.

"They were saying that he was responsible for those deaths in New Haven," Eve said, then quickly added, "I know it isn't true and I set them straight, I just thought you should know it's out there."

"Goddamn gossip mongers," Delta snapped. "Nobody bothers to fact check anymore."

"I appreciate you telling me about it, Eve. But if you don't mind, let's drop it. Taggart dislikes it when people he trusts talk about him when he's not around."

"Nobody is keeping him away," JJ said. "I mean, he's downstairs right now, just hanging out, when he could be here with us."

I could understand why JJ said what she did. Much like Delta, JJ was a social butterfly that thrived around people. But unlike my best friend, JJ was unable to comprehend what social anxiety really was and how debilitating its effects could be.

"JJ, I think you need to freshen your makeup, your ignorance is showing," Delta commented, which elicited chuckles from everyone but JJ.

"Bite me," JJ responded, leaning forward to look up at my roommate.

"JJ, are you making a pass at me?" Delta answered back.

With that, JJ shot off the bed and stormed out of the room. Seconds later, the door to the suite's other bedroom slammed shut.

"Thanks for that, Delta," Eve said with a fake smile. "She'll be a barrel of laughs for the rest of the night now."

"She asked for it," Delta replied, rolling onto her back.

Although I appreciated the way Delta stuck up for Taggart, and by association, me, I also found it interesting how the two party divas in our group, Delta and JJ, butted heads so often. It seemed contrary to how things should go.

"As much as I'd love to stick around and talk shit—" Brent said, pushing himself off the wall and heading toward the door, "—I have a test at seven o'clock in the AM."

Tony followed him. "I need to get back to it as well."

When the boys were gone, Eve stood up, preparing to leave. "Are you going to be okay? That couldn't have been easy finding Jim like that."

The image of Jim hanging there, his eyes open but unfocused, flashed across my mind.

"I'm fine," I lied. "Once I dive back into studying, I'll be able to push it out of my thoughts."

"Okay, but if you need to take a break or blow off some steam, let me know. I'm here for you."

"Thanks."

After the door closed behind Eve, I turned in my chair and stared at the course books on the desk. I needed to get back to reading chapters, but I just couldn't bring myself to get started. I rose to my feet and headed for the door.

"Where are you going?" Delta asked.

"Downstairs to see if Taggart's still there."

I took the stairs down the four flights, and when I exited the stairwell on the main floor I glanced right. I didn't spot Taggart among the numerous people milling around, but when I looked left, I saw him sitting by himself in the corner. His eyes were closed, no doubt listening to the techno-pop he was so fond of pumping through his earbuds. I walked over and stood in front of him, marveling at the fact he could be so relaxed after what we had found in his apartment. I guess that's one of the things that I found fascinating about him, his ability to remain level-headed and centered—no matter how crazy things got. Things have been pretty crazy over the last six months. Considering what he had been through during his childhood, his personality could have easily gone in a completely different direction. On the flip side, I sometimes missed the uninhibited outburst of joy that other guys our age displayed. It's not that Taggart didn't know how to have fun, because he did in a distinctly Taggart sort of way, but his highs were as limited as his lows.

I extended my foot and tapped Taggart's sneaker. His eyelids popped open and he immediately went through the motions of pausing his music.

"Everyone is gone upstairs. It's just Delta and me if you want to come back up."

Taggart glanced at the wall clock.

"I'll return to my apartment. The police should have completed their examination by now."

"Okay."

Taggart rose from the chair and gave me a tight hug, as was our habit whenever we parted. But instead of letting him go, I held onto his hands.

"Is something wrong?" Concern etched on his brow.

I debated voicing what had been bothering me ever since returning from his apartment, but I was afraid of how it would make me appear. Frightened.

"It's nothing. I'm just tired. You should head back before it starts raining."

This time it was Taggart who wasn't letting go.

"Something is bothering you."

I allowed myself an awkward smile. "Let me guess, you can hear it in my voice?"

He shook his head. "I can see it in your eyes."

I tried to widen my smile, but it wasn't one of my best efforts. "I don't want to sound paranoid or anything. Who knows, maybe I am. But you don't think Jim being found dead in your apartment has anything to do with your mother, do you?"

I could tell by his reaction that what I said took him by surprise, which made me feel like an idiot.

"Why would you think that? My mother is dead, and she had no accomplices."

Now I wished I had kept my mouth shut. How I felt made no sense, but still, I couldn't shake it.

"I know, I know. It sounds crazy. But what are the odds that after going through what we did this past winter that a dead body would mysteriously appear in your apartment? You're the genius, so explain that to me."

Taggart let go of my hands and slid them into his hoodie pouch. "I must admit the circumstances are comparable, but I fail to see a connection to my mother's activities."

"I agree, but it still has me spooked."

"You are allowing unsubstantiated concerns to affect rational thought."

I couldn't help but smile. "Ya think? Just tell me that everything will be okay, and I'll be fine."

Taggart looked confused when he said, "Everything will be okay."

I gave Taggart another hug. "Thank you."

He didn't look any less confused when he departed.

And I wasn't any less concerned.

Four
Friday, July 12ᵗʰ 6:45 AM

I'd taken up running during my final months of high school, as a last resort.

Back then, my life felt like it was spinning out of control as I tried to deal with my sister's death, schoolwork, a new relationship with Taggart, and above all else, the media circus that had befallen New Haven after the news of Taggart's mother broke. I couldn't turn my brain off at night, and my sleep habits suffered as a result. My mom had been a jogger for as long as I could remember, and I had always resisted her attempts to get me to join her, but when she suggested it as a way to dump all the excess baggage accumulating in my head during the day, I said I'd give it a try.

It worked better than I hoped, and I'd been running ever since.

I'd had to switch my exercise routine to the morning hours when I'd come to Truman because it fit my schedule better. I never was much of an early riser at home, but I found sacrificing a little sleep came more naturally than I thought it would, and now it became challenging to stay in bed after the sun rose. There was something satisfying about getting the blood pumping while the rest of the world was beginning to stir. Now, I can usually knock out three miles in thirty minutes, but on the occasional morning when there was just enough chill from a light breeze to require a light jacket, I could stretch it to four miles. The campus had numerous hiking and jogging trails, spanning all levels of experience, so I rarely took the same route on back-to-back days.

This morning I was running on one of my favorite trails, the Possum Gap. Not only did it offer a balanced combination of gradual inclines and challenging hills, but the scenery was breathtaking. It had rained the night before, so the plants and trees glistened with a sparkly sheen in the morning sun as I trotted past them. I didn't even mind that the moisture evaporating in the rising heat made the air heavy and clung to my skin.

I had the trail all to myself, which wasn't unusual for a Friday. The musical score to the latest Disney movie played in my earbuds as I breezed past the halfway point. My other friends who exercised used playlists filled with songs designed to get the heart pumping, but I preferred to listen to relaxing music. It helped me empty my head, allowing only the exertion and the landscapes I passed to occupy my brainwaves. Unfortunately, none of it was working today.

My relationship with Taggart was foremost on my mind. Although he seemed more like himself yesterday and said some beautiful things, one good day couldn't erase the weeks of distance I'd felt building before that. Maybe Delta was right, and I needed to let him adapt to this new world and not worry so much. Unfortunately, my DNA wasn't configured that way. I kept thinking about a play our literature class read in high school, *Pygmalion*, by George Bernard Shaw. In a similar way, I had transformed someone on the outside of society into a pseudo-functional young man by helping him tweak and adapt his social skills, and somewhere along the way, I fell in love with him. Now my handiwork was going to use his newfound confidence to venture out and explore the world—leaving me behind.

I shook my head, and when I did, I almost tripped over a fallen branch on the trail. I told myself I was getting worked up over nothing, but I wasn't convinced. And if I was wrong and we were fine, then there was Jim Book's body turning up in Taggart's apartment. What was that about? Taggart had been seeing people on his own, though he tells me they are fellow intellectuals he enjoys sharing ideas with. Could he have seen Jim on his own about something else?

No. I couldn't believe that. Taggart is incapable of telling a lie. There must be another reason the body ended up there.

I reached the end of the trail and stopped, checking the time on my phone in my armband. Satisfied that my pacing was reasonable, I put my hands on my hips and continued walking past the trail map towards the street. I had ninety-minutes before my first mid-quarter test of the day, which was plenty of time to shower, dress, and grab a bite to eat while I cram in some last-minute studying.

When I reached Holland Avenue, I glanced across the street where Evans Hall—an all-girl dormitory—bordered Truman Chapel. Foot traffic was still light as students and faculty made their way around campus, but one figure caught my attention. Someone was leaning against the wall next to a side entrance into Evans Hall, and whoever this person was, they seemed to be staring directly at me. They were too far away and obscured by shadows for me to tell if it was a man or woman. I paused momentarily, expecting the person to look away or move in some other fashion, but they continued looking at me. I shook it off and turned left, heading for Barksdale.

I was halfway across the Commons, which was a wide-open field in the middle of campus encircled by a row of eucalyptus trees, when I felt an eerie urge to look behind me. The Commons was used for any number of school functions, but its most frequent use was for informal study-picnics when the weather cooperated. There was hardly a day when I didn't find someone spread out on a blanket in the field, but at this time of morning it was usually deserted. I didn't expect to see anybody when I turned my head, despite the funny feeling in my gut.

I was wrong.

Leaning against one of the eucalyptus trees I had just passed was a dark figure. Again, shadows hampered my vision, but I was confident it was the same person I saw standing next to Evans Hall.

My heart began to race. I wanted to shake it off as coincidence, as if it was the same person walking behind me, simply heading in the same direction. But the person was just standing there. Staring. I was the only one out here in this field. I thought about calling Delta, or even Taggart, but decided against it. I could see my dorm on the other side of the Commons and would be there in less than two minutes. Surely nothing was going to happen to me out here, in broad daylight. I quickened my pace and continued on my way.

My body relaxed when I reached the steps of Barksdale, and I blew out the breath I'd been holding. When I pulled open one of the swinging doors, a hand fell on my shoulder from behind.

The shock that coursed through my body in that moment was electric, and just as traumatic. I shrieked and pivoted, instinctively swinging my right arm in a wide arc.

My open hand struck Taggart on the shoulder.

When I realized who it was, I hit him again several more times.

"Jesus Christ, Taggart! You scared the shit out of me!"

"I'm sorry," my surprised boyfriend said, barely noticing the blows I was delivering.

"You can't sneak up on people like that."

Taggart pointed to the bottom of the stairs I'd walked up to get to the door. "I was standing right there waiting for you. I'm at a loss to understand how you didn't see me."

"You didn't follow me here?"

"No."

I looked past him to the Commons, but there was nobody in sight.

"I think I was being followed."

Taggart followed my gaze across the Commons. "Go inside and wait for me in your room."

I watched Taggart run off toward the Commons before I headed inside, then upstairs.

Our room was dark when I opened the door, which meant Delta was probably still asleep. I went to the window and pulled the curtain aside. Our window overlooked the Commons, but when I looked outside all I could see were a few random people meandering across the field. Taggart, or my mysterious follower, were nowhere to be seen.

"What's going on," Delta's sleepy voice came from her bed.

"I think I was followed by someone after my run."

Delta sat straight up. "For real?"

"For real. Taggart's out there looking for them now."

Delta was out of her bed and by my side in a flash, throwing open the curtains. "What did he look like?"

"I'm not sure if it was a he. The person kept to the shadows, and I never got a good look at them."

"But you're sure they were following you?"

I recalled the image of someone seemingly staring at me from Evans Hall, then again from the trees bordering the Commons. I was performing my own version of an internal self-check for doubt.

"I'm sure."

A knock came from the suite's hallway door. I closed our bedroom door behind me when I stepped into the common room, then went to answer it. It was Taggart.

"I didn't see anyone acting suspicious," he said as he entered.

"You do believe me, don't you?"

"Why wouldn't I?"

"Right, it's just… after what I told you last night; I thought you might think I was acting paranoid."

"Just because your paranoid doesn't mean they aren't after you. Joseph Heller. A brilliant novelist."

"That doesn't make me feel any better."

Delta came out of our room wearing nothing but an oversized sweatshirt. "Did you see anyone?"

"No."

"Probably some creep getting his jollies scoping out sweaty young coeds," Delta said, crossing her arms across her chest.

"I don't sweat. I glisten."

"That's even worse, eyeballing glistening young coeds."

Now that the adrenalin from being followed and the scare Taggart gave me was wearing off, I was starting to feel annoyed. "This pisses me off. Now I'm afraid to go running, and I love to run."

"Isn't there anybody you can run with?" Taggart asked.

I looked at Delta, who quickly threw up her hands.

"Don't look at me, you know I'm allergic to running."

"There's nobody I can think of. I'll post something on the bulletin board at the FLEX." FLEX was the nickname everyone used for the school's athletic center, where I worked three days a week.

The door to the other suite room opened, and Eve stepped out. Her hair was pulled back into a ponytail, but otherwise, she appeared to have been awake for a while. She was already dressed for class.

"What are all of you talking about out here?"

"Cassie had some creep follow her after she ran this morning," Delta stated.

"You're kidding," Eve said, laying a hand on her throat. "That's awful. Do you know who it was?"

"No, but I'm okay. Taggart was right there, thankfully." Then a question popped into my head and I turned towards Taggart. "Which reminds me, what were you doing waiting for me in front of the building anyway?"

"I wanted to wish you good luck on your tests today, and I knew that's when you usually get back from your runs."

"Awwww," Delta and Eve said in unison.

"That's sweet," Delta added.

"You don't believe in luck," I pointed out to Taggart.

"But you do."

"I'm more of a karma over luck kinda girl, but I'll take it. Do you think I should call campus police and report it?"

"Definitely, yes," Eve said.

"But I can't give them a description or anything useful."

"Still, they can increase the patrols in the area during this time of morning," Delta said.

I felt my phone vibrate on my arm, and when I looked I saw that I'd received a text. At the same time, Eve reached into her back pocket to pull out her phone and a deep female sigh came from inside our room, which was Delta's inappropriate ring tone for the receipt of a text. As Delta went after her phone, I removed mine from the armband and opened the text.

"It's a text from the school administration informing us that there is an important email waiting for us about a recent death on campus."

"I got the same one," Eve commented after looking at her phone.

"Me too," Delta said when she returned.

Eve fired up her laptop that was on one of the study desks. Within minutes we were all reading the email over her shoulder.

Dear Members of the Truman College:

I am deeply saddened to inform you of the tragic loss of a member of our Truman family.

On Thursday, July 11th, Jim Book took his life. We offer our deepest condolences to his family, friends, and loved ones. During this time of great loss, we are reminded of the importance of community. Losing a fellow student and member of our university can be very difficult. I encourage those who feel they may need additional support to contact the Counseling Center (518-555-2741), the Interfaith Center (518-555-2758), as well as our office (518-555-2700) for any emotional or academic assistance you may need.

Many of you may feel very sad. Others may feel emotions such as anger or confusion. It's okay to feel this way. When someone takes their own life, it leads to a lot of questions, some of which may never be completely answered.

While we may never know why Jim ended his life, we do know that suicide has several causes. In many cases, a mental health condition is part of it, and these conditions are treatable. If you're not feeling well in any way, it's really important to reach out for help. Suicide is not an option.

Rumors may come out about what happened, but please don't spread them. They may turn out to be untrue and can be deeply hurtful and unfair to Jim's legacy and his family and friends.

Since Jim was also a Residence Assistant in Barksdale Hall, we will be holding a short assembly at 9 AM this morning for all Barksdale residents. Classes will be delayed by one hour to accommodate this meeting.

Dr. Evan Asmuchin
President of Student Affairs
Truman College

Delta was the first to comment. "Awesome, I get to sleep in this morning."

I turned to face my best friend and cocked my head to the side, frowning. "That's what you take from that? A guy took his own life, and you're thrilled that classes start an hour later."

Delta at first looked confused by my remarks, then that changed into annoyance. "Cass, I didn't even know the guy. All of you did. Look, I'm sorry that his life was so messed up that it ended the way it did, I really am, but don't expect me to mope around about it. People I don't know die every day, too many because of suicide I'm sure, but I'd be curled up in our room in the fetal position if I let all that get to me."

"She has a point, Cassie," Eve said softly.

Now I felt as crappy as I was expecting my roommate to feel. "I get it. But maybe let's not say it's awesome?"

The tenseness around Delta's eyes disappeared, and her smile returned. "Understood."

Eve closed the lid of her laptop. "What do we think this dorm meeting is about? I mean, they said pretty much all that needed to be said in the email. Surely, they're not going to talk about the gory details. So, what then?"

"I would assume they want to reinforce the main message of the email with the people who had contact with him the most, but also take the opportunity to be present and observe," Taggart suggested.

"Observe? Observe what?"

"This is standard protocol at most universities and schools when a death by suicide takes place. I assure you there will be one or more mental health professionals at this meeting to assess how the population is reacting to the event," Taggart stated.

"I'm sorry, what?" Delta asked.

"Simply put, the school is attempting to minimize the risk of a contagion."

Delta held up her forefinger and waved it back and forth as she spoke. "Maybe I didn't make myself clear before, so let me rephrase. What. The. Hell? Suicide is contagious?"

"I've heard about this," Eve commented with a long face.

I, on the other hand, had no idea what my boyfriend was going on about and wasn't sure I wanted to.

"It's not contagious in the way you're thinking about it. Suicide contagion is the exposure to suicide or suicidal behaviors within a peer group. It can result in an increase in suicide and suicidal behaviors. Direct and indirect exposure to suicidal behavior has been shown to precede an increase in suicidal behavior in persons at risk for suicide, especially in adolescents and young adults," Taggart explained.

"Wow, that's nuts."

"I second that opinion," I said.

"How would you even know that?" Delta asked.

For a moment, I didn't think Taggart was going to answer Delta.

"It's a fascinating topic," was his response.

Five

Friday, July 12^{th,} 8:50 AM

Barksdale Hall was unique in several ways. First off, it's a freshman-only dorm. Aside from the RA's supervising each floor, typically 3rd and 4th-year students, the only occupants in this dorm were 1st-year undergraduates. I'm not sure why, but I found it comforting knowing that everyone else here was on the same level as me. The other thing setting it apart was the full lecture-style classroom in the basement.

Some genius, and I don't use that word lightly, thought that the freshman year was such a culture shock, they wanted to do something to ease the transition for the newbies. To that end, a classroom was built in the same building where they slept. That way, for at least those challenging early morning classes, all the freshman students had to do was roll out of bed and stumble down to the basement. There was no chance of getting lost and a much shorter prep time was needed, so it was ideal.

Unfortunately, none of my classes were scheduled in that room.

The secondary use of the space was to conduct dorm meetings when it was needed, such as today.

At ten minutes to nine, JJ, Eve, Delta, Taggart, and I walked through the classroom's basement entrance. Taggart wasn't a resident, but he insisted on tagging along to hear what the administration had to say. As soon as we entered the room, we knew we should have left our suite earlier. All of the seats in the half-moon shaped space, with ten rows of stadium seating, were occupied. Scores of our fellow residents already stood at the back of the room and up against the walls bordering the aisles.

JJ, never the shy one, marched in front of the gathering and plopped down on an open area against the far wall, crossing her feet in a lotus position. The rest of us followed her example.

Standing at the head of the room were two men, both dressed in suits, a rarity on our small campus. I recognized one of them as Dr. Asmuchin, President of Student Affairs, and the author of this morning's email. The other man was unfamiliar to me.

I felt Taggart nudge me with his elbow, and when I looked at him, he nodded his head towards the back of the room. Following his eyes, I spotted what he was gesturing at. Leaning casually against the wall in between a couple of male students was the detective we'd talked with outside Taggart's apartment yesterday.

"What's he doing here?" I whispered in Taggart's ear. He responded with a shrug.

"Okay, why don't we get started," Dr. Asmuchin began. "I'm sure each of you read the email that was forwarded to you earlier, but to be 100% sure, I'm going to reread it right now."

Dr. Asmuchin read the contents of the message from this morning, word for word. When he was finished he laid the paper down on a table and interlocked his fingers at his waist.

"As Jim was the first-floor RA here at Barksdale and had interactions with many of you from other floors, we felt that it was prudent to personally explain how serious the university takes this matter. I have with me Dr. Tanner Shaw, the school's clinical psychologist, and he will be spending the day here at Barksdale, going floor by floor, answering your questions and listening to your concerns."

"Do you know why he did it?" a girl from the third row blurted out, which elicited a murmuring amongst the gathering.

"The answer to that question died with Jim," Dr. Shaw said. I found the pitch and tone of his voice calming. "We will never know why, which only complicates the grieving process."

"How'd he do it?" a male voice from the back of the room called out.

"I'm not sure that information is helpful to you right now," Dr. Asmuchin said.

"He hung himself," Dr. Shaw answered, which drew a furtive glance from the president. "But we are not here to focus on Jim. Our purpose is to support you and ensure that this tragedy doesn't have a detrimental impact on your experience at Truman. Listen, suicide is complex. There are almost always multiple causes, including psychiatric illnesses, that may or may not have been recognized or treated. These illnesses are treatable. You should know that 90% of deaths by suicide involve mental disorders and substance abuse. If you or someone you know is struggling here at Truman, there are ways we can help. This is a caring community. We need to be supportive of each other."

"What's he doing here?" came a male voice from somewhere in the multitude of people.

Dr. Shaw looked confused. "I'm sorry, what?"

A boy I recognized from my Urban Studies class stood up and pointed in our direction. He was someone I had taken an instant dislike to because, even with temperatures in the nineties, he was always wearing a Bob Marley style beanie cap. Today was no exception.

"I said, what is he doing here? He doesn't stay in Barksdale."

My ears turned hot as I realized who he was referring to. Taggart shifted his position beside me as the room grew very still.

President Asmuchin took a step forward, signaling he was assuming control of the meeting again. "This is not a closed forum. Everyone is encouraged to seek out whatever help –"

"They found Jim in that guy's apartment, and from what I hear, people have a habit of dropping dead around him."

Delta shot to her feet. "You're talking out of your ass, you pretentious dick-wad!"

The assembly exploded into a mass of voices with Dr. Asmuchin trying his best to wrestle back control. Taggart rose from his seat and rapidly headed for the exit, with me and the others right behind him.

"Taggart, slow down," I cried out as he burst through Barksdale's doors into the courtyard.

He came to a stop a few feet ahead of me but didn't turn around. When the group from our suite caught up to him, his eyes were focused on the ground near his feet.

"You shouldn't let what they say bother you," I said.

"This is high school all over again," Delta said, pacing back and forth. "When do people grow up?"

"I'm not sure some of them ever do," Eve said.

"True dat!" JJ agreed.

"Their false narrative doesn't bother me," Taggart said, his voice so quiet I could barely hear him. He still had not raised his head.

"Then why are you so upset?"

"I'm a distraction."

"I don't understand. A distraction to what?"

Then he looked me in the eyes. "I'm a distraction… for you. This unwarranted attention is distracting you from your studies. I know how much doing well here is important to you. I'm interfering in that."

He was right. I was determined to get off to a good start my freshman quarter. I was driven even. I wanted to prove to my parents, to the friends I'd left behind in New Haven who remembered me more as a party girl than an intellectual, and to myself, that I belonged.

"You're right. This is important to me. But I also don't think you're giving me enough credit. With everything I went through my senior year, what we went through together, I still managed an A average. You shouldn't worry about me. I've got this."

"Absolutely. This girl studies enough for two people," JJ remarked.

"And nobody listens to beanie boy anyway," Eve added. "He's always whining about something. I bet this will all blow over before the end of the day."

When Taggart returned my smile, I relaxed. "Speaking of which, I've got some last-minute studying and then a pair of tests to get to." I leaned in and gave him a quick hug. "Are you going to be okay?"

"I am if you are."

"Good. See you afterward?"

He nodded, and after throwing a wave to everyone else, I headed down the sidewalk towards the west side of campus.

***

Ten minutes later, I was approaching Grayson Hall, where Economical Theory among other courses was taught. A group of my classmates were milling around outside the entrance, but there was one woman who caught my attention. She looked a couple of years older than me, dressed in conservative tan pants and a yellow polo shirt, seated on the bench against the building. She was scanning the faces of those approaching the building, appearing to be waiting for someone. Apparently, I was that someone because when she spotted me her eyebrows rose and she stood up.

"Cassie Underwood?"

"Who's asking?"

The woman smiled and reached into her rear pocket to extract a business card.

"My name is Jaime Henson. I'm a contributor to a daily podcast called The Grind, and I was hoping I might talk to you for a moment."

My landmine detector started going off. "You're a reporter?"

Jaime scrunched up her face. "You say that like it's a bad thing."

"Let's just say I've had lots of experience with you people taking facts out of context and sensationalizing them."

"I'm sorry to hear that. Reporters such as the ones you're referencing give our industry a bad name and make it so much harder for the rest of us. At The Grind we take pride in our ethical standards."

"And the fact that you accessed my private class schedule to know where I'd be at demonstrates that so perfectly. If you'll excuse me, I need to get to my class."

The reporter blocked my path. "I promise this will only take a minute."

"Listen, let me save you some time. I know you really don't want to talk to me. The person you want is Taggart McGill, and I can guarantee he won't talk to you."

"He will if you say it's okay."

"And why on earth would I do that?"

"Because I have information about his sister."

That stopped me cold.

"What kind of information?"

"The good kind."

"Do you know where she is?"

The reporter grinned. "It's not that good."

"Why do you want to talk to him anyway? It's been months since everything happened. He's old news."

"That's true, but he's never given an interview about what happened with his mother, and I believe that's a story people would like to hear."

"And you think this information you have will get you that story?"

"I'm so confident that I'm willing to give it to you right now. No strings attached. I'll let you be the judge and trust that you'll do the right thing."

I thought about this, and about what Taggart would want. I knew he was desperate for information about his sister, but would he be willing to sit through, what for him would be, a torturous interview for it?

I glanced at the time on my phone. I still had thirty minutes before the test began.

"Okay, go ahead. Give it to me."

"Let's sit."

I took a seat on the bench the woman had previously occupied. Before she sat down, the reporter reached into her other back pocket and handed me a flash drive.

"Everything we have is on here, but I can tell you the Cliff Notes. How much do you know?"

"Only that his sister is three years older than him. His grandparents knew when the girl was born, but little else and they never bothered to follow up."

"Okay, from the beginning then. Taggart's grandparents are Petulia & Stephen Hamilton, which you already knew since you've spoken to them. Before Petulia was married, she was raised in less than ideal conditions, mostly in the various trailer parks where her parents lived. When she was eighteen she had an affair, a one night stand I guess you could call it, with someone she only knew as John. That union gave her a child—Rachel—who you eventually came to know as Miss Worthy, Taggart's mother. Petulia eventually married Stephen Hamilton three years later, and the two of them had a second daughter. That was Taggart's aunt, and the woman who brought him to New Haven. Her real name was Terri Hamilton.

According to the Hamilton's, Rachel was a problem child from the very beginning. Always in some sort of trouble. Petulia relayed to us an account where Rachel—who was eight at the time—stabbed a classmate in the eye with a paintbrush when the girl made fun of her painting. I have a notebook full of stories like that one. Ultimately, Rachel was kicked out of the house by Stephen when she was a senior. Seems that she tried to set fire to her high school. After that her parents lost track of her until she mysteriously showed up on their doorstep nine years later… a widow and eight months pregnant. She had been married to a man by the name of Sylvester Tinge, someone who was almost twice her age and very rich. Supposedly, he left her a considerable inheritance when he passed. However, the money was held up in probate court and Rachel was broke and needing a place to stay. Rachel delivered a daughter, but as you know, never told the Hamilton's the girl's name. We found it in the records at the hospital where she was delivered. The girl's name is Bella Tinge—Taggart's half-sister. There is some doubt about whether Rachel's husband was Bella's actual father, given his age. Rachel and the child disappeared without a trace shortly after the birth, and that was in 1997. After that, no one knows what happened to Bella. When Rachel showed up in Atlanta and married Preston Jenkins, there was never any mention of a daughter. I believe you know the rest."

They finally had a name. Bella. One step closer and yet so much farther to go.

"There's a copy of Bella's birth certificate on that drive."

"Thank you for this."

"I trust I'll be hearing from Taggart soon?"

"Yes."

"Great."

I shoved the flash drive into my pocket. "When you first told me who you were, I was sure you were here about what happened yesterday."

"Ha. I'm pretty sure I'll be tackling that story soon enough."

"Oh, there is no story there. Taggart has nothing to do with that."

"Are you sure?"

What she told me next made me question that belief.

Six
Friday, July 12ᵗʰ, 2:45 PM

As I approached Taggart's apartment, I told myself I should be excited, but I certainly didn't feel that way. Listening to what the reporter from The Grind had to say earlier put a damper on the good feeling I had about my mid-quarter exams. Instead of reveling in my accomplishment, I was instead confused and worried about this latest development. Things were no longer as straightforward as we had assumed and now there were more questions than answers. It felt as if the 500-piece puzzle we were working on had been swapped for a 2,000-piece version. What did it mean? I doubted that Taggart had the answer, but he still needed to know what was going on.

Seconds after knocking on his door, Taggart opened it. His face told me he must have already heard the news, that or something else was going on.

"Detective Moss is here," he said quickly, which explained the look. Taggart turned to the side and behind him

I could see the detective standing beside the room's lone table and chairs. He was again wearing a white dress shirt, but this time his sleeves were rolled down and he sported a red tie. I'm not sure why, but he looked more official today and I wasn't sure how to interpret it.

"Maybe you could come back later, Miss Underwood?" the detective called out.

"Not necessary," Taggart responded as he put his hand on the small of my back and ushered me into the room. Try as I might, I couldn't stop myself from glancing at the spot where Jim's body had been hanging a mere twenty-four hours earlier.

"I want Cassie here for this," Taggart said.

Detective Moss frowned, but I couldn't care less. What the detective didn't know was that in the end, he'd probably be grateful I was here.

"How long have the two of you been talking?" I asked.

"I only just arrived. Your timing's perfect. Almost too perfect," the detective responded.

I put my hands on my hips. "I just came from taking an exam. This is totally coincidental."

"I'm sure," the detective said, but his face told me he didn't believe me.

"Why are you here?" I asked. "I thought you said the other night that Jim's suicide was—how did you phrase it— by the numbers?"

"That's still true, but additional information has come to light that raises some concerns and bears further exploring."

"What would that be?" I asked, feigning ignorance.

"Mr. McGill, the other night you stated that your only contact with Jim Book was through Miss Underwood's freshman orientation group."

Taggart remained silent, so I followed his lead.

"Aren't you going to comment?"

"On what? You made a simple statement, one that didn't require a response."

The muscles in the detective's jaw rippled. "There's no need to make this contentious."

"Boy, did you come to the wrong address," I said.

"I'm simply verifying the information I took down that night is correct," the detective said.

"Your statement was accurate."

"Thank you."

"We did also mention that we went to high school with Jim," I interjected. "Although we didn't have contact with him back then."

At this point, the detective removed his notepad from his pocket and flipped the pages until he landed on the appropriate one. "The truth is that Mr. McGill was in the same class as Jim Book three years ago. American Literature. Jim was a senior, and you were a freshman, isn't that right?"

I remembered that American Literature was a senior level class at New Haven. Placing a freshman in that class was a little unusual, but with Taggart being so advanced it made sense.

"I'll have to trust your information, detective. I don't recall any of my fellow students from that class."

"Not one?

"Not one."

"Okay. Do you remember turning in a paper entitled *Literature's Obscuring of Gender into Oneness?*"

Taggart's eyebrows furrowed. "I do."

"What do you remember about it?"

"Nothing out of the ordinary."

"Really? Aren't you being a little modest?"

"I don't follow."

"Didn't the teacher comment on how extraordinary the paper was? Praising you and calling it college-level work?"

From the way he shifted his position I could tell what the detective said bothered Taggart. I was beginning to wonder if not pulling him aside when I first arrived to tell him what I learned was a mistake. Doing so would have undoubtedly made the detective even more suspicious than he already was, but right now I wasn't sure which was worse, the detective's mistrust, or Taggart's discomfort.

"How could you know that?" Taggart asked.

"Because the teacher wrote his comments on your paper."

"I repeat, how could you know that?"

Smugness was all over the detective's face. "Because I've seen the paper."

I could almost see the gears turning in Taggart's head as he began putting things together.

"Melvin Book was the teacher of that American Literature class. Am I to assume he's Jim's father?"

"He is. Here are a few other things we found out. Jim Book was an English major here at Truman and somehow he got his hands on a copy of your papers from your time in that high school class, retyped them and turned them in as his own. He used the paper I just mentioned for an assignment in his freshman Introduction to Literary Studies and has sprinkled in others written by you for various assignments for the past two years. Unfortunately, those papers were the high point for Jim's academic career because he's been struggling in his other courses. I have it on good authority he was going to drop below a 3.0 GPA this quarter, and that would mean he'd lose his scholarship. So let me ask you, how do you think Mr. Book got those papers?"

"I would assume that Jim took them from his father. He had access. Undoubtedly he made copies, and then returned them before they were missed. Of course, this is only supposition."

"And you still claim you had zero interaction with the victim?"

Whatever unease I saw in Taggart before was gone now. "I stand by my previous statement. If you're a halfway competent detective, you would have spoken to various people by now who spent time with Jim and discovered that there's not a single witness who saw me having a conversation with him."

"That means very little. You say you barely registered Jim's existence here at Truman, but he was keenly aware of you. In his room we found copies of your original papers, your class schedule, news clippings from your escapades back home, and a Google Maps printout with this address on it. You could say he was obsessed with you."

The detective had now revealed everything The Grind reporter had previously relayed to me, so I felt free to comment without accidentally giving away my source.

"You think Jim took his life because he was depressed about losing his scholarship? Then why do it here in Taggart's apartment?"

"Who knows what goes on in someone's head. One theory is that Jim recognized his only success here at Truman was because of Taggart, and therefore his ultimate failure should be as well."

"That's sad."

The detective put away his notepad and placed his hands on his hips. "I have another theory. Would you like to hear it?"

Knowing Taggart the way I did, I knew he couldn't care less what the detective was thinking. The way the detective was looking at Taggart made me want to say no also, but I couldn't help myself.

"Sure," I said.

"Mr. McGill somehow found out Jim had been submitting his old papers as his own, and that made him furious. So he invited Jim over for a talk and extracted a little justice, making it look like a suicide. We found chlordiazepoxide in his system."

"What's that?" I asked.

"It's a sedative used to treat anxiety disorders," Taggart finally spoke up. "But the detective is already aware that many suicide victims take such drugs to lessen their fight response."

Detective Moss shrugged.

"But we told you the body was still moving a little when we arrived. That means Jim did what he did sometime close to when we arrived. Taggart was having dinner with me during that time and before that he was with his professor."

"The time of death hasn't been narrowed down yet, and we only have your word about the body moving when you showed up. I still have a few holes that need answers, but I'm working on it."

"You can't be serious. You really think Taggart killed Jim?"

"Let's just say we've not ruled it out."

"Well, there's a humongous hole in the middle of this theory of yours. You claim Taggart did this because he was mad at Jim for stealing his papers. No way. If you knew him at all, you'd know that Taggart couldn't care less about those papers or what Jim did with them. He's not built that way."

"People change, Miss Underwood, and sometimes not in a good way."

"I believe that detective, I do. But a change like the one you're talking about doesn't occur for no reason. Something happens in a person's life, something pretty traumatic, to cause that kind of change. That hasn't happened here."

"Are you sure?" The detective pointed at Taggart. "I've read about what went on in New Haven. It seemed pretty traumatic to me."

I couldn't help but think about how Taggart had indeed changed since we arrived at Truman. His socialization and growing independence, along with my mixed feelings about it.

"That might be true, but you're way off base in this case," I said.

"Detective Moss," Taggart said calmly. "I could tell you that your investigation will find no direct communication between Jim and myself, as there was none. We barely spoke. There were no phone calls, no text messages, no emails. You could get a search warrant to go through my laptop, though I doubt a judge would grant you one, and even if you did obtain one, you would not find any evidence I was aware of Jim's malfeasance. You would be wasting your and the taxpayers' time pursuing this line of inquiry."

The detective looked long and hard at Taggart before moving to the door.

"Do you remember what I said when we first spoke? I told you I thought there was more to this story. Seems like I was right then, and it feels right now. We'll speak again soon."

The detective let himself out, and when the door closed I could feel the tenseness in my shoulders evaporate.

"I don't think Detective Moss likes you."

"Obviously," Taggart stated. "You knew about Jim's plagiarism of my papers?"

"What?"

"You knew about the papers before Moss told us. I could tell by the way you reacted. How is that so?"

I slid into one of the two chairs in the room, buying myself some time. I was confident that my decision to talk with the reporter was a good one, but that didn't mean Taggart would feel the same way, or that his reaction would be favorable. I braced myself for anything.

"I ran into a reporter before one of my tests, and she told me."

Taggart's expression remained unchanged, apart from his eyelids fluttering briefly.

"How did you perform on your exams?" he eventually asked.

The change of subject caught me off guard. "Huh? Oh. I think I aced both of them."

Taggart rewarded me with a broad smile. "That's excellent news."

I soaked in the smile, but my curiosity made me press on. "So, Jim and your papers?"

His smile, as rare as a diamond in the wild and just as valuable to me, disappeared. "My reservations about him committing suicide have increased exponentially."

"Why?"

"Although I cannot see a motive for murder in his actions, nonetheless it adds a sense of mischief to the equation that points more towards foul play than self-harm. I can certainly understand the detective's suspicion."

"Well, he certainly has those about you."

"And that might be the murderer's intention, or part of it anyway. To cast suspicion, either at me or away from themselves."

I pulled my foot up and tucked it underneath my other thigh. "I can't believe this is happening again."

Taggart sat down in the chair opposite me. "Whatever is going on here has nothing to do with what happened in New Haven. I promise."

"You won't take it personally if I don't take your word for it, will you?"

"Tell me about this reporter you ran into."

My excitement grew as I remembered what I had to tell him, though I had to temper it. It was difficult to predict how Taggart would respond, and although I had a good feeling about this, I had been wrong before.

"She was from a weekly podcast called The Grind. Naturally, I blew her off at first, but she had some information to trade, so I listened."

"What kind of information?"

"About your sister."

Taggart had been sitting with his elbows on his knees, but now he sat up straight.

"The reporter didn't know your sister's location, but she had plenty of other information. In exchange for it she wanted to set up an interview with you about what happened in New Haven. I checked out The Grind between my two tests, and they're a reputable news outlet. I listened to several of their stories, and they were all fair and unbiased."

Taggart's blank expression wasn't giving me any indication of how he felt about this news.

"She gave me the information, as a show of faith, with no promises. But from what she told me, I think you should consider talking to her."

I pulled the flash drive the reporter gave me from my pocket and held it up.

"A copy of your sister's birth certificate is on here."

Taggart's eyes locked on to the USB drive.

"Her name is Bella."

Seven

Saturday, July 13th, 9:10 AM

The weekends were the only time I allowed myself to sleep in, forgoing my regular running routine, because in my mind Saturdays and Sundays were a time to rest. The timing was perfect because after yesterday's scare, I still wasn't ready to hit the trails yet. I hated how I felt now. Helpless. Unsure. Less safe. I chose to run in the morning because it fit my schedule. I could select a path, any path, where I'd be alone with my thoughts. Now that was no longer an option, it saddened me. One of the reasons I'd picked Truman was for its sense of community, much like New Haven, where 'stranger-danger' was a foreign concept. It was unsettling waking up to the real world and all its hidden dangers.

Even though my alarm was turned off, I still found myself waking up early. I quietly crawled out of bed, making sure not to disturb Delta, slipped on a pair of sweatpants, and grabbed my phone. The screen readout informed me it was just after eight, so I located the textbook I needed to prepare for my next exam and slipped out the door to the common room.

I was surprised to find Eve already sitting at one of the desks, looking at something on her laptop.

"Oh, hey," I said quietly. "You're up early."

Eve casually closed the laptop's lid and turned to face me. "Yeah, I couldn't sleep. I guess Jim's death bothered me more than I thought, and then there's the whole thing you went through yesterday with being followed. It's just a lot."

I gestured my head towards the bedroom. "It doesn't seem to bother either of our roommates."

Eve smiled. "No, not at all. Now, if they announced a ban on all sorority activities, that'd be a different story."

I chuckled while making my way over to the couch.

In the six weeks we'd been at school, I couldn't remember an occasion when Eve and I had spent time alone. We'd see each other in passing during the week, just enough to say "Hi" and complain about how tough our classes were, but other than that we were mostly strangers to one another. I sort of felt sorry for her. Coming from Florida, she arrived on campus without knowing a soul, which I'm sure was rough. Delta and Taggart were the only two people I knew at Truman, but that couldn't compare to settling into a new situation on your own. She seemed kind enough though, and thankfully she got along fine with her roommate.

In many ways the combination of Eve and JJ were a lot like Delta and me. One roommate is quiet, reserved, goal-oriented, and heavily invested in their schoolwork. The other outgoing, people-centric, the life of the party, with their studies considered more of an afterthought. Whatever the reason, Delta and I worked, and from what I could tell it was the same for Eve and JJ. At least that part of Eve's transition to life at Truman had gone well.

I knew I should be more sociable and help make Eve's move easier, but my ambition to prove myself at Truman resulted in me putting together an aggressive schedule that limited my social time. Everything I did know about her, aside from the basics of where she was from and her area of study, I learned at our freshman orientation group meetings. Even then, it was a bit like pulling teeth.

I decided I could sacrifice a little studying right now to make up for the time I couldn't spend with her before.

"How are your classes going?" I asked, setting aside my textbook and phone.

Eve pulled her feet up onto the chair and wrapped her arms around her legs. "Tougher than I thought they were going to be, but I'm doing okay, I think."

"What made you want to study nursing?"

"I've been around hospitals a lot, and, I don't know, it's kind of a way to pay it forward. What about you, how are your classes?"

It didn't go unnoticed how quickly Eve switched topics. It made me wonder if there was some kind of medical problem in her past.

"Pretty much the same. I was an idiot and loaded myself down with too many hours this first quarter. I should have taken my father's advice and eased into it."

"We can't have our parents thinking they know what's best for us."

I smiled. "Very true."

"And how are you and Taggart getting along with everything that's going on?"

That's a good question I wanted to say, but instead said, "We're good. Did you have a boyfriend back home?" Now it was my turn to abruptly switch subjects.

Eve shook her head. "Haven't run across anyone I've clicked with yet. Besides, most boys shy away from the circus surrounding my family."

"That's right. If I remember correctly at one of our group meetings you said your father was a politician, right?"

A subtle change came over Eve's face, and it wasn't a nice change. "I did. He's currently a state representative, but he's running for a seat in the Senate this November."

"That's got to be exciting."

"I stay as far away from all of that as I can. I called it a circus before, and I wasn't joking. It really is."

"What does your mom do?"

"Nothing. You can say she's a stay-at-home mom, but mostly she just fills the role of the idyllic wife in my dad's campaign."

I could sense some friction there and wasn't sure how to proceed, so instead I allowed an uncomfortable silence to fill the space between us.

"Can I ask you something?" Eve rubbed the tip of her nose.

"Sure."

"You don't have to answer if it makes you uncomfortable."

Now I was starting to wonder what I had opened myself up to. "Go ahead."

"It's just—he seems so—the two of you seem so different—I mean every time I've been around him—"

"You want to know how Taggart and I make things work?"

Eve smiled awkwardly. "I was trying not to sound so blunt."

I returned her smile. "It's okay. I get that a lot. I think most couples would say that no one really knows their partner as well as they do. To some extent that's probably true, but in Taggart's case it is absolutely, one-hundred percent accurate. No one knows the real Taggart except me."

And maybe his therapist—I thought to myself.

"I know him because he's allowed me in. That person, the one that nobody else sees, is the one I've fallen for. But since I'm the only one who gets to see the real him, to everyone else it's hard to understand what it is that keeps us together, and I'm okay with that."

"I dated Jim," Eve blurted out suddenly.

That took me by surprise. "Wow. I didn't know that."

Eve looked worried. "I don't think anybody did. We only went out a couple of times. He asked me out after our first group meeting. I thought it was weird that group leaders were allowed to date members of their group, but he said it was fine. We just didn't hit it off, know what I mean?"

"I do."

"I know it was weeks ago, but I keep going over the time we spent together to see if there was anything I missed, any clues about the way he was feeling."

"You shouldn't do that to yourself, Eve. People who've known people for years, up close and personal, can't see the signs sometimes. You barely knew him, so don't beat yourself up over this."

Tears pooled in Eve's eyes. "But I should have seen it."

The way Eve was acting made me wonder if she believed her nursing training should have somehow made her more observant.

"Listen, just because—"

My phone started ringing. I intended not to answer it, but the name on the caller ID changed my mind.

"Chewy?"

"Hey, Cass. I found you. Surprise. I'm downstairs in the lobby."

"You're here? At Truman?"

"Yep. Right here in the lobby. I just stopped in to say hi."

"Your timing is terrible, but I'll be right down," I said and disconnected the call. I rose from the couch and pointed a finger at Eve. "We're not through with this conversation. I'll be back in a few minutes."

I felt awful for leaving Eve like that when she was obviously struggling with Jim's suicide, but I was super-excited to see my old friend and told myself Eve could wait for a couple of minutes. After bounding down the stairs, I burst out into the lobby area, searching for a familiar face.

"CASSIE."

The boy I knew from New Haven was standing in front of the check-in desk. Chewy would be a high school Sophomore this coming year, all five foot ten inches of him, thin with bony shoulders, unusually bushy eyebrows, and a pointy chin. He had a habit of wearing his dark-framed glasses low on his nose to look over the top.

I gave him a bear hug, and then held him at arm's length.

"What on earth are you doing here? Is Tunes with you?"

"Nah, he couldn't come. My mom had to be here in Atlanta for some special cancer treatment, so we're living in an apartment near the hospital," Chewy explained. "School's on summer break, so I came along to help out after her therapies. Tunes might come up later to visit."

"That's good. How is your mother doing?"

"Good, I guess. She never tells me much, but she seems positive."

"That's great. Man, you are a sight for sore eyes. I can't tell you how good it is to see you."

"Are you rooming with Delta?" Chewy asked eagerly.

I suspected that since Tunes was Chewy's best friend, and Tunes was still carrying a torch for Delta, Chewy would no doubt report back to him on how Delta was doing.

"I am, but she's asleep, and you don't mess with Delta's sleep."

Chewy's smile dimmed. "Oh, okay."

"How'd you get here?"

"I drove," he answered, pride evident on his face. "I got my license last month."

"Good for you. And your mom let you drive all the way out here from Atlanta?"

Chewy pushed his glasses up on his nose at the same time he became very interested in my shoes.

"The day after she gets treatment she's always wiped out and sleeps the whole day. I know she wouldn't mind."

"Chewy," I admonished. "You shouldn't take advantage of her like that, especially with what she's going through."

"I know, but it was the only way I could get over here, and I really missed you guys. Does Taggart live in this dorm also?"

I had half a mind to send him right back to Atlanta, but I didn't know how much I missed him until he was standing there in the lobby. We had all been through so much together. Chewy's father died in the same accident that took my sister, and it was that disaster that ultimately uncovered the murderous activities of Taggart's mother.

"No, Taggart lives in an off-campus student apartment. He'll be excited to see you."

"Excited? This IS Taggart we're talking about?"

"You're right, pleased then. Listen, I need to go back upstairs and finish something, it should only take a couple of minutes. Why don't you hang out down here until I come back, and then we'll go see Taggart. We can all have breakfast together somewhere?"

"That sounds great," Chewy said.

"I'll be back as soon as I can," I said as I started towards the stairs.

When I let myself back into our suite, Eve was no longer at the desk where I left her. Her laptop was gone as well. I knocked on the door to her bedroom and waited. When nothing happened, I knocked again. Finally, I heard movement from inside the room. The door cracked open and JJ's wild hair and squinting eyes peered out at me.

"What do you want?" JJ croaked.

"I need to talk to Eve," I replied.

JJ looked over her shoulder, then back to me.

"She's not here," she said, closing the door in my face.

I stood there, dismayed. Why had Eve split like that?

Eight

Monday, July 15th, 7:00 PM

I'm not sure why I was so apprehensive about going to the first group session since Jim's death, but I was. Holding a meeting at all wasn't a given since Jim was the group's leader, but the text we received that morning informed us that it would go on as scheduled, with a new leader. I tried to understand the school's position. Attendance at these meetings was mandatory, part of the school's efforts to combat freshman fallout, and I'm sure the school couldn't let the tragedy derail those efforts. The powers that be probably didn't want to allow the shockwaves from what happened to linger as well. Allow a respectful amount of time to mourn and come to terms with it, then move on. Anyway, I'm sure that these sessions were a great way of allowing people to express the shock and grief they felt about Jim's death.

During our first group meeting at the start of school, held in the basement classroom at Barksdale, Jim suggested moving our meetings to Hard Bean to facilitate a more open and relaxed atmosphere. It was a popular hangout in Wolfs

Head, for students and locals alike. Although it was known primarily as a coffee shop, their food offerings were just as impressive. The only person who complained was JJ, because even though it was a short walk away, it was still farther to go and that seemed to bother her. She was out-voted by a landslide, and we've been meeting here ever since.

The café was well-designed so that it could accommodate all sorts of customers. For folks who only wanted to dash in to satisfy their morning, noon, or night elixir cravings, the ordering line was set up for max-efficiency. The area closest to the serving area was a careful mix of comfortable chairs and couches with plenty of wall-outlets for laptops and other personal electronic devices. The back half of the café contained both long and short tables, all hand-made, for their dine-in customers.

It was there that our group started to assemble.

I had walked over from the dorm with Tony and Brent. I'd intended to go with Eve and JJ like we usually did, but the two of them had already left when I checked. Eve had been avoiding me since our talk Saturday morning, or at least that's the impression I got. She wasn't in the dorm after I took Chewy to have breakfast with Taggart. It must have been late when she returned because I didn't hear her come in, nor did I hear her leave early the next morning. Eve was gone that entire day as well. I finally did see her in the food court this morning, but she was deep in a conversation with another girl I didn't know, so I left her alone.

I could take a hint. If Eve wanted to continue the conversation we started Saturday morning, she knew where she could find me. Still, why was she ignoring me? What had really gone on between Eve and Jim that caused her to feel such a sense of responsibility?

When we entered the Hard Bean, I spotted Eve and JJ sitting at our regular table with Lisa French. As I approached, Eve and I exchanged cordial smiles, but she quickly looked away.

Lisa was painfully thin, so much so that eating disorder popped into my mind whenever I saw her. Her frizzy brown hair was rarely combed, and she always wore high neck outfits no matter how hot it was. She was rooming in a suite like ours with two other girls, but she had lucked into a room by herself. Apparently, there were some last-minute dorm assignment moves, which quite possibly could have involved Delta's late enrollment, and she was the beneficiary. Lisa rarely spoke out at our meetings. The most I ever heard her talk was when she voiced displeasure about Taggart sitting with the group, despite him not being officially part of it.

Thinking of Taggart, he was nowhere around. He always arrived for our meetings before I did, though he waited outside and wouldn't join with the others until I was there. I hadn't seen him since our breakfast with Chewy on Saturday, which wasn't unusual. After Chewy went home, Taggart and I had gone our separate ways so I could return to my room and sequester myself for the remainder of the weekend to study. I assumed Taggart returned to his apartment. On class days, we usually had lunch together in the food court, but he didn't show up today, which concerned me, so I resorted to sending him an email. It was times like this when his refusal to carry a cell phone really irked me. I still hadn't received a response. Now he was a no show for the group, and I was officially becoming worried.

Maybe Taggart changed his mind and decided to investigate Jim's death? It was plausible, but it didn't explain him not answering my various attempts to contact him, unless he was pulling the "I didn't want to worry you excuse".

That would really piss me off. How could anyone think that was a valid rationale for avoiding being open and honest? An even more worrisome thought was that if Taggart's theory about Jim's death being murder was correct, then maybe Taggart himself was in danger. For a millisecond "the vision" of Taggart dangling by his neck flashed through my mind, which I rapidly shook away like my brain was recoiling from a red-hot iron.

Forcing myself to concentrate on my surroundings, I slid into the chair next to Lisa, across the table from JJ. Eve was next to JJ. Brent and Tony showed up and took their regular seats. Everyone had just settled in when Brandon and Angela appeared. Brandon sat down next to Tony and Angela next to Brent.

Ugh, Brandon. Not my favorite person, and as awful as it sounds, the one person I really hoped wouldn't show up tonight. I usually prided myself on getting along with just about anybody, but he was the exception. He was always belligerent, to everyone, ridiculing all of our opinions and making fun of our inner-most worries. As moderator Jim did his best to muzzle him, but it was like trying to contain a leaking sieve with a layer of tissue paper. His presence tainted the whole orientation experience. The thing is, Brandon was so small in stature, just five foot six and barely a hundred pounds, that even Lisa could pin back his ears if things turned physical. But it was apparent to everyone that this bully preferred to unleash his inner rage verbally.

"I don't know about anyone else," Brent said to kick off the conversation, "but this feels weird."

"Everything feels weird to you, Rosen," Brandon said. He addressed everyone by their last names, and not in a 'part of the team' way. He wasn't wasting any time tonight spewing the insults.

"Give it a rest, Brandon," Tony snapped. In the past when Jim had failed to get Brandon to keep his toxic remarks to himself, Tony would get in Brandon's face, which only seemed to spur Brandon on even more.

Brandon opened his mouth to respond, but then seemed to think better of it and stayed silent. This was almost as unnerving as his toxicity because it felt like he was recoiling only to strike harder the next time.

"It feels weird to me, too," JJ commented.

"I don't understand it. I mean Jim seemed perfectly fine at last week's meeting. Cracking jokes and cutting up, just like he normally does," Angela said. At the groups first meeting she told us about her plans to become a lawyer, yet she looked anything but. A tad on the plump side with freckles covering her cheeks, a small pudgy nose, blonde hair that she always wore with twin pigtails, and the most evenly cut bangs I've ever seen. I commented to Delta once that she reminded me of a lifelike cabbage patch doll. Her personality, on the other hand, was ideally suited for the law. She was very level-headed and pragmatic, which went along with her conservative attire and no-makeup looks.

I ventured a glance at Eve, who was nodding her head.

"I heard you found the body. That right, Underwood?" Brandon asked.

I wanted to kick Brandon in the shin for putting that image of Jim back in my head. "Yeah. Not a pleasant sight."

"Did he shit himself?" Brandon continued.

"What?" I said. The others voiced their shock as well.

"I heard that when people hang themselves, they lose control of their bowels."

"Brandon, you're a troglodyte," Eve said, a look of disgust on her face.

"I'm certainly hung like one," Brandon replied with a creepy smile.

"I've had enough of this," Tony said, looking around the inside of the café. "I thought we were supposed to get a new group leader. So, where are they?"

Tony was studying to be an architect and rumored to be from a family who was either very rich, very connected, or both. Our reasons for thinking that were tri-fold. First, he was the best dressed—male or female—of anyone who lived in our dorm. The contents of his closet, which had to be stuffed, were from stores most people had never heard of or had only seen in magazines. Second, he resided in one of only two solo rooms in Barksdale, which were impossible to get assigned to. And finally, he reacted so negatively to Brandon's taunts, much more than anyone else, that it made me believe he had to come from some sort of position of entitlement.

"It's only ten past seven," Angela pointed out.

"My father would say early is on time, on time is late, and late is unacceptable," Brent said.

"That explains a lot about you," Brandon said.

"Brandon, why don't you go—"

"Guy's—" I cut Brent off before he could finish. I suddenly had an idea. "Listen, we all have to be here, but that doesn't mean we have to engage with everyone. Brandon brings nothing useful to any conversation we have, and his only purpose seems to be to stir shit up, so I propose that from now on we ostracize him from the group."

"Who put you in charge, Underwood?" Brandon asked.

"What does that mean, exactly?" JJ asked.

"It means we act like he's not even here. You want to put out a fire, take away the fuel."

"You can't do that," Brandon said.

"I like it," Tony said, smiling.

"So do I," said Brent.

"All in favor of ostracizing Brandon from the group?" I asked, raising my hand in the air.

Everyone except Brandon raised their hands.

A young woman who looked only a couple years older than us with short blonde hair, wearing a yellow long-sleeve V-neck t-shirt came rushing up to the table.

"I'm sorry I'm late," the woman said, trying to catch her breath. "I wasn't told you were meeting off-campus, so I was waiting at Barksdale. Are we voting on something?"

Everyone lowered their hands.

"Just an internal matter. It's all resolved now," I said.

"Like hell," Brandon said.

"You must be our new leader?" Tony asked.

"That I am," she said, taking a seat at the end of the table. "My name is Talia Davis."

"Well, you should know that I think my fellow team members just staged a coup or something because they're trying to ban me from the group," Brandon said hurriedly.

Talia bit her lower lip. "First off, I don't think you mean coup. You are?"

"Brandon Carter."

Talia's concerned face turned into recognition. "Ah. Brandon. Why doesn't everyone else introduce yourselves so I can put a face to the names?"

The way Talia blew off Brandon made it obvious she'd been pre-briefed about the personalities in our group. My guess was that part of Jim's duties was to make notes about us and report back to the university. That made sense, so when situations like this occurred—when a leader needed to be replaced mid-quarter—the new leader could be prepared.

After going around the table and introducing ourselves, Talia laid her hands flat on the table.

"I'm sorry to be taking over your group under such tragic circumstances, but I'm going to do my best to see that the remainder of the year goes smoothly for all of you. A little about me. I'm a grad student seeking my doctorate in Psychology. I'm originally from—"

"Are you not going to do anything about what I just told you?" Brandon interrupted.

Talia smiled at Brandon. "Let's just get on with the meeting and see how things play out. How about that? Now, as I was saying I'm from Chicago originally but moved—"

Brandon pushed back his chair and stood up. "I don't need to be here if I'm just going to be ignored."

Talia smiled again, but this time I could see no warmth behind it. "You're not being ignored, Brandon. I'm listening to you, but as team leader, I set the agenda and when we discuss items. I'm happy to meet with you one-on-one after group. For now, I'm afraid you do have to be here. You cannot move out of the dorms next year if you do not complete an orientation group, so unless you want to remain in Barksdale until you graduate, I suggest you take your seat."

I was beginning to like Talia Davis. A lot.

Brandon pointed at me. "Her boyfriend is a freshman, and he doesn't have to live in the dorms. He lives off-campus."

Talia didn't even bother to look at me. "Yes, well, I guess there are exceptions made. Unfortunately, you're not one of them."

"Then I want to move to a different group," Brandon continued, still standing.

"That request would have been considered if it came during the first week of the quarter, but seeing that we are at the midway point, that is impossible as well. Now, shall we continue?"

Brandon glared at us all, then retook his seat.

"Good," Talia said. She pulled out her phone and checked the time, then laid it on the table.

"I'm afraid more than a quarter of our time is already gone, and I wanted to discuss how everyone is doing given the events of the last week and the fact it's mid-terms, so how about I save my biography for next time. Is anyone feeling like the stress is starting to overwhelm them?"

I stared at the top of the table, waiting for someone else to speak up.

"It is a lot," Angela said. "I feel guilty whenever I'm not studying or in class. Like school is all there is… or should be."

A lot of heads around the table nodded in agreement, my own included.

"I thought part of what school was about was the social experience. Personal growth. But with all this school work, it's hard to enjoy it," JJ added.

"From what I hear, you enjoy it plenty," Brandon said.

JJ shot Brandon a look, but when she saw me looking at her, she remained silent.

"Brandon, I'm not sure how this group was run before, but in my groups, only positive remarks are welcome. Anything else should be kept to yourself."

Brandon smirked. "I thought that was positive."

Talia returned an empty smile. "I'm sure you do, but it's my definition that counts. If you continue to detract from the group's purpose in this manner, I will have you removed and you'll have to start this all over again next quarter."

Brandon's smirk disappeared at the same time several smiles like my own appeared around the table.

"I hear what all of you are saying. You should know that you are not alone. High levels of stress are very common among first-year students. Just remember to keep your social and educational options open. You are not locked into any specific field of study, so consider trying out a variety of academic areas or hanging out with different peer groups to find the right fit for you. Homesickness, especially for those of you who have never lived away from home, is common, and adjusting to living with roommates isn't always easy.

"I recommend to all of you that you practice something called self-compassion," she said smiling at each of us. "I see a lot of blank faces. What is self-compassion? In basic terms, it's a way for someone to avoid negative self-judgment and cope with feelings of inadequacy—perfect for those of you who feel you aren't performing up to your usual standards. Different factors are involved, including self-kindness, common humanity, and mindfulness. Having self-kindness means that a person is not overly critical of themselves, common humanity consists in accepting that failure is a part of life that everyone must deal with, and mindfulness is described by living in the moment and staying calm and collected. Studies have found that students who have high levels of self-compassion are more energetic, optimistic, and motivated than those with lower levels.

"Most importantly, if things continue to feel overwhelming, I encourage you to visit me or any of our school counselors for personalized help. I can't stress that enough."

As much as I hated to admit it, I had gotten more out of thirty minutes with Talia than I had during our entire time with Jim.

Things were looking up.

Nine
Thursday, July 18^{th,} 2:14 PM

"We need to do something to celebrate," I announced, letting my backpack fall to the ground as I tumbled onto my bed.

Delta turned around from her seat at the desk and smiled at me. "Somebody is in a good mood."

I rolled onto my side and propped my head on my hand. "I took my last mid-term this morning. It feels like a bag of bricks has been lifted off my back."

"That IS a reason to celebrate, but then again, you know I never need much of a reason."

"Let's do something together tomorrow. Heck, you can bring Jon along if you want."

Delta pinched her lips together. "Jon's history."

I sat up. "Oh, I'm sorry. What happened?"

"He told me he was dropping out of school, so I pulled the plug. He wasn't too happy about it either, but I told him it was for the best. I think he's working for his uncle at a hardware store now. That's probably not a surprise to you."

"Not entirely, but to be frank, he didn't seem to be right for you."

"I thought you felt that way, and you're probably right."

"I'm just glad he didn't get a job at some restaurant. Can you imagine him stealing food off of customers' plates?"

Delta burst out laughing. I did the same.

"He was pretty bad about that, wasn't he?" Delta asked when she regained her composure.

"I'll say."

"What about Taggart? You're not inviting him to our celebration?"

That dimmed my smile, but I felt too good to let it wipe it out altogether.

"I'm tired of trying to figure him out. He's gone back to being a ghost again. We have a couple of days where he's all sweet and caring, and then poof, he disappears for days. At least he's returning my emails now. I don't know. I'm starting to wonder if I'm not smart enough for him."

"Smart enough?"

"Delta, you know how intelligent he is. I think maybe he's bored when he's with me. That's why he's spending so much time with his professors."

"Listen, there are different kinds of smarts. There are book smarts, and then there is being witty, clever, and funny. Maybe you're not on the same level as Taggart as far as book smarts go, not many are, but in the other categories you rock it big time. That's what Taggart sees in you, and that can never be boring. I'm going to repeat what I told you last week. In the span of a year, he has gone from being a virtual recluse to being here with us, soaking up knowledge and interacting with it. He just needs time."

I reached out and took hold of Delta's hand. "Thank you. I know you're probably right, but it's so hard—feeling ignored."

"If that's what he's doing, I promise you he's not doing it consciously."

"I hope you're right," I said, then sprung off my bed. "And that's enough of being weepy. What are we going to do tomorrow?"

"Well, my sorority is throwing a mixer, and we're allowed to bring guests. I know you're not into the whole Greek thing, but maybe you can think of it as a party."

"I'm in," I replied without hesitation, which was so unlike me. Delta was a born sorority girl, and she'd recruited me hard at the beginning of the year, but she backed off once she realized I wouldn't change my mind. I left my days as a party girl behind me in high school, and although I wasn't thrilled about going to a sorority gathering, spending time with my best friend was more important right now.

"Awesome. We may have to blow off class tomorrow afternoon to prep."

"Yeah, that's not going to happen," I replied.

A knock on the hallway door interrupted us. I stepped into the study room and opened the door to find a man facing away from me, looking down at a clipboard in his hands. When the stranger realized the door had opened, he spun around, looking surprised.

"Hello there, sorry, I wasn't sure if anyone was home," the man said. He was six-foot tall, older, late forties or early fifties, but in good shape for his age. He was wearing a light-yellow polo shirt with the Truman logo embroidered on the chest, and khaki pants. His sandy hair was cut short, but his eyebrows could use some trimming. "Are you alone?"

"My roommate is here with me," I responded, my curiosity rising.

Looking at the clipboard, the man said, "Are you Delta, Cassie, Eve, or Jennifer?"

"I'm Cassie. My roommate is Delta."

"Excellent. But your other suitemates aren't here?"

"They're in class. What's this about?"

The man smiled again. "I'm sorry, I should have led off with that. My name is Gerald Batiste, and I work with the university's outreach division. We are going door to door to make sure our residents are aware of the services the school has at its disposal, given the recent circumstances."

"Hello," Delta said as she appeared beside me.

"Good afternoon," Gerald said, displaying his tooth gap yet again.

"This is Mr. Batiste—"

"Gerald, please."

"Gerald is from the school and he's going around making sure everyone is coping okay."

Gerald smiled and tapped his clipboard against his chest. "We find that sometimes students are hesitant to come into the offices to seek the help they need, so we're trying the one-on-one approach. Extraordinary times need extraordinary measures, and all that."

"I think that's great," Delta said. "But we're all fine here. Nothing to worry about."

I thought I caught a brief flash of something odd on Gerald's face, but whatever I saw was quickly replaced by another smile.

"And you feel the same way, Cassie?"

"I do."

"And how about your suitemates? Do you know them very well?"

"I wouldn't say we're close, but I haven't seen anything that would concern me."

"Have they expressed—"

"Mr. Batiste, I'm sorry, Gerald, I hate to be rude, but I really need to get ready for my part-time job. They don't like it when we're late," I said.

Gerald became concerned. "Absolutely. We mustn't have that. Thank you both for taking the time to talk with me."

Gerald reached to his back pocket and came back with one of the brochures people were handing out at the dorm meeting.

"We already have one," Delta explained.

"Excellent. Well, I'll be moving on. Enjoy the rest of your day."

I closed the door and Delta busted out laughing.

"He looked like Alfred E. Neuman with those teeth," she said.

"I have no idea who you're talking about, but either way, it's not nice to make fun of him. Listen, I'll need your help picking an outfit for our night out, but right now I have to head to work. We'll talk about it tonight?"

"Count on it."

I quickly changed into my white FLEX polo shirt, my part-time job's mandatory work attire, and headed out. As I made my way to the stairs, I noticed some sort of commotion behind me, taking place at the opposite end of our floor. I thought briefly about backtracking to see what was happening, but I only had ten minutes to make it to the FLEX, and I couldn't afford to be late.

The FLEX was the nickname for Truman's athletic center that both students and faculty used to work out. I was lucky enough to land one of the coveted jobs that opened up every quarter and didn't want to do anything that might jeopardize it. The managers were strict about tardiness and absences. They could afford to be because there was a long list of students waiting for the opportunity to work there. I had missed my shift the previous week because of Jim's suicide and the questioning by the police, which my manager excused, but I didn't want to push my luck.

Walking through FLEX's main doors, I found myself still impressed with the facility. In addition to the two pre-existing, re-finished full-sized basketball courts, a recent expansion and renovation project included an approximate 7,500 sq ft. weight room, a 3,000 sq ft. cardio room, and a group exercise studio, including one dedicated to spinning classes. Windows surrounded one whole side of the second-level indoor track encircling the basketball courts to allow exercisers to take in the nature reserve that backed up to the rear of the building. Though I'd hated to do it, I moved my morning runs to the track for the increased security. I was usually one of the first ones through the doors in the morning, so the traffic on the circuit was minimal.

Other FLEX features included lounge areas, recreational game space, two racquetball courts, and an outdoor recreation center, where the campus community could check-out kayaks, canoes, camping equipment, and even get essential bicycle services and repairs done.

The job I was given—front desk receptionist—was highly sought-after because it paid well, there was very little actual work involved, and the dead time made for lots of opportunities to study. I said hi to Teddy—the day shift attendant—as I walked past the reception desk and through a door leading into a smaller room behind the greeting area. That's where the time clock was, along with a coffee pot on a stand and a circular table with two chairs.

Returning to the reception desk, I found Teddy squeezing one of the FLEX's promotional rubber balls in his left hand and holding open a paperback novel with his right. When I first met FLEX's dayshift worker, I thought he was more interested in increasing his biceps than his GPA. The same type of shirt I was wearing strained to contain his bulky muscles. I even heard he had been reprimanded for sneaking in some bench presses during his shift. But after talking with him, I learned he was, in fact, a very dedicated student.

"Busy today?" I asked.

"About normal," Teddy said, climbing down off his stool. He tossed his ball into the bucket with the others, grabbed a half-empty protein drink, then strolled past me.

"Adios."

I settled onto the same padded stool Teddy had just vacated and scanned the check-in register on the computer. There were only a dozen people currently using the facility, which was about average for this time of day, but one name stuck out at me. Brent from our orientation group was on the list, which was a bit of a surprise because I'd not seen him at the FLEX before. It wasn't a complete shock because Brent looked like he took care of himself, but I would have thought he wouldn't have waited until mid-quarter to stop in.

Prior to me getting to know Taggart, Brent would have been the type of guy I could see myself going out with. He had a laid back personality, but with a quick wit. I got the impression he was only going to college because his family expected it from him. He was the type of guy who was self-assured enough to do well in the world. He just wasn't in any rush to do it.

On a typical day, things didn't pick up at the FLEX until five, so I decided to try and get in a couple of chapters before then. I pulled my Social Economics book out of my backpack and settled in.

Sixty minutes later, Brent exited the swinging door leading from the men's locker room. He was drenched in sweat, soaking through the grey Adidas t-shirt he was wearing, making me wonder why he wasn't using the towel sticking out of the black gym bag he was carrying.

"Hey, I didn't know you worked here," he said as he approached. Call me suspicious, but the way he subtly hit on me all the time made me not believe him.

"That I do. I've not seen you here before, though."

He stopped in front of me, finally pulling out his towel and wiping his brow.

"It was crazy the first half of the quarter, and I needed to concentrate on my classes. I've finally found a rhythm and it felt like it was time to hit the weights again."

"I get it. Looks like you got your money's worth."

He smiled as he hung the towel around his neck. "I did. You look like you spend a fair amount of time here as well, off the clock."

I'm never comfortable on the receiving end of compliments, especially about my looks, which was why I know my face was turning red. "Actually, I run."

"Really, I like to run also. We should run together sometime."

The sound of someone clearing their throat drew both of our attention to the entrance, where Taggart was standing.

"Oh, hey, Taggart," Brent said.

The nod of Taggart's head was barely noticeable.

"So, I gotta head back. Let me know about the run," Brent said to me.

Taggart watched Brent walk past him out the doors, then stepped up to the desk.

"What are you doing here?" I asked.

"I've been otherwise engaged and not had the opportunity to see you, so I came by to do that."

"Do what?"

"See you."

Try as I might, the cavalier way he treated being apart from each other bothered me. I know it made me seem like a twelve-year-old and I could feel the bitchiness surging in me. I didn't like it, but I couldn't help it either.

"Oh. Well… we're not allowed to have visitors when we're working."

Taggart glanced back at the door Brent just exited, then returned his gaze to me.

"I'm not a visitor. I am a student here at Truman, and I've come to make use of the facility, and talk to you at the same time."

I couldn't help but smile a little. "You've come to work out?"

"Indeed." Taggart wasn't smiling, but you could see the amusement in his eyes. I had never seen him do anything remotely athletic, yet his body was in excellent shape, and there wasn't an ounce of fat on him.

"Okay. You'll need to scan your student ID."

He produced his ID from his wallet then let the scanner read the barcode on the back.

"Are you going to work out in that?" I asked.

Taggart looked down at his Converse tennis shoes and faded jeans. Beneath his partially zipped hoodie I could see a solid black T-shirt.

"Is that a problem? I didn't see a dress code."

"No. No. It's just that you might get hot in what you're dressed in."

"Temperature regulation. I understand. I assume cold beverages are provided to help in this regard."

"You can purchase some at the health bar. Do you have any money?"

"I have a debit card."

"Then, you're good."

Taggart looked down the corridor into the weight room, then back at me.

"Perhaps you can recommend a type of workout I might enjoy."

"That depends. What type of training are you interested in? Cardio, resistance, strength, maybe endurance training?"

Taggart stuck his hands in his back pockets. "Which one is the closest? I'll probably be taking numerous breaks."

I was about to answer his question when my phone chirped, signaling the receipt of a text message. I swiped the screen and after reading a couple of sentences, my focus switched to the sender identification, which read BLOCKED. Returning to the text, I felt goosebumps rising on my arms as I continued to read.

PLEASE RELAY THIS TO TAGGART.

TAGGART - YOUR SISTER IS COMING FOR YOU. I DON'T KNOW HER PLANS BUT KILLING HER MOTHER PROBABLY WASN'T A GOOD IDEA.

"Taggart, you need to look at this," I managed to say, holding out my phone for him to see the screen.

I watched his eyes as they read the text, then he took the phone from my grasp.

"Who do you think it's from?" I asked.

He shook his head without taking his eyes from my phone.

"Very few people have this number after I had to get a new one because of all the reporters hounding me."

"I'm aware."

"Well, whoever it is obviously knows about you and your sister, and where she is, or rather where she's heading."

"And quite possibly with bad intentions," he replied, handing back my phone.

A disturbing thought popped into my head. "I hadn't considered it until just now, but your sister might be cut from the same cloth as your mother."

"You mean a murderous psychopath."

"I wasn't going to be that blunt, but maybe, yeah. What are you going to do?"

"Not sure what I can do since we know very little about her. She's three years older than me, and according to my grandparents, she has hazel eyes and blonde hair, but those can be easily altered."

"It's kind of creepy when you think about it. I mean, she could walk right up to you and you'd never know who she was."

My phone chirped again, sending a cold chill down my back. I hesitated a moment before swiping the screen.

"Oh no," I said as I read.

"What is it?"

"It's another mass text from the school. They sent out an email about another death on campus."

My fingers fumbled as I opened my email app. When the screen loaded, an email header from the school was at the top. I quickly opened it and began reading.

I could feel the blood drain from my face. Tearing my eyes away from the screen, I stared into Taggart's anxious eyes.

"There's been another suicide."

Ten
Thursday, July 18th, 7:00 PM

That old quote by some ancient baseball player kept rolling around in my head. Deja Vu all over again. What was happening right now definitely felt a lot like that.

Piling into the basement in Barksdale, the events of the previous week were heavy on my mind. The dorm meeting was set for 7:00 PM, and this time we made sure to arrive early, securing seats in the front row. I had to leave my shift at FLEX early to make it, but my manager said he understood. I wasn't doing much good there anyway because I was too upset to concentrate. Taggart had stayed and walked with me back to the dorm. He did his best to get me to engage with him, to pull me out of my head, but I felt numb. Like a walking zombie.

Sitting in the freshman classroom, I felt myself starting to emerge from that funk. Delta occupied the aisle seat, with me next to her, Taggart on my other side, then JJ and Eve. I noticed the guy with the Jamaican beanie, the one who'd called out Taggart last week, making his way up the aisle with a group of other boys. I caught his eye and he paused, causing the procession of people behind him to back up, and for a second I thought he was going to make a scene. But then Delta rose from her seat and crossed her arms. She was staring directly at him. He must have decided against whatever he was thinking of doing because he lowered his head and continued up the aisle.

New to the room this week was a table directly inside the entrance covered with suicide prevention pamphlets. I looked at my hand and discovered I was holding one, but had no memory of picking it up. I saw Tony enter the room and he spotted us in front, claiming a seat next to Eve. A few minutes later Brent arrived, followed closely by Brandon and Angela, but by then all of the front row seats were taken, so they kept moving towards the back of the room.

I watched the faces of everyone as they made their way into the classroom. It was a solemn mix of the morbidly grim or utterly shocked, with a few annoyed looks sprinkled in. There wasn't much conversation as I'm sure nobody knew what to say. Two students in less than a week had decided to end their lives. What could you say?

Dr. Asmuchin and Dr. Shaw were once again standing at the head of the class. I didn't think it was possible, but they both looked even more somber. Someone else had joined them for this meeting—Talia Davis—the new leader of my orientation group. The school's administration was well-represented.

After a few stragglers wandered in, Dr. Asmuchin closed the door behind them.

"I want to thank everyone for being here tonight. These are trying times, but together we will overcome the confusion and uncertainty to forge a path forward. Once again, I will read the official statement we released earlier this afternoon.

"I am deeply saddened to inform you of the tragic loss of another member of our Truman family. Lisa French took her life sometime during the night Wednesday evening, July 17th. We offer our deepest condolences to Lisa's family, friends, and loved ones. During this time of significant loss, we are reminded of the importance of community. Losing a fellow student and member of our university can be very difficult.   Losing two in such a short period of time is unthinkable. I encourage those who feel they may need additional support to contact the Counseling Center 318-555-2741, the Interfaith Center 318-555-2758, as well as our office 318-555-2700 for any emotional or academic assistance you may need. Many of you may also feel very sad. Others may feel emotions such as anger or confusion. It's okay to feel whatever emotion you might be feeling. Lisa's reasons for ending her life may never be known.

"In many cases, a mental health condition is part of it, and these conditions are treatable. Rumors may come out about what happened, but please don't spread them. They may turn out to be untrue and can be deeply hurtful and unfair to Lisa and her family and friends."

As Dr. Asmuchin was reading the announcement, I replayed all of my interactions with Lisa in my head. It depressed me even further to realize how few there were. She was in my orientation group, we were supposed to be helping each other acclimate to college life, and I'd barely talked with her. Yes, she was shy and standoffish, but I should have tried harder. Shouldn't I?

Dr. Asmuchin lowered the paper he was reading from. "I plea to every one of you, it's crucial that if you're not feeling well in any way, you reach out for help. Lisa neglected to do so, and therefore, one of God's special gifts was lost."

The room remained quiet. I knew how everyone felt. We all were desperate for answers and didn't know where to get them.

"Dr. Shaw and Miss Davis, both from our Social Services department, will remain here after the meeting to answer your questions or to just talk. Please make use of their time. Everyone can return to their rooms now."

As soon as people started moving, I made a beeline for Talia Davis before anyone else could reach her.

"Talia, tell me this isn't happening. Lisa was quiet and shy, but suicidal?"

Talia took me by the elbow and led me to the corner of the room. "Yes, I found her sullen and withdrawn, but in our brief interaction Monday I didn't see any signs this was a possibility. She had good grades and no problems with any of her instructors. But Jim—"

"What? Jim, what?"

When Talia spoke again, her voice was softer. "It's possible that Jim's suicide triggered Lisa's."

Taggart's comments last week about a suicide contagion popped into my head.

"That's really a thing?"

"A very real thing. You need to watch the people on your floor, or anyone you come in contact with. Listen for anyone talking about killing or harming themself, even jokingly. Or pay attention for anyone exhibiting behavior such as hopelessness. It's a strong predictor of suicide. They may talk about 'unbearable' feelings, predict a bleak future, and state that they have nothing to look forward to. Dramatic mood swings or sudden personality changes is another indicator. They may lose interest in day-to-day activities, neglect their appearance, or show significant changes in eating or sleeping habits."

"I'm not trying to be funny, but almost everyone I know jokes about that stuff."

"I understand, but we have to take everything seriously, especially now."

"What do we do if we suspect someone is considering it?"

"Ask them. You can't make a person suicidal by showing that you care. In fact, giving a suicidal person the opportunity to express their feelings can provide relief from loneliness and pent-up negative feelings, and may prevent a suicide attempt. Beyond that, just offer to help them find the support they need and of course report any concerns to an appropriate staff member."

"Okay, I will. Thanks, Talia."

I returned to the others, still standing in front of their seats.

"What did you ask her?" Eve spoke first.

"Let's go back to the room first."

Back in our suite, I hurried into our bedroom and grabbed the desk chair. If everyone I expected showed up, we were going to need more seats. I dragged the chair into the common room and gave it to Taggart, then took a seat in one of the desk chairs next to him. Eve caught on to what I was doing and disappeared into her room, returning with their chair. JJ and Delta sat down on the couch. A couple of minutes later I answered a knock on the door.

Tony, Brent, Brandon, and Angela were all standing there.

"I think we need to talk, don't you?" Tony asked.

I opened the door wide and ushered everyone in. JJ looked like she was trying to use mind-control to influence Brent to sit next to her, but instead Angela squeezed onto the couch between her and Delta. The three guys took up various positions leaning against the wall.

"I just wanted to say before we get started that this isn't an official school meeting, so if we hear any of your lip Brandon, I'll deck you, swear to god," Tony stated.

Brandon held up his hands. "Chill, dude. I'll be quiet as a mouse."

"What were you talking to Talia about," Angela asked, looking directly at me and ignoring the blatant demonstration of testosterone.

"I wanted to know what she thought about Lisa's suicide."

"I heard she hung herself with some speaker wire," Brandon said, which drew a sharp look from Tony. "What? That's not lip, that's facts."

"What did Talia say?" Eve asked.

"Pretty much what we're all thinking… disbelief. But she did say something interesting, and it ties into something Taggart alluded to last week."

"What did you say?" Angela asked, looking at Taggart.

Taggart looked around the room, then settled his attention on me before speaking.

"It has been shown that the suicide of a student has a rippling effect in the school environment as well as in the greater community, as a single adolescent death by suicide increases the risk of additional suicides. The process by which a completed suicide increases the suicidal behavior of others is called contagion. When multiple suicides occur close in time and geographical area, at a rate greater than normally would be expected in a given community, it is considered a cluster. That's a term created by the Centers for Disease Control in 1988. I believe the administration is concerned that the previous death triggered Lisa's act, and therefore a suicide cluster might be forming here at Truman," Taggart explained.

"I'm calling bullshit on that," Brent said. "Where are you getting this from?"

"Numerous published papers, news articles, investigative reports. The CDC studied the phenomenon after a rash of teen suicides in Palo Alto. Approximately one to five percent of teen suicides occur in a cluster after a youth dies by suicide. Though they are rare, contagion results in approximately 100–200 seemingly preventable deaths annually."

"I just Googled it on my phone and got page after page of hits," Tony said. "It's a real thing."

"I did too," Delta said, still looking at her phone. "Listen to this… research has found that a death by suicide may touch approximately 135 people, one third of whom experience a severe life disruption as a result. Exposure to a peer's suicide has been found to be associated with suicidal ideation or behavior in adolescents that can persist for up to two years. Studies have supported the fact that it is not the closest friends, but rather the less close friends who knew the deceased who have the highest rates of suicidal ideation or behavior as a result."

"Which is why the school is holding these meetings and handing out all these pamphlets," I said, wanting to steer the conversation in a more positive direction. "They're trying to prevent a cluster from forming. I mean, this is a perfect breeding ground, isn't it? High stress and the incredible pressure to succeed. Most of what Talia wanted to tell me was to keep an eye out for suicidal behavior, so they could get people the help they need."

"What kind of behavior?" JJ asked.

I relayed everything Talia told me that I could remember. "I checked, everything and more is in those pamphlets. You can find one anywhere. They're all over the dorm now."

"There is one other possible explanation for these deaths," Taggart said.

"Taggart don't," I said.

Angela shifted forward in her seat. "Taggart don't what? What don't you want him to tell us, Cassie?"

The cat was out of the bag now, and there was no going back, not without me looking like an idiot. I trusted Taggart's instincts and the way he could read people, for the most part, but I wasn't 100% in agreement with his—or detective Moss's—theory about Jim being murdered. I was ashamed to admit that Jim committing suicide was so much simpler.

"Taggart has a theory, but it's really thin. We would be better off concentrating on what Talia told me."

"I want to hear it," Angela pushed.

"Me too," Brandon added. "I'm all about conspiracy theories. You know that Michael Jackson was actually murdered, right?"

"Tell us what your theory is, Taggart," Eve asked.

Taggart's eyes met mine, and then I slowly nodded my head.

"I don't believe that Jim's death was suicide. Someone took his life and arranged the elements to look like a suicide."

I looked around at the gaping mouths in the room.

Brandon spoke up first. "That's awesome."

"Who? Why?" Tony asked.

"Undetermined," Taggart answered.

"What would make you think that?" Delta asked.

Taggart gave them the same spiel about his listening abilities that he gave to detective Moss and received almost the same response.

"That's it? You didn't hear suicide in his voice?" Brandon asked.

"And the fact the body was left in my apartment. It's presence there was meant to send a message, and not some final emotional statement."

"Then what about Lisa?" Brent asked. "Do you think she was murdered also?"

"Unknown. It's possible she only reacted to what she thought was a suicide."

"But isn't it strange that two people from our group have been found dead," Brandon stated. "And one of them was found in your apartment, and the other didn't like you sitting in on our meetings."

While everyone was staring at Taggart now, my eyes locked on Brandon.

"I fail to see the correlation between those two observations," Taggart said calmly.

Brandon must have felt the cold glare from my eyes on him because he looked back at me and shrugged. "I told you, I like conspiracy theories."

"I don't know about anyone else, but murder is a whole lot easier to understand than suicide," Angela stated. "I just don't get it. To me, suicide is quitting, pure and simple. Life isn't going your way, so you chuck it all away. No regard for the people you leave behind and the pain it causes. It's the ultimate act of selfishness if you ask me."

"You have no idea what you're talking about, Angela," Eve shouted, surprising all of us by her intensity.

"What, I'm not allowed to have an opinion?" the wide-eyed Angela responded.

"Not when it's so ignorant. It's like you're giving us an opinion about a foreign film and you don't even bother to learn the language it's in. You try to put yourself in these poor people's place, and you fail miserably. Just do society a favor and keep your ill-informed mouth shut."

"So, you're the expert now?"

Eve shot out of her chair like it was on fire.

"I guess so since I tried to kill myself once," Eve half-cried. She spun on her heel and disappeared into her room, slamming the door shut behind her.

Eleven
Thursday, July 18^{th,} 7:50 PM

The sound of the slamming door reverberated in the room, though I doubted any of our neighbors took much notice. The stunned faces looking back at me now must have matched my own.

I looked at JJ. "Did you know?"

The blank expression on JJ's face provided my answer before she spoke. "She never said anything."

"I feel like I'm two feet tall," Angela said, clasping her head between her hands.

"Maybe more like two inches," Brandon added.

"Maybe we should go get Talia," Tony suggested. "She's probably still downstairs."

I thought about the suggestion, then shook my head. "We need to talk to Eve first."

"But who's going to go in there?" Delta asked. "We can't all go. She'll freak out."

"I recommend anyone but Taggart," Brandon said. "I think about jumping out a window every time he opens his mouth."

Taggart leveled his gaze in Brandon's direction, but remained silent.

"You're not helping, Brandon," Brent said.

"Is there a way we can give this contagion to Brandon?" Tony growled.

"Don't talk that way, Tony. It's not even funny," Angela said.

"Yeah, low blow dude," added Brandon.

I looked over at JJ again, who still looked shaken. "She's your roommate, JJ."

JJ's eyebrows shot up and she hugged herself with her arms. "But I don't know what to say. This is freaking me out."

I can't say that I blamed JJ for her reaction; this had shocked all of us. But burying our heads in the sand would not help Eve. Somebody needed to step up.

"I'll go in there with you if you want?" I offered.

The relief that came over JJ was instantaneous. "Yes, please."

"I'll go too," Delta chimed in.

"That'd be great."

"Maybe you don't need me at all?" JJ suggested. "The two of you can talk to her."

I rose from my chair. "You're coming, JJ. I also think everyone else needs to clear out. We don't want Eve worrying that you're all out here trying to listen in on what we're saying."

"But that's exactly what we plan to do," Brandon said.

Brent pushed off the wall where he was leaning. "Let's go, everyone. They need their space."

One by one, the group departed. Taggart was the last one to the door.

"I'm going to attempt to gain access into Lisa's room, just to satisfy my curiosity."

"Okay, but don't get caught. You're already on detective Moss's bad side."

The grin he gave me did little to reassure me. When he was gone, I knocked softly on Eve's door.

"Come in," came the muffled reply.

Opening the door, I saw Eve sitting in the middle of her bed, her feet crossed in front of her, hands in her lap. Eve and JJ had chosen not to go with bunk beds in their room, arranging their beds so the heads met one another at the far corner of the room instead. I sat down next to Eve, Delta and JJ taking seats on the other bed.

"The three of you drew the short straw?" Eve asked. It was apparent that she had been crying, but she made a decent attempt at a smile now.

"Nope, we're all volunteers. Everybody else has gone, so it's just us," I said.

Eve reached out with one of her hands and toyed with her blanket. "You should know that I am not suicidal, far from it, so get that out of your head right now. My episode was years ago. I've been through more therapy than I care to mention, and I'm completely fine now—well, as fine as anyone can be in this world."

"I'm sorry for what Angela said out there," Delta commented. "And she's sorry too."

"I'm sure she is. It just gets under my skin when people assume they know what other people are going through."

"The other day, when you were beating yourself up about not recognizing what was going on with Jim, it was because of your past. You've been where he was."

Eve's forced smile retreated somewhat. "Yes. I know that our circumstances were completely different, but I still feel that I can recognize the signs more than most."

"Do you mind if I ask—" JJ spoke hesitantly. "—I mean if it's not too painful—"

"Let me guess. You want to know why I tried to kill myself? Or maybe how. It's usually fifty-fifty when people find out," Eve said.

"Why would you mention something like that?" I asked in a huff, staring at JJ.

JJ looked hurt and confused. "I don't know. I'm out of my depth here. I feel like I should be walking on eggshells around Eve now."

"Please don't feel that way," Eve said. "I'm as mentally and emotionally strong as anyone else now. And although it is a raw subject, I feel like I owe you the truth. I really, really like you and I want us to be friends, not just two girls forced to be roommates."

JJ smiled brightly. "I'm not too much of a ditz for you?"

"Don't call yourself that and stop selling yourself short."

JJ lowered her gaze. "I'm not the one saying it."

"Then maybe you should take Talia's advice," I interjected. "Monday night she said to try different peer groups to find the right fit. If the people you're spending time with treat you that way, maybe it's time for a change?"

"You'd be more than welcome to hang with us," Delta said, which surprised me. She and JJ never really clicked and thinking about that now, I think I suspected why. Could it be that when the two party-girls looked at each other, they saw themselves, and they didn't like what they were seeing? Or, was it possible they saw one another as competition?

"Thanks, I appreciate that. But how did this therapy session get focused on me anyway? We're here to make Eve feel better."

The three of us chuckled.

When things grew still again, Eve started talking.

"When I was sixteen, I was messed up. Royally. On the outside I worked really hard to appear like everyone else, you know, playing the part of the average American teenager. I was good at it too. I was always on time with my hair and makeup done. I participated in class and laughed at people's jokes. But it was a mirage. I had good grades in school, which made my parents happy, but little else. No friends, no social life, no hobbies. I take that back, I did have one hobby. My hobby was making sure nobody knew how empty I was on the inside."

I had no reason to doubt the truthfulness of what Eve was telling us, but a part of me had a hard time reconciling how this attractive and intelligent young woman could have no friends. The boys should have been chasing her non-stop.

"I can see by the look on your face Cassie that you're having a hard time believing me. Let me clarify something for you. It's not that nobody wanted to be friends with me, or date me, because they did. It was me. I didn't want to be around them. And it wasn't a social anxiety thing like your boyfriend Taggart has. With me, I never felt like I deserved their attention, so I rejected it. Everyone my age assumed I was chasing a 4.0 GPA and all-consumed with schoolwork. And my parents were clueless, like everyone else."

"That sounds so lonely," JJ said.

"You have no idea. Just because it was self-imposed didn't make it any less painful either. And the twisted thing is, I began to enjoy that pain. You sort of become addicted to it because it's the known quantity. I would go to school functions like a dance or a big sport thing and just stand outside, watching everyone else enjoy themselves. Of course I was disgusted with myself, which only added to the pain. It was a vicious cycle."

"I can't even imagine," I said.

"No, and I wouldn't want you to. Even me telling you about it now doesn't properly describe what it felt like. Cassie, you lost your sister. Do you remember the pain you felt when that happened?"

The heartache erupted inside me as soon as the memory hijacked my brain. "I do."

"Take that pain you felt then and multiply it by a hundred. That's how bad you have to feel to consider taking your own life."

None of us spoke for a couple of seconds.

"And nobody knew what was going on with you?" Delta asked.

Eve's expression changed. Her eyelids drooped and forehead creased.

"There was one person," Eve said. "Her name was Theresa Battle. She was a grade ahead of me. I could tell she was in pain, and she could see the same in me. I don't know why, but somehow damaged people have a way of finding one another. Maybe we gravitate to people with similar issues because it helps us not feel like utter freaks."

"She was depressed, like you?"

Eve nodded. "We were both going through the same thing, in our own way. You know, I bet the person who came up with the phrase misery loves company – had never been miserable. You don't wish that shit on anybody. Anyway, we both decided that life had become unbearable, so we made a pact. A suicide pact. We would help each other end it all."

I noticed that Eve's eyes had glazed over, and she was staring straight ahead, unseeing. Her voice had become almost robotic, locked on one tone without the typical beats and rhythms.

"We debated back and forth about how we would do it. I wanted to use pills, but Theresa wanted us to hang ourselves. She said it would make more of a statement, as if killing ourselves wasn't enough. Finally I gave in and agreed. I got the rope from our garage and learned how to tie the correct knot, and Theresa stole pills from her mother that would help us relax. We picked a tree that was near a spot we would usually meet and selected a day. October thirteenth. But when that day came, it was raining. Neither of us wanted to go out of the world on a rainy day, so we decided to delay a week. On October twentieth, there wasn't a cloud in the sky, so right after school we walked together to the tree. I still remember the clothes we wore. We tied off our ropes and threw them over a big branch, swallowed the pills, slid the ropes around our necks, then climbed up the cheap wooden ladder we each had purchased from the hardware store. When we felt the pills starting to work we said goodbye, then stepped off the ladder."

Eve stopped talking. For the first time I noticed that tears had formed in her unfocused eyes.

"But something went wrong?" I prodded.

"Right… wrong… I guess it depends on your perspective. Our necks were supposed to break from the fall after stepping off the ladder, but that didn't happen. My rope was too far away from the base of the tree and the branch gave too much. We also didn't wait long enough for the pills to really take effect because I was able to fight like hell as I was choking, so much so that the branch ended up breaking. We miscalculated how much weight the branch would hold.

Some kids found us sometime after that and an ambulance rushed us to the hospital. I was in intensive care for two weeks with a crushed larynx and recovering from the effects of oxygen deprivation. Doctors said it was a miracle that I survived and didn't suffer any brain damage."

"But everything turned out okay?" JJ remarked.

Eve finally came out of her trance and looked at JJ. "Yes, for me. But Theresa wasn't so lucky. Her neck did break in the fall, and she died lying right there next to me."

I was speechless. To go through a traumatic experience like that, both physically and emotionally, was mind-numbing. But to also carry around the guilt of another person's death was incomprehensible.

Eve looked at each of us, one at a time, then started playing around with her blanket again.

"I was in a bad place. We both were. Afterwards, my parents got me help, an excellent therapist that I still see from time to time, but nowadays just to say hi and do a check-in. I came to grips with how wrong it was to do what I did, what we did, and I've made peace with the role I played in Theresa's death. It took me a long time to move on, but I haven't forgotten. I owe Theresa that much. I only hope that now that you know what happened, you won't see me as some kind of monster."

An uncomfortable silence settled in between all of us.

"I don't know what the right words to say are," JJ said to break the quiet. "Only that I don't think you're a monster. The opposite, actually. I can't imagine going through all of that and still being able to function. That's the stuff that nightmares are made of, or so I'm told because I don't think I've ever had one, which should give you a clue just how sheltered a life I've led. But not you, Eve. You've been to hell and back, and still here you are. You're one of the most put-together persons I've ever met, and for some reason you want to be friends with me. Whatever the farthest thing from monster there is… that's you."

After a couple moments of silence Delta said, "Those were some pretty good words, JJ."

Eve slipped off the bed and met JJ as she stood, embracing her tightly.

"Well, I know what we need to do next." My comment made the other girls look at me. "I heard the Hard Bean Café just came out with a Banana Fudge smoothie that's to die for. Sorry, poor choice of words. Anyway, I say we all head down there and get one."

Delta grinned. "I'm in."

"I'll even buy," JJ added, smiling now.

We all looked to Eve, who still had her arms around JJ. Her eyes were moist and her bottom lip was quivering.

I jumped off the bed. "That's settled, let's go."

Twelve
Thursday, July 18^{th,} 8:44 PM

Stepping through the entrance at The Hard Bean Café, it was apparent that a whole lot of people must have had the same idea we did. Every sofa and comfy chair was occupied. The glow from laptop screens and tablets being used created an odd techno atmosphere that contrasted sharply with the café's homestyle décor. Looking towards the dine-in area in the back, we could see that it was as packed.

The four of us just stood there, immobilized by indecision, when I heard somebody call Delta's name.

Turning around we encountered a girl I didn't recognize who must have been coming from the restroom. She was wearing a t-shirt emblazoned with Greek symbols, the same sorority Delta was a pledge of.

"Hey, Fran," Delta replied.

"Let me guess, you heard about their banana fudge smoothie and had to come check it out?" Fran asked.

"You know it," Delta said, glancing around the interior. "Although it looks like we might have to come back later."

"No, you don't. Our group is leaving, we'll let you have our spot," Fran said.

We waited as Fran and her friends vacated their table, thanking them as they moved past us. Everybody gave their orders to JJ and the rest of us claimed the newly opened space.

"Looks like a lot of people had the same idea we did." Delta slid into her chair.

Taking my seat, I noticed that despite the café overflowing with people, the noise level remained subdued. I guess no one wanted to be alone with their thoughts given what had recently happened, so they flocked to a place like the Hard Bean to find comfort in the presence of others, but it wasn't your typical rowdy atmosphere.

"I know. Truman ought to open their own café at the student center. They're missing out on a lot of business," I said.

"I don't know, I think I'd still come here," Eve said. "I like getting away from campus now and then, just to recharge my batteries."

"Good point. Me too," Delta said.

"Jim had a good idea, moving our meetings here," Eve said.

The three of us fell silent. I glanced over at our group's regular table in the corner, imagining Jim sitting there with a smile on his face. Knowing now what he had been doing with Taggart's papers painted all of my memories of him in a different light. I'd admonished Brent the night we found Jim's body for calling him 'sketchy', but the truth was, I felt the same way (though I would never say so out loud) and it had since been proven true. Were his actions that of an unstable mind, or just a misguided one?

"It's all so surreal. First Jim, now Lisa," I said.

"What was Lisa like?" Delta asked. She had never met our deceased group member.

"She was quiet. Introverted. But really nice when you got her to talk." I allowed myself to internally pout as I thought about how I let another opportunity to connect with someone slip by due to my insane schedule.

"She could have been pretty, but she was so darn thin," Eve added. "I wondered if she suffered from an eating disorder."

"I thought the same thing," I said.

"You remember Julie Glick?" Delta asked me. "She was in our biology class at New Haven last year. She's a senior this year."

"Vaguely."

"Sure, you remember her. We always thought she had bulimia or something because she was so thin."

Then I did remember her, or more accurately, I recalled how some of our classmates made sport of her thin appearance. It wasn't something I enjoyed being reminded of because of the way I'd turned a blind eye to the way she was teased. Thinking back on it now, I wished I could go back in time and say or do something.

"Oh, yeah," I said.

"Turns out, she had diabetes."

Now I felt like an even bigger failure than before. All I could do was take solace in the fact that I would never let that happen now. Somewhere along the line I grew a backbone, and wishing it had happened sooner wouldn't do me any good.

JJ arrived with our orders and, after passing them around, took a seat. "What are we talking about?"

"Well, we kind of took a detour, but we were talking about Lisa," Eve answered.

"She was nice," JJ said before putting her lips on the straw extending from her drink.

After a deep pull from my drink, I was engulfed by a rapture of glorious sweetness.

"Oh.My.God. This is sooooo good. Almost orgasmic," Delta so eloquently stated what I was already thinking.

"I felt that shoot straight to my hips," Eve joked.

JJ shook her head. "I don't care."

"They must lace this with cocaine or something. It's too good."

"Lisa should have ordered one of these Monday. It might have changed her mind," JJ said.

I forgot about the decadence in my plastic cup and stared at JJ. I saw that the others were doing the same.

"Too soon?" JJ asked, offering a weak smile.

"Too soon," Eve said, then attacked her straw again.

"Hey, ladies," a male voice came from behind me. I turned to see Brent emerging from a crowd of people.

"Hey, Brent," JJ was quick to respond with a smile.

Brent took up a position standing to my right, between Delta and me. I watched as he nodded at Eve, but then quickly turned his attention to me.

"Our minds must be on the same wavelength," he said.

"No doubt," I said.

"What's everybody drinking?"

"Their new banana fudge smoothie."

"Is it any good?" he asked.

"Delta said it's orgasmic," JJ said with a sly smile.

"Almost orgasmic," Delta corrected.

Brent's eyebrows rose. "Sounds like I need to get me one of those. Mind if I join you?"

"Sure," JJ said before anyone else had a chance to object.

"I'll be right back." Brent headed towards the ordering line.

It irked me that JJ had invited Brent to sit with us. It derailed the whole reason I'd suggested coming here in the first place—showing Eve that her past had no bearing on our friendship. But nixing the invitation for Brent to join us now would be awkward and might even make Eve uncomfortable.

JJ borrowed a chair from another table and set it between herself and Eve. When Brent returned with his drink he paused momentarily when he saw how JJ had arranged the chairs, then went ahead and sat down.

We all watched him with anticipation as he took his first sip.

"Well, what do you think?" JJ asked.

Brent considered his response. "I guess Delta and I have different definitions of orgasmic."

Everyone around the table burst into laughter.

"I'm pretty sure we differ on a lot of things," Delta observed after the hilarity died down.

Although Delta and I had never talked about it, I'm pretty sure she picked up on Brent's subtle interest in me and she was none too happy about it. She could be intensely protective of her friends.

"I'm glad to see that everyone's mood has improved from earlier. It got pretty heavy there."

The levity around the table disappeared like the ocean receding at low-tide.

"Nothing that a good talk couldn't cure," I said, wishing more than ever that JJ hadn't invited Brent to join them. The sour expression on JJ's face made me think that she was of the same opinion.

"So you girls came here to blow off some steam?"

"The banana fudge smoothie isn't reason enough?" Eve asked.

Brent placed his drink on the table. He had taken only the one sip.

"I guess. But if you're really interested in blowing off some steam, there's a club over on Revere Street that's pretty rocking," Brent said, looking directly at me. "It's ladies' night too."

"That sounds like fun," said JJ eagerly.

"I'll pass. This is as strong of a drink as I want tonight," I said.

"I'll second that," Delta said.

"I'll third it," Eve said, then added. "Don't you think it's a little insensitive going out to party after finding out someone we knew took their own life today?"

Brent was unfazed. "What do you call this? Anyway, it was only a thought. Life goes on, as does school, and you have to find a way to release that pressure. What does everyone do to vent?"

"I read," Eve answered. "I'm a big Diana Gabaldon fan. I've read her Outlander series several times."

"Between school and my sorority, I don't have time for much else," JJ said. "But I'm open to anything."

"I'm in a sorority also, but when I get time, I like to write short stories," Delta said.

"Really?" Eve said. "What kind?"

"Mostly fantasy – and a little romance."

Brent looked at me, waiting for my answer.

"I run."

"That's right. You mentioned that this afternoon. We were going to see about running together sometime."

I had hoped he might have forgotten about that. "I like to run early in the morning."

"How early?"

"I'm there when the FLEX opens."

"That is early. Oh, what the hell, I can give up some sleep. How about tomorrow morning?"

I was getting uncomfortable the way Brent was making the conversation about just him and me.

"No offense, but I enjoy running by myself. It helps clear my mind."

"I get it. I'm like that too. We can both run by ourselves, at the same time."

"Dude, can't you take a hint?" Delta blurted out. "She wants to run alone."

I could tell I was fighting a losing battle with Brent's persistence. Maybe it would be easier if we did run a couple of times, and then he'd get tired of me ignoring him.

"It's fine, Delta. I'll see you in the morning, Brent."

Delta crossed her arms across her chest and sat back in her chair.

"I'm going back to the dorm," JJ announced, standing up in a huff. "Anyone want to walk back with me?"

"I'll come," Eve replied. "Thanks for suggesting this, Cassie."

"We need to do it more often. Be careful going back."

As I watched my two suitemates depart, they ran into Taggart coming in through the door right as they were about to leave. I watched them exchange pleasantries, Eve pointed in our direction, then Taggart made his way towards us.

"Hey, Taggart," Delta said when he sat down in the chair next to me. "How did you know we'd be here?"

"Cassie left a note on the door," he explained.

All of the suites in Barksdale had a dry-erase board hanging on the outside of their door. A low-tech way of leaving messages for one another. Thinking about that now,

I wondered if that was why Brent coincidentally showed up when he did.

Turning towards our other tablemate, Taggart said, "Brent."

"Taggart."

"Cassie just made a date with Brent to go running together in the morning," Delta stated flatly, which drew a death-stare from me.

Taggart's face was unreadable as he looked at me, then at Brent.

"Okay."

"Okay?" I replied. I felt heat rising on the back of my neck. "That's it? Just okay?"

"I can't fault the logic. Running in pairs, given your recent scare, seems prudent."

I was furious, and when I get that mad, I say things I later regret, which is why I stood up.

"I'm leaving," I stated, then looked at Delta. "You coming with me?"

"Sure," she said, snatching her phone off the table.

Taggart looked confused. "I was going to inform you of what I found in Lisa's room."

"Tell Brent," I shot back at him. "I'm sure he'll be happy to hear all about it."

I stormed off with Brent yelling after us, "See you in the morning."

Thirteen
Tuesday, July 23rd 5:50 AM

It had been four days since Taggart pissed me off, and just as long since I had spoken with him. He repeatedly tried to see me at the dorm, but I refused to go to the door. He showed up outside my classes, and I just walked by him. He popped up at the food court and I left as soon as he sat down, sometimes leaving a full plate of food behind.

Let him feel what it's like to be ignored.

If I'm being honest with myself, the first couple of days was because I was still angry for the way he'd acted—or didn't act—when he heard Brent wanted to run with me. After that I couldn't face him because of the way that I acted.

I was ashamed, pure and simple. I had allowed my immaturity, my irrational emotions, to take over and it caused me to blow up and act like a spoiled child. The fuse had truly been lit when we arrived at Truman and he started spending less and less time with me, and it finally went off when he didn't blink when hearing Brent was becoming my running buddy. Sometimes, anger and rational thinking seem like foreign concepts to each other, at least in my experience. Once the anger bled away, which I'm embarrassed to admit took two full days, it was replaced by cold hard logic, and I finally realized I was expecting something from Taggart I had no right to. On some level, I wanted him to be jealous of another boy, and that's just not the way he was wired.

I also realized something that Delta had been trying to tell me all along, but I just couldn't see it. I have a long history of struggling with impatience, something else I'm not proud of, but what Delta was trying to tell me was that I needed to give Taggart time to adjust to this new life at Truman. But she had it backwards. I was the one who needed to change, just as much as Taggart, and I wasn't being patient enough.

This was on me.

On a good note, the whole thing with Brent turned out better than I hoped. He showed up that Friday morning as promised, and other than saying good morning to each other, I paid no attention to him at all. I was a much better runner than he was, and he couldn't keep up with my pace, which made it even easier to ignore him. He quit before I did but was waiting in the lobby when I came out of the locker room. To avoid him I ducked back behind the check-in desk and struck up a conversation with Debbie, the morning manager, discussing the upcoming schedule. I rambled on until finally Brent gave up and left.

When I showed up for my run yesterday morning, Brent was nowhere to be seen. At our group meeting last night—which was even more somber than the week before—he didn't say a word to me or even look in my direction once.

Mission accomplished.

The sun started to peek over the horizon when I rounded the corner on my way to the FLEX. It struck me that the morning pause, that limbo time between waking up and eventually crawling out of bed, seemed to match the mood of the entire campus these past two days. The pause was a time when you would just lay in bed and contemplate the day ahead until something prompted you to get moving. That's what everybody seemed to be doing now, milling around, waiting for some kind of sign that it was time to return to normal. It was as if the two deaths had put the campus on pause.

Of course, given my present state of mind, that could just be a depressed way of looking at things.

I walked past the edge of head-high bushes outlining the front of the FLEX and I could feel the anticipation building within me. My morning runs had turned into much more than a way to get exercise, they'd become almost therapeutic. So much so that I'd begun extending how long I'd spend circling the track, soaking up the blissful exhaustion that held my troubled thoughts at bay.

Once I cleared the bushes, I noticed someone standing by the front entrance. It was Taggart. I shouldn't have been surprised because this was the one place he hadn't turned up yet. I almost gave in to my impulse to turn around, but I didn't.

It was time to face the piper.

As I approached, Taggart spoke first. "It's not open yet."

"I know. Six o'clock. Promptness isn't one of the morning managers' strong points."

We just stood there, neither saying anything. Taggart was wearing his same ole clothes. His cargo pants, the solid black hoodie. There was a time I was bothered by his lack of variety in the way he dressed, but this morning I found it oddly comforting.

"I think—"

"No, let me talk first, okay?" I interjected.

Taggart nodded his head.

"I am SO sorry. Sorry for the way I acted the other day, for the way I've acted since then, and basically for the way I've been acting since we arrived here at Truman. I've been wallowing in my own self-pity about not seeing you enough, worrying that you're drifting away from me, and I haven't been considering how new and different this is for you. I've not been patient enough, and I took it out on you. That's not right, and I'm very sorry. I've been avoiding you for the last couple of days because I was too ashamed to tell you that."

Taggart smiled, but I could tell it was half-hearted.

"I accept your apology—" Taggart said softly. "—though I need to apologize as well. I assumed you understood that even though our time together here at Truman has been limited, that my feelings for you have remained unchanged. In fact—"

"I did know—"

Taggart held up his index finger and I fell silent.

"In fact, my feelings have grown exponentially. Every conversation with one of my professors, every debate I've undertaken with other faculty members, every shred of knowledge I've absorbed while I've been here at Truman, has been because of you. You showed me how to relate to the world, a gift that I didn't know I needed. So whenever we're apart and I'm doing what you've enabled me to do, I am thinking of you. But I've come to realize that isn't enough. My assumption that you understood things between us remained unchanged was incorrect. I worried about how you were doing academically, because I knew how important that was to you, but I failed to consider your feelings. I am sorry for not doing a better job of communicating my own feelings to you."

Tears were flowing down my cheeks. "Taggart, you didn't do anything wrong."

"Untrue. I did something that under the correct circumstances can prove invaluable, but when it comes to emotions and understanding what others are feeling, it is a gross error in judgment. I assumed. Assuming should be listed among the top five reasons civilization will one day crumble. The semi-raunchy urban definition that states assuming will make an ass out of you and me, is surprisingly, paradoxically, accurate. I will refrain from doing it with you from now on."

Just then, Debbie, the FLEX's morning manager, rounded the hedges. She was flipping through a bunch of keys on a ring when she looked up and saw the two of us standing there. A look of concern appeared on her face when she noticed the tears in my eyes.

"Do I need to call campus security?"

I half-laughed and wiped my eyes. "Good morning, Debbie. No need, we're good."

"Morning to you, Cassie," Debbie said, giving Taggart a wary eye. She slid her key into the deadbolt. "You know you should be the one opening up since you're always here so early."

"Then I wouldn't be able to run."

We followed Debbie into the dark FLEX lobby and waited while she disappeared into the back office. A couple of seconds later, the lights flickered to life.

"Give me a couple of minutes to get everything fired up," Debbie said as she reappeared and headed towards the still unlit exercise area.

Taggart and I found ourselves standing there alone, again.

"Will Brent be making an appearance?" he asked.

"No, I think he finally lost interest in me."

Taggart frowned. "That's unfortunate. I don't like you running alone."

I reached behind me and picked up my right foot to start stretching. "I haven't seen anybody strange in days, and this is a secure facility. I'm okay."

"I'm not so sure. I now think that both Jim and Lisa's deaths were definitely not suicide."

I dropped my foot. "What?"

"Since we haven't spoken, I wasn't able to tell you what I ascertained in Lisa's room. While her roommates were asleep she supposedly tied a speaker wire to the outside knob of her door, looped it over the top, then tied it around her neck while standing on a chair. She kicked away the chair and then choked to death."

"That's awful. What about that makes you suspicious?"

"The door remained partially open. If she did as they say, the door should have been completely shut. I suspect it was open because somebody needed to let themselves out afterward and they failed to close it behind them."

I thought about it for a second. "Maybe Lisa couldn't close the door because the wire draped over the top was too thick?"

Taggart shook his head. "I checked. The door can close that way. But there is something else. A note was found on Lisa's laptop."

"What did it say?"

"It was typed on a blank word document. Anyone could have put it there. It read simply - *It's all too much*."

I let that sink in for a moment. "It still doesn't mean—"

A bloodcurdling scream chilled me to the bone, coming from somewhere inside the FLEX. Taggart immediately sped off down the hallway, with me close behind. A second scream directed us towards the door leading to the basketball courts. When we burst inside, I almost ran into Taggart's backside when he came to a complete halt.

Debbie was on the other side of the court where the main light panel was, her face buried in her hands.

The object of her distress was a body hanging from the railing bordering the upper-level track.

It was Brent Rosen.

Fourteen
Tuesday, July 23rd 7:05 AM

I remembered studying the symptoms of shock in health class back at New Haven High. We even had a pop quiz on the topic. That type of stuff fascinated me, so much so that I briefly considered going into the medical field. Cold and clammy skin, a bluish tinge to lips or fingernails, rapid pulse and breathing, nausea, enlarged pupils, and weakness or fatigue. I'd nailed the pop quiz, but as I was quickly finding out, recognizing that you were the one experiencing shock was an entirely different matter.

Taggart noticed it first. He had taken my phone to call 911 while I stood there staring at the body. Brent was wearing a Radiohead t-shirt, jeans, Nike running shoes, and a pair of brightly colored socks. The socks stuck out in my mind because one of Brent's shoes had slipped off his foot—exposing the sock—and was lying on the court beneath him. When Taggart tried to return my phone I vaguely remember him saying something about shock. He ushered me back to the front of the building, sat me on a bench in the lobby, then covered me with towels. I'm not sure where the towels came from, nor did I really care.

I felt light-headed for a while and time passed in odd spurts. I remember seeing Taggart escorting Debbie, having her sit next to me. I remember blue, flashing lights. Then a man in uniform, campus police I think, bending down in front of Debbie and me to say something. I don't recall what he said. More people arrived, shuffling back and forth. At some point, I noticed that Debbie was no longer sitting next to me.

I didn't start feeling like myself again until Taggart sat down next to me and took my hand.

"How are you feeling?" Taggart asked when he noticed me looking around.

"Better, but now I feel stupid."

Why I suffered from shock after finding Brent, and not Jim, I couldn't explain. Maybe it was because I knew Brent better? I was around him more. Or perhaps it was the circumstances of how we found him, or where he was found? I hadn't had breakfast yet, so maybe that was a factor. I didn't really know. Why the brain acts the way it does is a complete mystery to me.

"Where'd Debbie go?" I asked.

"Detective Moss is here. He took her into the back office for questioning," he answered. "I imagine we'll be next."

There was a police officer stationed just outside the entrance, and beyond him I could see an ambulance in the parking lot with its rear doors open.

"Do you feel well enough to answer a few questions?" Taggart asked.

"I don't think the police will really give me a choice, will they?"

"I mean from me."

I looked into his probing eyes. "Okay."

"How could someone gain access to this building after hours?"

I thought about his question for a second. "The main door is dead-bolted. We both watched Debbie open that, so nobody came in that way unless they had a key. There are two other emergency doors to the outside, push doors that don't open from the outside, and they have alarms on them. I guess if you knew how to disable the alarm and prevented the door from locking in place, you could get in that way."

"How thorough is the staff about ensuring the facility is empty at night?"

"You mean if somebody wanted to hide out and purposely get locked inside?"

Taggart nodded.

"I've only closed a couple of times, but from what I witnessed, yeah, it could happen."

Taggart seemed to be considering this.

"Taggart, what's going on?"

"I'm not sure."

"Do you think somebody did this?" I asked.

"It's a distinct possibility," he replied.

"But who? And why would—" I paused as I suddenly remembered something. "That text warning we received about your sister. Do you think it could be her?"

"I have a hard time believing a woman could have staged these deaths, but on the other hand, we do not know her physical attributes, nor do we know if she's working alone. What baffles me, if it is indeed her, what is the reasoning."

"Isn't it obvious? Payback for killing her mother."

"On the surface that seems reasonable, but it's not logical. Why not come after me directly? Why did these three people have to die? Also, why stage them to look like suicides?"

"Logic has very little to do with how people act sometimes, especially if she's anything like your mother. Maybe she's punishing you by killing the people you know?"

"I don't know these people. You and Delta are the only two people I care about."

"But how could she know that? Think about it, the only people you've talked to here at Truman have been various faculty members and the gang from our orientation group. If she has been watching you—"

The realization sent shivers down my spine.

"What is it?" Taggart asked.

"The person who followed me after my run that day. I bet it was her."

Taggart squeezed my hand. "Do not worry. You'll not go anywhere alone, and when one of your roommates cannot be with you, I'll be there."

"You cannot skip classes just to watch out for me."

"Yes, I can."

I knew that was true. Attending classes was nothing more than a formality for Taggart. He could do well in his courses by just reading the textbooks. But Taggart knew that the instructors often included questions on their exams based on material they only discussed in class, as a way to encourage attendance, so that was the only way to guarantee a perfect score.

"Fine, but we have to tell detective Moss so he can warn everyone else in the group. If we're right and they're being targeted, they have a right to know."

"We can warn the others, but telling the detective our suspicions would be a waste of time."

"Why?"

"Because I'm confident when it comes our turn to talk to the detective, he will be intent on placing the blame for these deaths on me."

"That's crazy."

"Indeed, but I fear we are victims of the detective's lack of imagination. Furthermore, there is no proof my sister is behind all of this."

"We have the text message."

"First, the text was from a blocked number and could have come from anywhere. We could have sent it to ourselves. Secondly, are you sure you still have the text?"

"I didn't delete it."

"Check."

I fumbled with my phone, scrolling through my received texts.

"It's not here. How can it not be here?"

"Your phone was probably hacked, and the message removed shortly after it was received."

I tried to think if there was a time that I'd left my phone unattended since receiving the text, and I couldn't. Then I thought about how Taggart had used my phone to call 911 after we found Brent. Could he have deleted the text? But why would he do that?

"Mentioning my sister to the detective now will seem like a desperate attempt to direct his investigation away from me. I think it's best we keep that to ourselves for now. And on that subject, might I also offer a piece of advice?"

"Always."

"When we talk to the detective, be truthful, but do not present information he doesn't specifically inquire after."

I opened my mouth to say something when the detective and Debbie appeared from the back office. Debbie gave Taggart and me a nervous glance as Moss escorted her out of the front door. When he returned, he placed his hands on his hips.

"This is becoming all too familiar," the detective said.

Instead of responding, Taggart looked at me and tilted his head slightly. If I could read minds, I'm sure his would be saying, "I told you so."

"Follow me," the detective said, then moved towards the back office.

I shrugged the towels off my shoulders and walked with Taggart, hand-in-hand, trailing several steps behind the detective.

Inside the small office we were told to take a seat, which we did. The detective closed the door and then leaned his back against it.

"I understand you work here, Miss Underwood?"

"In the afternoons."

"Your co-worker tells me you jog on the track here every morning at this time, although that's a fairly recent habit."

"I used to run on the trails but switched to the indoor track instead."

"Any particular reason for the change?"

"It's been raining a lot lately." The statement itself wasn't a lie, just not the reason for the change.

"Why were you here this morning, Mr. McGill?"

"I needed to discuss something with Cassie."

"At six o'clock in the morning?"

"She keeps a rigid schedule. I knew she would be here."

"What did you need to discuss with her at that time in the morning?"

"That's private."

"Is that so? Miss Underwood?"

"Like he said, it's between the two of us and no concern of yours."

"You'd be surprised what concerns me. During our first encounter, you described Miss Underwood to me as an acquaintance. According to people I've talked to since then, I understand the two of you are more than that."

I remembered Taggart's advice about not offering facts the detective didn't ask about, so I remained silent. When neither of us responded, the detective folded his arms across his chest.

"Our victim… I'm sorry, our latest victim was here last week, and according to Debbie, she had the distinct impression he was—and these are her words—sniffing around Miss Underwood. Were you aware of that?"

"I had knowledge that the two of them would be running together, yes," Taggart answered flatly.

"I'm curious Taggart, how did it make you feel knowing that Brent was interested in your girlfriend?"

"My interpretation of their encounter was the two of them ran at the same time, but separately, and that was all. Brent may have been interested in developing a relationship with Cassie, but it was unreciprocated. Also, I'd prefer it if you'd address me as Mr. McGill, detective."

The detective dropped his arms and began pacing back and forth in front of us, a scowl on his face.

"Where were you last night, MR. MCGILL, from six p.m. on?"

"In my apartment."

"Alone?"

"Yes."

"And how about the night of the seventeenth? Last Wednesday?"

"The same."

The detective came to a halt in front of Taggart.

"I have three suspicious deaths, and all three of the victims had some sort of issue with you. Can you see how that might be a problem for me?"

"I can, considering your limited intellect, narrow focus, and inability to conceptualize."

The detective balled his fist and took a step in Taggart's direction. "You smug little—"

I shot to my feet and placed myself between the two of them. "I think all he's saying is that maybe you're jumping to conclusions."

"Detective, can you tell me what makes these deaths suspicious to you?" Taggart asked.

That seemed to take the detective by surprise. He stepped to the side so he could look around me at Taggart. "What?"

"I asked what is it about the deaths that make them suspicious?"

The detective regarded Taggart for a moment before finally answering. "First off, the people who knew them hadn't noticed any suicidal tendencies. You said so yourself about Jim Book."

"You've only just found Brent," I interjected. "How many people could you have spoken to about him?"

"Sure, I've only spoken with your co-worker so far, but I have a feeling that I'll be hearing the same thing from others. Do you deny you didn't feel the same way?"

"No, it's true, I didn't think Brent was suicidal," I answered honestly. "But not everybody gives off signals."

"Is that the only reason you classify them as suspicious? Is there any physical evidence that suggests anything but suicide?" Taggart continued.

"No. Brent Rosen's ID was scanned into the building last night. It's plausible he could have hidden until everybody had left to do what he did. But why end his life here?"

"He had a roommate. Maybe he needed a place he could be alone?" I suggested.

"True, but anybody could have scanned his ID last night when the desk was unattended. Even your boyfriend. Then his body could have been brought in later and staged."

"Even if we played out this fantasy and said Taggart did kill Brent, why would he do it here?"

"Maybe he was sending you a message, Miss Underwood."

"That is so far beyond nuts. Were there any signs of a break-in?"

"No, but that doesn't mean anything."

It was Taggart's turn to stand. "Detective. It is my opinion that the only thing you find suspicious about these deaths is my so-called relationship with the three victims, that along with your clear dislike of me. Sometimes a coincidence is just that, detective, a coincidence."

"Hardly ever in my business. That first night you tried to convince me it wasn't a suicide, now you're saying they are?"

"You've not been listening, detective. What I'm saying is that on one level, your instincts are correct. These are not suicides. Still, you are letting yourself adopt a pedestrian, and certainly predictable, investigative approach, one that has you mistakenly pointing the finger at me. Frankly, I could care less about your accusations, as you'll clearly be unable to prove something that did not take place; however, your misdirected attention could place somebody else at risk. Your efforts would be better rewarded by focusing your attention elsewhere. Now, if there's nothing further, we'll be going."

Taggart put his hand on the small of my back and guided me towards the door. I didn't let out the breath I was holding until the FLEX entrance doors swung shut behind us.

Fifteen
Tuesday, July 23rd 10:15 AM

I'd blown Brent off as an irritating distraction—and now he was dead.

All morning that thought kept buzzing around my head, like a bumblebee hopping from flower to flower. Except in this case, instead of collecting a life-sustaining substance when the bee landed, it would plunge its stinger deep into my brain and release a wave of regret. When I finally allowed myself to really think about who it was we'd found that morning, that's when the guilt crept in. A large part of me wanted to believe what Taggart was saying, that Brent's death was not suicide and someone—or several someone's—were responsible for stealing his life. If that was true, then Taggart's insistence that the proper response should be anger, not sorrow, was right. My pent-up emotions needed to be directed somewhere, because someone needed to pay. I managed to hold onto that train of thought—most of the time—but every now and then a tiny sliver of doubt snuck in. I wondered if Taggart could be wrong, that Brent had been depressed and chasing after me was really a cry for attention. And even if the chance of that being true was small, minuscule even, it meant my last interaction with a troubled soul was to basically treat him like shit.

God damn bee!

After we'd left the FLEX, Taggart and I had walked back to my dorm in silence. At the entrance he'd said, "Get dressed, then instruct your roommates they need to accompany us to the student center. Don't tell them what's going on, but don't take no for an answer."

I looked at the time on my phone. "Eve might already have left for class."

"Then send her a text instructing her to leave class and meet us at the Hideaway. Impart upon her the gravity of the request."

"Why the Hideaway?"

"You received quite a shock this morning and need food to help you recover. Also, we'll be asking the other members of your orientation group to join us as well. As they also may be in class, the student center is more centrally located and better suited for our purpose."

After that, I did as Taggart instructed. Delta and JJ were still asleep—big shock there—and less than enthusiastic about surrendering their beds for a trip to the student center. But when Delta saw how serious I was, she eventually got on-board and helped me wrangle JJ. We all got dressed and right before leaving the room, I sent a group text to everyone in our orientation group that read:

Emergency Meeting at the Hideaway RIGHT NOW! This is NO SHIT! Get up and walk out of your class and get to the Hideaway ASAP.

When the four of us arrived at the student center, Taggart bought me a bagel and a cup of coffee at the food court, despite my objections that I wasn't hungry. It turns out

I actually was, and I devoured the bagel in three bites and gulped down the coffee.

That was just over thirty minutes ago and still no one else had shown up. I was on my third cup, and the jittery sensation I was starting to feel told me it needed to be my last. Looking around the Hideaway, which was a pseudo-lounge area located between the food court and the bookstore in the student center, I tried to gauge everyone's temperament. They all looked as jumpy as I felt—except for Taggart of course.

"I can't believe you yanked me out of bed for this," JJ said. She was spread out flat on her back on one of the couches in the Hideaway.

The spacious room was designed for the students—and faculty—to relax and escape to between classes. For that purpose it was furnished with loads of comfortable chairs and sofas. Sunlight from the outside bathed half the room, leaving the other half shaded, but there were plenty of lamps if needed. The four of us had settled in the farthest corner of the room away from the entrance, though at this time of morning no one else was in sight.

"At least tell us what the deal is," Delta said. She was sitting next to Taggart and me on a couch facing the one JJ was lying on.

"Let me see the text you sent," Taggart asked, ignoring Delta and holding out his hand.

I gave him my phone and watched him check my sent texts.

"That seems adequate, though I suggest you send another," he said when he handed my phone back to me.

I typed – THIS IS NO JOKE. COME TO THE HIDEAWAY ASAP!! LIFE OR DEATH!

I showed Taggart the text before sending it. He nodded his head, so I tapped send.

"Hello? You did hear me ask a question just now, right?" Delta said, clearly irritated.

I had just shoved my phone into my back pocket when Angela walked through the door.

"What's all the drama about?" Angela said before pausing to look at her phone. Her eyebrows shot up as she read. "Life or death? What the hell?"

JJ had the same look as she sat up, her eyes glued to her phone. "Cassie, what's going on?"

I briefly wondered if I might have gone a little overboard in my desire to get everyone to respond, but quickly squelched that worry. If Taggart was right, then everyone had a reason to be concerned.

"Take a seat, Angela. We need to wait until everybody else gets here before we start."

Through the glass walls encompassing the Hideaway, I spotted Eve as she ran into Tony in the hallway. They exchanged a few words before walking our way.

As Eve and Tony entered the Hideaway, Delta received a text.

"I'll be right back," she said as she bolted out of the room.

"What's going on, Cassie?" Tony asked.

"That's a popular question right now," JJ said.

"We're still missing Brandon. We need to give him a couple more minutes."

"Brent's not here yet either," Angela pointed out.

I kept my body turned away from the group so they couldn't see the pain in my face.

"He wasn't in our English class this morning," Tony said. "He might be sleeping in."

"Does this have anything to do with the commotion down at the FLEX center this morning?" Eve asked, slipping into a spot on the couch next to JJ.

"Guys, please—"

"I know everyone is curious," Taggart cut me off, "but it is important that everyone be present for this."

"Present for what?" JJ asked.

"Yeah, you're starting to scare me, Cassie," Angela said.

Delta reappeared at the door with a guest in tow.

"Chewy? What are you doing here?" I asked.

Delta and Chewy took up a spot near the end of the couches so they could see everyone seated on both.

"Are you kidding?" Chewy responded. "It's all over the news. I had this hunch that Taggart was involved somehow, and I had to come find out."

"What's all over the news, and who the hell is this guy?" Tony asked.

"This is Chewy. We went to school together in New Haven," I answered.

"What kind of name is Chewy?" JJ asked.

"It's a nickname. It's my favorite character in Star Wars."

"You shouldn't be here," Taggart said with an edge in his tone.

"What are they talking about being on the news?" Eve asked.

"We need to wait for Brandon before—"

"Screw that. Brandon's probably jerking off somewhere. I want to know what's going on NOW!" JJ said.

I looked at Taggart and we exchanged a silent acknowledgment.

"All of you will soon be receiving a mass text from the school informing you that another one of your classmates has committed suicide," Taggart said.

I'm not sure what kind of response I was expecting, but what we got was stunned silence. So much so that I started to wonder if they heard what Taggart had said.

"A third one?" Angela asked slowly.

"That's what's on the news," Chewy said. "Three suicides in less than two weeks will kinda make headlines."

"How do you two know about it already?" Tony demanded.

"Yeah, why are you telling us this and not the school?" JJ added.

I took a deep breath. "Because the classmate who is dead is Brent. Taggart and I found him."

Angela's hand flew to cover her open mouth. The color drained from Eve's face, but her eyes remained fixed on me.

"The three deaths are connected in some way?" Chewy asked.

"They're all part of the same freshman orientation group," Delta answered. "But that's not all, is it, Taggart? There has to be some other reason why you brought us all here, isn't there?"

Taggart didn't bat an eye. "It is my belief that these are not suicides, but in fact, murders. There is a good chance somebody is targeting the members of this group."

Chewy punched the air. "I knew something was up."

That's when everyone started talking at once. JJ leapt up from the couch and got right in Taggart's face.

"Why on earth would you think that Taggart? What are the police saying?" Eve asked, managing to talk over everyone else.

"They believe the same thing, kind of," I answered.

"Kind of the same thing?" Tony said.

"The detective on the case thinks these might be murders as well, but only because all three victims had an issue with Taggart. He's their number one suspect."

A subtle change appeared on Tony, JJ, and Angela's faces. It was a look I knew all too well because I'd witnessed it every time my parents questioned me when they thought I was hiding something from them.

"What kind of issues?" Tony asked.

"Jim stole a paper I had written in high school and submitted it as his own for a class here at Truman. Lisa voiced her displeasure about my attendance at your group meetings, and Brent was attempting to form a romantic attachment with Cassie."

"Those are pretty weak, as far as motives go," Chewy offered.

"Even I can see that. So, why do you think we're being targeted?" Angela asked.

"Wait a minute—" Delta interrupted. "I'm not even part of your group, so why am I here?"

Taggart gave Delta a half-smile. "I should amend my earlier statement. It appears the person responsible is targeting people that I have spent the most time with while here at Truman, which includes you."

"No offense, Taggart, but you're not even part of the group," Angela said.

"That is true, however, if the person responsible for these deaths has been observing me, then other than a few professors, you are the ones I have spent the most time around."

"So, who do you think is doing this?" Eve asked.

Taggart considered this for a moment. "I have my suspicions, but until I have more proof, I will keep that to myself. I also ask that you do not communicate this theory to anybody outside of this group until I have more evidence."

"But what do we do in the meantime? According to you, we're targets, right?" JJ asked.

"Simple logistics. No one goes anywhere or spends time in their rooms alone. No exceptions."

"That's going to be a problem for me," Tony said.

"Why?" Taggart asked.

"I'm in a single room. No roommates or suitemates."

"Can you stay with someone, or have someone stay with you until this is resolved?"

"I probably could, but I won't. I value my privacy."

"More than your life?" I asked bluntly.

That gave Tony pause. "Almost as much. Don't worry, I'll be careful."

Taggart shrugged his shoulders. "Of course, I cannot force you to follow these recommendations, only warn you of the potential consequences."

"Consider me warned."

"I'm going to have a problem too," Angela stated. "My classes are in the south part of campus and none of my roommates go anywhere near there. How will I get to class?"

"I can help," Chewy said, raising his hand. "I can be an escort for whoever needs it."

"You'd do that?" I asked.

"Sure. All I'm doing during the day is playing video games and trolling Instagram anyway. It'll be kinda cool to be a bodyguard."

"What about your mom? Doesn't she need you," I said.

"She doesn't have another treatment until next week, and right now we're really getting on each other's nerves."

"Who are you?" a new voice said from right inside the door. Everyone turned around to find our orientation group leader—Talia Davis—leaning against the door with her arms crossed. I didn't hear her come in, nor did I know how long she had been standing there.

Chewy looked embarrassed. "I'm friends with Taggart, Cassie, and Delta."

"Are you a student here?"

"He's just visiting," Delta answered.

Talia regarded him for a few seconds more before turning her attention to Taggart.

"We've not been officially introduced. You must be Taggart McGill? I'm Talia Davis, this group's leader. I believe I saw you at the dorm meeting last week."

"I am, and you did."

Talia turned her attention to me. "What was the meaning behind those texts, Cassie? Pretty dramatic stuff."

"How did you know about those?"

"I guess you forgot you added me to your group contact list at our last meeting."

She's right, I did forget. Now I was left scrambling to think of an excuse to explain the messages. As they say, the best lies contain a bit of truth in them.

"Have you heard about Brent?" I asked.

Talia's face softened and she dropped her arms. "I have. In fact, I was in a meeting about that when I received your texts."

"I just felt that everyone should hear about it from Taggart and me instead of a group text from the school. That's all."

"That's commendable, but life or death? Really?"

"I admit that was overdramatic, but I was getting impatient, and nobody was showing up. I thought the school text would come at any time."

Talia stepped further into the room and stood beside the chair where Eve sat.

"I understand completely. Now that everyone's here, I think we should talk about Brent's death and how you feel about it."

The sound of beating feet proceeded Brandon bursting into the room, gasping for air.

"Thank god, you guys are still here," he said, struggling to catch his breath. "My phone died, and I didn't have my charger. What's up?"

"I'm afraid there's been another suicide," Talia said.

Brandon leaned over and placed his hands on his knees. "I've heard about that already."

"You heard it on the news?" I asked.

"No, it's all anybody was talking about in my first class this morning. Apparently, whoever the girl was, she left the water running and because it was a second story off-campus apartment, the water overflowed into the apartment below. They found her when they broke in to stop the water."

"Brandon, what are you talking about?" Eve asked.

"The suicide. The girl slit her wrists in her bathtub."

Sixteen

Tuesday, July 23rd 3:00 PM

Lockdown.

Truman was calling it a suspension of classes for the day due to, in their words, the unfathomable tragedy that has descended upon the school. They informed us that the administration strongly suggested all students living on campus return to their dorms and stay there for the remainder of the day. Campus services such as the library, FLEX, and the student center were being suspended. Movement around the school grounds—though not strictly prohibited—was discouraged.

In high school, we called this what it was. A lockdown. I called it something else—a mistake.

"CNN pulled up," Delta announced. From our room's window we could see the administration offices, and that was the only place on campus with any sort of activity today. "All of the major news services have vans here now."

After Brandon surprised us with the information of a fourth apparent suicide, which caught Talia off-guard as well, we were all instructed to return to our dorms and wait for a communication from the school. Since Angela lived in a different hall than the rest of us, Chewy volunteered to escort her back, wait for her roommate to arrive, then come back to our suite. The rest of us came straight back to Barksdale, but as soon as we arrived Tony broke off and headed to his own room.

"You really shouldn't be by yourself, Tony," I called after him.

He swung around and continued walking backward. "I'll be fine. Call me if anything significant comes up."

After I watched him disappear around a curve in the hall, I looked at everyone else.

"If this were a movie, he would have the words victim number five stenciled on the back of his shirt," Brandon commented.

"That's not funny, Brandon," Eve said.

"Would it be funnier if I said it was a Netflix movie?"

Delta chuckled until she caught the look I was giving her. "Don't encourage him. Come on, let's get back to the room."

Our room was where we remained for the rest of the day, watching the news coverage on every conceivable channel. The official communication from the school arrived at the same time Chewy did after escorting Angela. Unlike the first two emails, this one was short and direct to the point. Apart from relaying instructions about how the rest of the day would go, it contained the bare minimum of facts.

The name of the other suicide victim, the one other than Brent, was Pauline Rome. She was a second-year economics major from Arkansas who lived by herself in an off-campus apartment. Other than going to the same school as us, she had no connection with our orientation group or anyone associated with it.

The news on TV was much more revealing, but unfortunately, it was doing exactly what I felt shouldn't be happening—sensationalizing the suicides. Mini-biographies on all of the victims scrolled across the screen accompanied by commentator analysis, all of them searching for clues to explain the deaths. Almost every broadcast had its own subject matter expert on suicides, and the phrase suicide cluster was batted around like a new toy given to a box of kittens. Something that was noticeably absent, at least to us, was any talk from the police about a murder, instead of suicide.

The topic of the news broadcast would eventually turn to the school itself, dropping subtle hints about how Truman was somehow responsible for fostering an environment that could lead to what we were experiencing. After seeing how the media coverage was painting the school, I understood why they did what they did with the lockdown. It was damage control. They knew what was coming and they took steps to limit the exposure to the student population, and by extension, themselves.

Though I grasped the reasons behind the school's actions, and why they thought they were necessary, I disagreed with the focus. Right now I felt the school should be trying to quell the epidemic, if there was one, by identifying students at risk and getting them help. That was kind of hard to do when everybody was shut away in their rooms.

At some point during the day, everybody—except Taggart and me—received a concerned phone call from parents. Delta had just been contacted by her parents and was speaking to them using hush tones in the corner of the room away from everyone.

My phone call was delivered in person.

When the knock on our suite door came, I expected it to be Tony checking in, but instead I found my dad looking back at me when I pulled open the door, an awkward smile on his lips. He was dressed for work, shirt and tie with dark slacks and old school penny loafers.

"Dad? What are you doing here?" I asked, stunned.

"Waiting for a hug from my girl to start with," he said, holding out his arms. "—then maybe to be invited in."

Embarrassed, I embraced him and squeezed tightly. The smell of his aftershave reminded me just how much I missed home.

"And I'm pretty certain you know why I'm here," he said as we parted and stepped past me into the common room.

"Hi Mister Underwood," Delta said, standing in the door to our room.

"Hey, Delta. Have your parents called you yet?"

Delta nodded. "Yes sir. Just got off the phone with them. I'll let the two of you talk."

The way Delta abruptly closed the door gave me cause for concern. She and my dad got along great, so for her to cut things short like that told me something was up.

Dad took a seat on the couch and patted the spot next to him.

"What's going on?" I asked without moving.

"Sit down so we can talk," he replied.

Now I was really anxious. My dad was using his serious tone, which was usually reserved for the times I got into trouble, or he had to relay bad news.

"Listen… I know why you're here," I said as I took a seat next to him. "You and Mom have concerns."

"That we do."

"But why didn't you just call?"

"Because I wanted to see your face when we talked."

"You could have facetimed me."

"Not the same, besides, depending on how this conversation goes, you and Delta might need help packing up your stuff."

The back of my neck began radiating heat, which happened anytime I got into a serious argument.

"Dad, I'm not coming home," I stated flatly. "And what does Delta have to do with anything?"

My dad sighed. "We talked things over with her parents before I came up here. They agreed to go along with whatever we decide."

"But why would you even think I needed to be brought home?"

"If it were up to your mother, there wouldn't even be a discussion. We've seen the news. Four suicides in a couple weeks? Any parent who isn't concerned should be ashamed of themselves. What is even going on here?"

There was so much I could say, but I didn't dare because my fate would be sealed then. I couldn't risk saying anything that would add to my parents' worries and give them cause to drag me home. Not because it would be a severe over-reaction on their part, but because I needed to help Taggart see this through. I could kick and scream all I wanted about how I was an adult and how unfair it would be, but the hard fact was they paid my bills at Truman. And no matter how much Taggart cared for me, if I went back to New Haven he would remain at Truman to find his sister, and I wouldn't blame him.

"It's an unfortunate situation for sure, but I'm doing okay. Delta is too. There is no reason to be worried about us."

"Is the school too hard? Are you feeling too much pressure?"

"I'm not going to lie and say it's not tough, because it is, but not unreasonably so. I'm making good grades in all my courses. And I really like my suite-mates. We all get along and support each other. Besides, I have Delta and Taggart, so there's really no reason you and mom should be worried."

Dad smirked. "Those two aren't the best examples of emotional stability."

That made me smile. "Maybe not, but I'm fine. Really."

Dad looked me in the eyes, searching for the answer to a question only he was privy to.

"How are you and Taggart doing?"

I was extra-careful to not let the doubts about our relationship reach my face. It would only serve as fuel for my dad's concerns and distract from the real issue. "We're great. He's really coming out of his shell here."

My dad nodded, but something in his expression told me he had more to say.

"You look like you want to say something else," I stated.

He shifted his weight so he was facing me more directly. "I wasn't going to. In fact, your mother told me I should leave it alone and mind my own business, but you know me, I'm not one to shy away from hard conversations."

I swallowed in anticipation. My dad's *hard conversations* usually meant I was in for a lecture that undoubtedly would be unpleasant. "What is it?"

"Cassie, I've really admired what you've been doing for Taggart. Helping him become more social, adapt to his surroundings. I know it hasn't been easy."

"But…"

"But… I think maybe it's time for you to take a step back. The dynamic between you has changed. You've developed something like the Florence Nightingale syndrome. You've been nurturing him, sheltering him, and protecting him because you think he needs you… and maybe he did at first… but now that he's in college and interacting with his peers… I don't know, I just think you need to re-evaluate what it is between the two of you."

I was so stunned I couldn't speak at first. My father has never voiced his opinion about any of my boyfriends, much less lectured me, and I didn't know how to process it. It didn't matter that some of what he mentioned touched on things I had worried about myself. What bothered me the most was the lack of trust. Maybe trust wasn't the right word. No, a better word would be the lack of confidence.

"Dad, I evaluate my relationship with Taggart **every single day**. What girl doesn't? It hurts me to think you don't believe I'm self-aware enough to consider something like that."

My dad's face fell. "Oh, honey, don't be mad at me. I just want you to be with someone for the right reasons is all."

"And the only reason I would ever be with Taggart is if he was damaged and needed fixing, is that what you're saying?"

"Not at all. But you do have to admit that the two of you are so different from each other."

"I hate to point this out, because it sounds so cliché, but what you're talking about is only what you see on the surface. We connect on an emotional level, and isn't that where it really counts?"

Dad seemed to consider this. Finally, he nodded and put his hand on my knee. "You're right, I'm an idiot, and I'm sorry. And I guess your mother was right also, I should have kept my big mouth shut."

I showed him a cautious smile. "I know you and mom worry, but I'm a big girl now, even if you forget that now and then."

"Noted. Well, your mother's not going to be happy that I'm not bringing you home, but I trust your judgement."

I secretly breathed a deep sigh of relief. "Thank you."

"You could come home more often on the weekends. That would help calm her."

I made a face. "I've had mid-terms and needed to study. But I'm done with them now, so maybe this weekend?"

"Good." The smile on his lips disappeared. "Were you friends with any of the victims?"

"I knew some of them, but I wouldn't say we were friends. Doesn't make it any less disturbing though."

"I imagine. Do you want to grab a late lunch with your ole man before I head back?"

I was tempted to take him up on the offer, but then I remembered everyone still hanging out in my bedroom. "I wish I could, but I gotta get to my part-time job soon."

"Oh, okay," he replied. The disappointment on his face almost made me reconsider.

"I'm sorry you had to drive all the way here. You took off of work too, didn't you?"

Dad pulled me into another hug. "Honey, none of that matters when it comes to making sure you're safe."

When he left, a wave of guilt swept over me. I did my best to alleviate my parents' fears, but all I did is put a band-aid on a gaping chest wound. Since losing my sister Becca, the fear of something terrible also happening to me was ever-present. To their credit, they recognized early-on how they behaved towards me and allowed me the freedom I needed.

But I knew what a strain it was for them. What was going on now could only be intensifying their fear.

I headed toward my bedroom knowing that if more deaths happened, a very different conversation would be in my future.

Seventeen
Tuesday, July 23rd 3:45 PM

"What he say… what he say?" Delta was in my face as soon as I stepped into the bedroom.

"He's letting us stay," I replied.

Delta tilted her head towards the sky. "Thank god! I was sweating bullets in here. You didn't tell him anything about what we really think is going down, did you?"

"Are you crazy? If I did, we'd be in the backseat of my dad's car, driving south right now."

Brandon blowing a raspberry in Taggart's direction, caught my attention. "It kinda blows your entire theory, doesn't it?" Brandon said.

"What are they talking about?" I asked Delta.

"Brandon was telling Taggart that the girl slitting her wrists throws a wrench into his theory of somebody killing the people he knows," Delta replied.

"It would appear so," Taggart said, though his face and posture didn't express self-doubt.

I caught Delta's eyes and we shared a silent thought.

"What was that?" Eve asked from her spot at the window.

"What was what?" Delta asked.

"That look."

"What are you talking about?" I asked, feigning ignorance.

"The two of you gave each other a look after Taggart admitted he might be wrong. What was that about?"

"Taggart didn't admit he was wrong," Chewy observed from his perch on Delta's top bunk.

"I said he might be wrong," Eve responded.

"He didn't say that either," Chewy insisted.

"Yes, he did. I heard him," Brandon said.

Chewy jumped down from the top bunk. "What he said was 'it appears so' when you stated he was wrong. That's not the same thing at all."

"We're arguing over semantics now?" Eve said.

"In this case, it matters," I said. "The look you saw between Delta and me, that was because we understood why he answered that way. He was trying to ease everyone's mind without actually lying."

"And how would you know that?" Eve asked.

"During the time that I've known him, I've learned two things that I'm one hundred percent certain of. The first, he never lies," I said.

"And what's the second?" Brandon asked.

"He's never wrong," Delta responded.

Brandon shook his head. "Everyone lies, even if it's just a white lie."

"Why do you think he pisses so many people off? He refuses to bend the truth or sugar coat things to avoid hurting someone's feelings," Delta explained.

"Even when he really should," I added, looking at Taggart and thinking about his interviews with Detective Moss.

Eve crossed her arms. "So, if you're not wrong, then how do you explain the girl's suicide?"

"I have a theory, but I'm withholding an explanation for now. Suffice it to say that my initial postulation remains unchanged."

JJ, who had been alone in her own room since we returned, suddenly appeared in the doorway holding an overnight bag. Her eyes were red.

"Are you going somewhere?" Brandon asked.

JJ nodded. "My parents are coming to get me. They're making me drop out of school."

Eve shot to her feet. "No!"

Having just finished the same conversation with my father, I couldn't say I was surprised. JJ obviously didn't have the same trust-factor with her parents that I did with mine.

Tears filled JJ's eyes. "I was on the phone with them for over an hour trying to talk them out of it, but their minds are made up."

"I'm so sorry, JJ," I said.

"Me too," Delta added, sneaking a look in my direction.

"Will you be back next quarter?" Brandon asked.

JJ offered him a weak smile. "I don't think so. My parents' opinion of Truman isn't very positive right now."

Eve moved to the door, JJ set down her overnight bag and the two of them embraced.

"We'll stay in touch though, right?" Eve said into JJ's shoulder.

"Count on it."

The two girls broke apart, both wiping tears from her eyes. JJ then reclaimed her bag.

"My parents should be here any minute. I'll come back for the rest of my stuff this weekend. Don't burn out the bulb in my makeup mirror before then."

"No promises," Eve replied, which drew a genuine smile from JJ.

"Bye, everyone. Good luck catching who's doing this."

We all waved our goodbyes and JJ started walking out of the hall door, then reversed course.

"I almost forgot. One of my sorority sisters texted me earlier. She knows a girl who attempted suicide last quarter. Fortunately, she pulled through. I thought that might be something you'd want to know."

I could see Taggart's back stiffen, suddenly interested in what JJ was saying.

"Indeed," Taggart responded.

"I'll text Cassie the details then. Ya'll take care," JJ said.

This time JJ didn't come back.

"Well, that sucks," Brandon said.

"I bet that's happening a lot today," I said, again thinking about my own situation with my parents.

"What?" Chewy asked.

"Parents taking their kids home."

Delta looked out of the window again. "Do you really think the girl JJ mentioned has anything to do with what's going on now?"

"Doubtful, but it would be negligent not to pursue it," Taggart said.

"Who knows, maybe she went to New Haven and Taggart knew her back then, like that Jim dude?" Chewy said.

"I'm sensing a theme," Brandon said. "Being friends with Taggart may be hazardous to your health."

"If that's the case, I'm telling everybody the two of you are BFF's," Eve directed at Brandon.

"Hey, another set of vans pulled up in front of the administration building," Delta exclaimed. "I can't make out the wording on the door though."

Everyone gathered around her at the window.

"It's those two black vans on the far right," Delta said, pointing.

"I can't make out the markings either."

"I'll be right back," Brandon said as he headed for the door.

"Where are you going?" I asked.

"I got to get something from my room."

"Chewy, please go with him."

Chewy nodded once and followed Brandon out the door.

They had been gone for just a couple minutes when Delta said, "That Brandon is a character."

"That's an understatement," I replied. Then after thinking about her comment some more, "Tell me you're not interested in him?"

"Is that so bad?"

"Do you want my opinion?" Eve interjected.

"No, thank you," Delta snapped back.

"Why am I not surprised you of all people would take a liking to him," I said.

"What? He's cute, that's all I'm saying."

"Like a leopard seal is cute. They're called leopards for a reason, you know. They rank up there with killer whales as the Southern Hemisphere's top predator. And it eats penguins, which are also cute."

"Hey, don't give yourself a wedgie. I won't talk to him if you're going to get all Mean Girls about it."

That gave me pause. I realized I was doing exactly what I told myself I wouldn't, influencing Delta in her choice of guys. I was her best friend, so naturally I want only the best for her, but it wasn't my place to decide what that was. Delta was her own person and no matter how much I disliked Brandon, which was a lot, she needed to form her own opinion about him without my persuasion.

"No, you're right. Just ignore me. If you want to go after him, by all means. Go for it."

"Are you sure? You seemed pretty wound up about him?"

I took Delta by the shoulders. "Girl, we have been best friends forever, and you know I love you, but we are two separate people who sometimes like different things. I would never stand in your way about this."

I glanced over at Eve. "None of us should."

"Okay, cool. I'm not saying that I will, and he's not really paid much attention to me. He seemed more interested in JJ. But still, just in case."

"Well, JJ isn't around anymore, and trust me, there isn't a boy on this campus who can resist you when you turn on the charm."

Delta smiled widely. "You think so?"

Before I could answer, there was a knock on the hall door. Taggart went to open it and Brandon and Chewy walked in. Brandon was holding something black in his hands.

"What's that?" Eve asked.

"Binoculars," Brandon answered matter-of-factly, holding them out for me to take.

I instinctively recoiled. "Why do you have those?"

Brandon looked confused. "Just to look at stuff. I don't have cooties, if that's what you're afraid of."

Still, I hesitated to take the looking glass, so Taggart stepped in and grabbed them instead. Using them to peer out the window he fiddled with the focus for a moment, and then stood there concentrating on something of interest.

"Well?" I asked.

"It's the Center for Disease Control," Taggart replied.

"The CDC? Why are they here?" Chewy asked.

"It's not unexpected. In 2014 the CDC was sent to Fairfax, Virginia to conduct an inquiry of youth suicides. Then again in 2016 in Palo Alto, California after two clusters of youth suicides occurred between 2009 and 2015. I hypothesize that because the CDC is based here in Atlanta and the speed at which this supposed suicide cluster has spread is faster than anything previously reported, they are taking an interest."

"So what, they're gonna come up with a suicide vaccine?" Brandon asked. "I hate shots."

"I'm sure they'll have a nasal spray version for you," Delta replied, which made Brandon smile, and me groan internally. It had begun.

A knock came from the hall door, causing everyone to look in that direction. Angela strolled in after Eve opened it.

"What are you doing here?" Eve asked.

"I got tired of just watching the news and I was curious about what you guys were up to?"

"Did you walk over here, unaccompanied?" Taggart asked.

Instead of Angela looking embarrassed, she seemed defiant. "Yes."

"That was incredibly irresponsible. You could be dead right now."

"I'm not so sure about that. Did you see the CDC vans out there? I think you have this whole thing wrong. There isn't some mysterious murderer that your over-active imagination conjured up. It's a mental health crisis, plain and simple.”

“I know you want to believe that, but—”

“Somebody told me Lisa left a note. Leaving a note says suicide to me. And now there's this girl who's not even part of our group,” Angela said, then turned to Brandon. “Tell me you're not buying all this?”

Brandon was caught off-guard. He glanced at Delta before shrugging his shoulders. “I don't know. Taggart does seem really smart.”

“Oh, and you've never heard of a smart person being delusional. Typical Brandon answer. Eve, what about you?”

Eve didn't hesitate. “I trust Taggart and Cassie.”

Eve's response seemed to frustrate Angela even more. She started becoming more animated when she spoke.

“Where's Tony and JJ? I don't see them here. I bet they're not buying into this conspiracy theory either.”

“I presume Tony's in his room, and JJ's parents took her home. They're forcing her to withdraw from school,” I answered calmly, hoping it would get Angela to act the same way.

Angela became still. “JJ's gone?”

After pondering it for a moment, she remarked, "That might not be a bad idea," speaking more to herself than to anyone else. Then she added, "Either way, I'm done with this group. You all deserve each other."

With that, Angela charged out of the room. Almost immediately after the door closed, Delta made her way for it.

“Where are you going?” I asked.

Delta opened the door before looking back. “Just because she doesn't believe someone is after us, doesn't mean it isn't true. I'm gonna follow her and make sure she gets back to her dorm okay.”

"Hang on, I'll go with you," Brandon said, moving in her direction. "That way you're not walking back by yourself."

The sly smile on Delta's face before they disappeared told me that had worked out exactly as she had hoped.

My phone chirped to tell me I received a text. Reading the screen, I said, "JJ sent me that info on the girl who tried to commit suicide last quarter."

Taggart set down the binoculars.

"Let's go talk with her."

Eighteen
Tuesday, July 23rd 5:15 PM

The name of the girl JJ had texted was Ginger Wood, and after a quick GPS search on her address we learned she was located on the far side of Wolfs Head. Despite Eve insisting that she wanted to come along, we left her behind with Chewy after convincing her it would be best to keep the number of people bombarding this possibly unstable person with questions to a minimum.

Thirty minutes later, my car pulled into the Place Du Plantier apartments. The dwellings were in a more rundown section of Wolfs Head and seriously overdue for extensive renovation. We navigated the parking lot so covered with cracks in the concrete that it resembled a patch of varicose veins. We spotted the right apartment number, parked, and then made our way to a solid green door that was missing several pieces of paint chips. I could hear a game show playing on a television inside. Taggart knocked three times.

Not long afterward, the door swung open to reveal a woman dressed in a uniform I recognized as belonging to one of the fancier restaurants in Wolfs Head. The name tag on her uniform read Ginger.

"I'm not buying anything," the woman said, not bothering to remove the lit cigarette from her lips.

"That's okay, we're not selling," I said, making sure to smile. "Are you Ginger Wood?"

"I am, who's asking," Ginger replied, looking at the two of us closer now.

"My name is Cassie Underwood, and this is Taggart McGill. We're both students at Truman."

"I'm happy for you both, but I'm still not buying anything."

I smiled again. "And we're still not selling anything. We were wondering if we might ask you a few questions?"

"Questions? About what? Is this some kind of survey? I really need to be getting to work."

"No, it's not a survey. Maybe you've heard about what is going on at Truman the last couple weeks?"

Ginger looked confused. "Come again?"

"The suicides."

Ginger's face fell and her posture stiffened.

"Are you here representing the college?" the woman snapped angrily.

"No. No. Nothing like that. We both knew the victims, well three of the four of them, and we're just trying to understand what's going on."

"Excuse me," Taggart interjected. "Where were you born?"

Ginger seemed to be thrown off by the question. "What's that got to do with anything?"

"Possibly nothing," Taggart replied.

The woman took a deep drag of the cigarette before taking it from her lips. "Orlando, Florida," she answered, smoke billowing around her reply.

I had wondered what Taggart was after with his question but given the fact Orlando was only two and a half hours away from Jacksonville, where Taggart's sister was born, I now knew where his mind was at. She looked to be the right age, but she also looked nothing like Taggart.

When Taggart didn't say anything, Ginger turned her attention back to me. "I'm sorry about those other people, but I can't help you."

"We just wondered if you knew any of them," I asked.

Ginger cocked her head to the side. "You think we're all part of some suicide club or something?"

"The timing between your—" Taggart began.

Ginger crossed her arms across her chest. "Listen, my situation wasn't anything like theirs."

"I'm confused. You didn't—I mean—didn't you try to take your life?" I asked.

"No. Well, not technically. Trust me, I have nothing to do with them."

"Please," I said.

Ginger stared back at me, then her eyes softened. "Listen, I can tell you my story, but it may not be the one you want to hear. It's all about how your wonderful Truman University is actually a back-stabbing piece of dog shit."

"I would like to hear that," Taggart stated.

"Why don't you come in then." Ginger stepped away from the door to allow us to enter.

The inside of Ginger Wood's apartment was filled with cardboard boxes and a few pieces of furniture. The television I heard playing was a medium-sized LCD atop of one of the boxes opposite a two-person love seat.

"Are you moving?" I asked.

"Moved. I've only been here a month, but I haven't found the time to unpack yet. Have a seat."

Ginger put out her cigarette in an overflowing ashtray then plopped down in a well-worn recliner. Taggart and I moved to the love seat.

"So, here's the deal. I've had issues with depression for most of my life, but I've managed it with medication. No one other than my family and my best friend knew about it. Last year my doctor switched antidepressant prescriptions because of insurance. The insurance company wouldn't cover the brand version of the medication I was on because a generic came out. The generic 'script gave me side-effects, mood swings specifically. This happens to many people, but doctor's don't inform patients that differences between brand and generic are allowed. Even from one manufacturer of the generic to another the differences can be enough to cause massive side effects. Anyway, it caused me to get into a fight with my boyfriend and afterwards the two of us sent some not very nice emails back and forth. After that, I'm ashamed to admit, I kind of overdosed. I was alone in my dorm room when I downed twenty pills. I knew it was a stupid thing to do, even as I swallowed the pills. I know what you're thinking, but I promise you I wasn't trying to end my life. I was just lashing out, you know?

"Anyway, I tried to make myself throw the pills up but couldn't, so I went to Truman health center. They sent me to the hospital, where doctors determined I posed an imminent risk of harm to myself or others because of the way I was mouthing off, so they placed me on a seventy-two hour hold to monitor me. As I was getting ready to leave the hospital, the director of student life left a voicemail message on my mother's cell phone. They had evicted me from my dorm room, banned me from attending classes, and prohibited me from setting foot on campus.

"I eventually filed a complaint with the department of education's office of civil rights. I claimed that my depression was a protected disability, and they were being prejudiced towards me. My point being that Truman treated me differently than a student with, say, mononucleosis, or a broken leg. The school told me that if I didn't voluntarily withdraw, I would be forced to as soon as I had missed enough of the classes which I'd been banned from. The school also told me that a mandatory withdrawal would be noted on my record and that my family wouldn't be refunded for the quarter's tuition or room and board.

"My parents hired a lawyer. Then, the university said it would only reconsider if I released several years of my confidential medical records. I did that and even offered to move off-campus with my mother for the rest of the quarter, but Truman still rejected my appeal and told me that if I didn't agree to withdraw, I would be mandatorily removed. So I did it. I withdrew."

I was stunned by what I had just heard. "Why would they do all that?"

"I might be able to answer that," Taggart said. "In the current climate, some college administrations worry about potential liability. They fear getting a reputation as a suicide school, or are concerned about the safety of the community, so they discipline students with mental health issues instead of giving them the help they need."

Ginger pointed at Taggart. "What he said."

Taggart continued on. "There was another case on the west coast where a freshman girl had also been on antidepressants for anxiety since her senior year of high school. That girl texted a friend after she cut herself deeper than she had intended in the shower, and that friend told their resident advisor. Soon after, housing and residential services slipped an envelope under the girl's door, notifying her of her alleged involvement in a housing policy violation. Their position was that by cutting herself in the bathroom, the girl had taken part in actions that disrupt the normal functioning and operation of the residence hall and actions posing a significant risk of harm to self or the community. They gave her three days to plead her case.

During the appeal the school's assistant director told her she could be suspended or expelled and that she had put the entire school in danger. He allegedly said it was possible the girl would become so emotionally unstable that she might start running around the halls, threatening her floormates with a knife. He told her she could only stay in school if she waived her confidentiality and allowed her therapist to provide weekly reports to the administration, which she agreed to."

"That's awful. How could you ever trust your therapist in a situation like that? They're basically spying on you for the school," I said.

"You couldn't. Schools like Truman are basically all about covering their asses. But you can see how my situation wasn't anything like what's happening now. Those poor souls."

"By chance, would you have known Pauline Rome? She was the latest fatality, and she would have been in your class."

Ginger shook her head. "Name doesn't ring a bell, sorry."

Taggart looked at me. "It appears there is nothing we can learn here."

We both stood to leave.

Ginger rose with us. "Were you close with any of the ones who—"

"Not real close, no. But it's still a shock even if you know them a little bit."

"I guess so."

"You mentioned earlier that your parents hired a lawyer for your appeal. Are they both your birth parents?" Taggart asked.

Ginger's head snapped back. "You're just full of odd questions. Yes they are. Been together for thirty-five years."

When Taggart turned and headed for the door, I quickly said, "Thank you for being so forthcoming with us. I hope we didn't disturb you too much."

"No worries. Best of luck with your studies."

We said our goodbyes at the door and strolled back to my car.

"She was enrolled at Truman before we even graduated high school, so she couldn't have been your sister. It would have been one hell of a coincidence if we ended up going to the same college."

"She could have been monitoring our activities and noticed our applications to Truman. We sent them in early enough that she would have had time to process a late-enrollment for the preceding quarter."

"Okay, but she has both of her birth parents."

"Which could have been a lie."

"So, what, you do think she's your sister?"

We had reached my car and we stood by our respective doors speaking over the roof.

"No. But it did get me thinking. My sister could be enrolled at Truman right now. There would be no better way to observe my activities then being a student herself."

Over Taggart's shoulder I saw someone I recognized heading straight for us.

"Did you ever contact that reporter who gave us that information about your sister?"

"The time has never been right," he replied, but I could tell he was being evasive.

"Imagine seeing you two here," the woman reporter from The Grind said as she appeared beside Taggart. Her hair was tied back in a pony-tail and she was wearing a faded jean jacket.

Taggart turned to face her and she offered her hand.

"I'm Jaime Henson. Hopefully, Cassie has told you about me?"

Taggart took her hand and gave it a perfunctory wiggle. "She did. I've meant to reach out, but I've been distracted of late."

"I can imagine. Four suicides, three of them with a connection to you, and you found the bodies of two of them."

"You could say the same thing about me," I quickly pointed out. "Have you been following us?"

The reporter shrugged her shoulders. "What can I say, I get a little impatient sometimes. Who were you here to see?"

"It's a private matter," Taggart said.

The Grind reporter frowned. "I thought we had an arrangement."

"We do about the events that occurred in New Haven. I will honor that agreement, but my thoughts about anything else are off-limits."

"Fair enough, but just answer me this. Does what happened in New Haven have anything to do with what's going on here? I'm not buying this whole business about suicide clusters the TV networks are pushing."

Taggart glanced at me before answering. "All I will say is that things are not always digital. Ones or zeroes. At times they can be both."

The reporter's eyebrows scrunched together. "Huh?"

Behind Taggart and the reporter, a van I thought I recognized pulled into the parking lot.

"Taggart, look."

We both watched as the van we identified earlier as belonging to the CDC slowly made its way in our direction.

"Listen, Jaime, we've got to run, but if you want a story that has some teeth to it, go right now and talk to the girl in apartment 10A. Her name is Ginger Woods, and she has a story that I think you'll want to hear."

Without waiting for a reply, Taggart and I slid into our seats and I had the car quickly moving in the opposite direction toward a different exit.

When we were a couple of blocks away I asked, "If you think your sister is enrolled at school, what are we going to do?"

"We need to get a look at school registration records."

"I doubt they're going to let just anyone browse through those."

Just because I anticipated his answer before he gave it, didn't mean I found it any less upsetting.

"Which is why we're going to break in."

I sighed before I gave him my response. "At least it's not a funeral home this time."

Nineteen
Tuesday, July 24th 7:22 PM

It was our good luck—if you could call it 'good'—that the school decided to cancel classes for a second day in a row. The notification came via email as we were driving back from our interview with Ginger Wood. The news media, in all its forms, was still a pervasive presence around all the primary gathering spots, so the school limiting their source of information was probably the right call. The free day would give us time to eyeball the layout of the admissions building inside and out before breaking in.

"Breaking into a university admissions office isn't the same," I pointed out while we drove back to the dorm. I was referencing our antics from last fall when we broke into a funeral home to obtain evidence of a suspected crime. "If you remember, we almost got caught then."

"The battery on our lookout's phone died. We will be better prepared this time."

"But this is serious. If we get caught, it will be a felony, and the punishment won't be a wrist-slapping."

"You are right. This is serious. People are dead, and I believe more will die unless we take steps."

I checked my rear-view mirror for the hundredth time since leaving the apartments. Now that I knew the reporter had followed us from the campus, I was more paranoid than ever.

"Then let's go to the police," I pleaded. "Tell detective Moss everything."

Taggart shot me a look as if I had suggested he start listening to Taylor Swift music.

"And tell him about a warning from a sister we know next to nothing about who possibly has ill-intentions towards me, delivered via a text message that no longer exists? Should we also mention that she is somehow overpowering people I've met and making their deaths look like suicides?"

"Okay, I admit it sounds silly when you say it like that."

"This is the only way. We will take the necessary precautions to ensure we are not apprehended, but we must look at those records. Along those same lines, I need you to drop me off in front of the admissions building on the way back. I'm going to monitor it tonight to see how frequent the security patrols are in the area."

"You're going to stay out there all night?"

"I am. After you drop me off, go straight back to the dorm and have Chewy and Delta meet you at your car. I don't want you walking in by yourself."

I did as Taggart requested, and when I pulled into the dorm parking lot, I couldn't help but notice how much emptier it seemed since we left. Were kids using the opportunity of a free day to get away for a while, or had they cut and run, deciding that whatever was going on at Truman wasn't worth the risk? I couldn't blame them either way.

As I walked back to our dorm room with Chewy and Delta, I explained to them what he was up to. It disappointed Chewy that Taggart hadn't asked him to join the surveillance, but he got over it quickly when I suggested he spend the night—which was totally against dorm rules—if his mom okayed it. We chose not to tell the others about Taggart's break-in plans though, deciding that it was smarter if we considered it a need-to-know situation.

Chewy ended up sleeping on the couch out in the study area, which I think made Brandon jealous. Brandon floated the idea of sleeping in JJ's empty bed next to Eve, which she quickly squelched, then he bitched and moaned to both Delta and me as we escorted him back to his room.

Taggart reappeared early the next morning. After rousing Chewy, the two of them came into our room and closed the door.

"Campus security makes a round at the top of every hour, but they only do a drive by. They do not check the doors. The windows and doors are all alarmed. Nothing extravagant. I should be able to unlock a window and disable the alarm when I visit later today."

"Then what?" Delta asked. "Can you break into their computer system?"

"Unknown. But if you'll recall the school required a paper admission packet, so even if I'm unable to access the computer records, those paper records should be available. I would surmise that the most recent enrollees would still be on-site and not in storage. I'll know more after my visit."

"I suppose I would be wasting my breath trying to talk you out of this again?" I asked.

"There is a recessed section by the auditorium across the street where someone could steal themselves away and provide us adequate warning should something unexpected occur. I'll need at least one person to accompany me inside to help locate the relevant physical records while I address the computer system. Two would be even better."

"You know I'll help," Chewy was quick to speak up.

"I guess I can be a lookout again," Delta said.

Everyone then looked at me.

"For the record, I'm not happy about this, but I'll help."

"This is so cool," Chewy bubbled. "It's like old times again."

A couple of seconds later we all turned and looked at Delta.

"What?" she exclaimed.

I heard someone knocking on our hall door so I moved to answer it. "Charge your phone," I said to Delta as I exited our room.

I opened the door to find Tony standing there in the hallway wearing a dark blue robe and grey slippers.

"I hadn't heard any updates from you guys, so I thought I'd stop by," he said.

"Come on in," I said.

As Tony stepped into our suite Eve appeared at her door. Her hair was disheveled, and the beginnings of dark circles were forming under her eyes. I guessed that sleep was hard to come by for her last night as well.

"Is Taggart here?" Tony asked.

"He is, why don't the two of you come into my room. We're all in there."

After we all piled into my room Tony started right in.

"What's the latest? Are we still thinking somebody is knocking off people Taggart hangs out with?"

"We do," Taggart answered.

"Despite that last girl not having anything to do with our group, or you?"

Taggart hesitated. "I believe Pauline Rome did, in fact, commit suicide."

Taggart had told me his suspicions earlier, but it didn't make it any easier to hear it again now.

"Why do you think that?" Eve asked.

"You've all seen the news coverage. Of the four victims, she's the only one that had a history of mental illness. Her stability was in question. It is my opinion the events of the past two weeks nudged her towards an outcome she was already teetering on. That is, in part, what suicide clusters do."

The room went still.

"If I understand what you're saying," Tony said, breaking the silence. "You think she was collateral damage?"

"In essence, that is correct."

"I feel like I need to cry," Eve said softly.

"So, what are you going to do?" Tony asked, more animated now. "We can't just wait around for somebody to pick us off."

"And there are even less of us now. JJ's parents took her home yesterday, and I'm not sure about Angela," Eve stated.

"Listen, we're going to talk to the police again today," I lied. I knew Taggart wasn't going to tell them about his real plan and he wouldn't be able to lie, so I had to say something that would calm them down. Taggart probably wouldn't approve, but at this point I was just trying to keep the situation under control and that was something he wasn't very good at.

"Should we all go to the police with you?" Eve asked.

"There's no need."

"I want to know more about this mysterious person who you say is behind all this. Who is it? How do you know them?" Tony asked.

"I am still unable to say definitively."

"You mean you won't say."

"That can obviously be inferred."

Tony grabbed his hair. "God. I should punch your lights out. You're so god damn arrogant sometimes."

"Careful, you wouldn't want to mess up your robe," Delta quipped. "Love the slippers."

Tony glared at Delta then marched out of the room.

"Call me and tell me what the police say after your meeting," he called out.

After hearing the hallway door open I was expecting it to slam shut, but instead I heard Tony say, "What are you doing here?"

"I could be asking you the same thing," a voice I recognized answered. "Isn't this Cassie and Eve's suite?"

"They're straight back," Tony said, followed by the sound of a closing door shortly after that.

Talia Davis appeared in the doorway, with Tony behind her. Our group leader was sharply dressed in a turquoise pants suit.

"Good morning. I see that everyone is up and moving early this morning."

A round of mumbled good mornings made its way around the room.

"I've just come by to see how everyone is doing. I heard about JJ. It's an awful shame, but obviously, her parents have to do what they feel is right."

"Have you heard anything about Angela?" Eve asked.

"I've not been by to check on her yet. Should I have heard something?"

"She was contemplating doing the same as JJ did yesterday, dropping out of school. Maybe she changed her mind."

Talia showed us an apologetic smile. "Unfortunately, there has been a lot of that happening. Let's hope she did change her mind. She'll be my next stop. But it's encouraging to see that you all have formed such a tight support group. It's an absolute must in times like this."

"We're kind of watching each other's backs," I said.

"And that's what I like to see."

"Except Brandon. He's only watching butts, the female kind," Eve said.

"Ahhh, well, you know what they say about karma."

That struck me as an odd response from somebody on the college payroll, which led me to ask my next question.

"Talia, at our first meeting, you told us you were a graduate student. Did you get your undergraduate degree here at Truman?"

"I did not. I obtained my undergraduate degree in Psychology from LSU. I transferred after that. This is my first year here at Truman."

"You also said you were from Chicago. Did you grow up there?"

"That's also a no. My father was in the Navy, so we moved around a lot."

"What about your mother?"

"What about her?"

"What did she do?"

Talia placed her hands on her hips. "My, my, you're just full of questions today, aren't you Cassie?"

"It's just that we never did get a proper introduction when you joined our group. I'm curious."

"Well, let's just make sure we take care of that at next week's meeting. For now, I gotta keep moving. Remember, my phone and office door are always open for any of you. Even you, Mr. McGill."

Taggart gave Talia a curt nod.

"Take care," she said, holding my gaze for just a moment before smiling at Tony, then walking off.

After the hallway door had closed, Tony stuck his head back in the room.

"Just FYI, when I was leaving before, I swear I caught Talia listening at the door."

Twenty
Wednesday, July 25th 2:00 AM

There's something about the wee hours of the morning that makes everything creepy, no matter where you are. That's just a thought in my head, of course, but knowing that doesn't help much. The Truman campus was no exception. In this case it earned an extra creep factor because of the English-goth style architecture everywhere you look.

The night sky was heavily overcast, which was helpful because behind those clouds the moon was supposed to be full. Since it was the middle of the summer, Taggart was the only one of us with a black hoodie to wear, because basically that was his entire wardrobe. Everyone else had to make do with dark color t-shirts and pants. After Taggart's reconnaissance visit to the admissions office this afternoon, we also went by a hardware store to pick up some compact flashlights and cheap work gloves, both of which I could feel in my back pockets as we made our way through the campus.

Delta and I had concocted a story to tell Eve that the New Haven group was having dinner with Chewy's mom, and since we might be back late and didn't want Eve to be alone, it would be a good idea if she spent the evening with friends. After a few phone calls, she made arrangements to spend the night with a girl one floor up from us who was from her history class. That girl's roommate was one of the ones who decided to bail on school, so it turned out she was eager for the company. After making sure Eve was settled in upstairs, the three of us walked over to Taggart's apartment. We needed to catch some sleep before it was time for us to become felons, which wasn't going to be easy since Taggart only had the one mattress and no couch. Delta and I shared the mattress, and Taggart and Chewy made do with some spare sheets and a couple of pillows.

When the time came, I thought about making one last plea for sanity, but seeing the look in Chewy and Delta's eyes told me I would be fighting a losing cause. We were doing this.

***

I'm not sure what the founders were thinking when they came up with the construction plans for the Truman campus, but the admissions office was located on the far east side of the property away from all of the other administration buildings. It was sandwiched between two female-only residence halls, adjacent to the alumni center, and directly across from the auditorium and its clock tower that could be seen from the rest of the campus.

Our destination was only a fifteen-minute walk from Taggart's apartment, and he said it would be easier for us to go unseen if we left the car behind and stuck as close to the buildings as possible. The campus was completely still when the four of us made our way to the auditorium across the street from the admissions office. Taggart showed Delta the spot he had picked for her lookout duties, giving her a direct line of sight to the office's main entrance.

Taggart checked his watch. "We need to get behind the bushes. A patrol will be coming by shortly," he half-whispered.

All of us ducked behind the waist-high bushes that ran in front of the auditorium and waited. Three minutes later a black, unmarked Ford Explorer rolled slowly past our position. As soon as the Explorer was out of sight, we hopped up and followed Delta to her observation spot.

"How much charge does your phone have?" I asked.

"Eighty-four percent."

"Is the speaker muted?"

"Affirmative," she said, smiling. "I've always wanted to say that."

"Gloves," Taggart said.

The three of us slipped on the work gloves we had purchased. The pair I was wearing felt a couple of sizes too big.

"Okay, stay alert. This should only take thirty minutes and we should be out of there with plenty of time to spare before the next patrol."

"Then get going. I got this," Delta said, making a shooing motion with her hand.

Checking one last time to make sure there were no random cars about, the three of us bolted across the road. Taggart led us to a window approximately thirty feet from the main entrance. Even though it was dark, and light from the closest lamp post didn't reach as far as we were, I still felt vulnerable standing there. I watched Taggart remove the outer screen and re-examine the layout, which felt like it was taking forever. Then he turned to face us.

"This window is in the men's bathroom directly off the lobby," Taggart said. "I disconnected the alarm this afternoon and it's doubtful anybody would have noticed, but there is always the possibility."

"Great," Chewy mumbled. I was too scared to say anything, so I just nodded.

Taggart pulled up on the frame and the window rose easily. The three of us stood there frozen for a moment, waiting for the sound of an alarm to shatter the nights silence, but nothing came.

"What if it's a silent alarm?" Chewy whispered.

"Only one way to find out," Taggart said before crawling through the window. I watched him feel along the inside frame of the window, then beckon me with his hand.

"It's still disconnected."

He offered me his hands and I quickly scrambled inside, making sure the flashlight in my pocket didn't slip out. I waited in the dark while Chewy did the same.

Inside we cautiously moved past the two stalls and two urinals on one side and a row of sinks on the other. At the door, Chewy and I waited for Taggart to open it. When nothing happened, I said, "Is something wrong?"

"The door is locked."

"Who locks a bathroom door?" Chewy wondered out loud.

"Somebody who works at the Truman admissions office," I replied sarcastically. Examining the door closer I saw that it was old with an old-style lock containing keyholes on both sides. "Can you pick it?"

"We'll soon see," he said as he reached for his tools in his back pocket.

Taggart had perfected his lock picking skills this past summer after the news about his mom broke and it became impossible for us to get around town without getting ambushed by reporters. To break up the boredom during our self-imposed isolation, after running out of books to read, he had ordered specialized tools off the internet and taught himself how to defeat most common locks. He even showed me how to beat a few.

"Shine your flashlight on the door handle," Taggart instructed, which I did.

After almost a minute of tinkering, the door popped open.

Chewy and I followed Taggart out into the main lobby. Even without lights, apart from the ones we were carrying, the large room was surprisingly easy to see. The walls and floor were light in color, which reflected the ambient light. Taggart quickly moved to the end of a long counter that ran almost the entire length of the room. It extended past a set of desks, and up to a door at the rear of the room. Turning the handle, he effortlessly opened the door.

Taggart pushed the door open and directed his flashlight inside. The small room contained a row of three-drawer filing cabinets along the left wall.

"This is where they keep the files with the current year's enrollees."

"They lock the bathroom, but this they leave unlocked. Go figure," I said.

"First, find all of the files for the people, men and women, in your orientation group. Take a picture with your phone of the contents and put them back where you find them. Work fast. I'm going into the next room to see if I can access the computer."

"Roger that," Chewy said.

When Taggart moved away, I shone my light on the nearest cabinet. The label on the top drawer read AA-AOF.

I mentally ran through the names of everyone in our orientation group.

"I'll get Brandon Carter, you find Lisa French," I said.

Without a word Chewy started moving down the row of filing cabinets, shining his light on the label on each drawer. I found CA-CO on the middle drawer of the second cabinet and pulled it open. Brandon's file was in the middle section. I slid it out of its slot, closed the drawer, then opened the file on top of the cabinet. I took out my phone, enabled the camera, then started snapping pictures. There was the school's application status sheet, the four-page application form, official ACT score report, high school transcript, letters of recommendation from teachers, and my personal favorite - the ulcer-inducing personal essay. Sometimes there would be a copy of the applicant's driver's license if they were requesting a campus parking pass.

When I snapped the last picture I put everything back in the order I found it and returned the folder into the proper slot. I glanced over at Chewy and saw him shining his flashlight on a piece of paper.

"Chewy, we don't have time to read. Snap the pictures and move on."

He put away his flashlight and picked up his phone. "Sorry."

Going through my mental checklist again meant Tony Greer was next. I moved behind Chewy towards the next cabinet when a noise from the outer room made me freeze.

"Did you hear that?" I whispered.

"Yes," Chewy replied with the same soft tone. "Sounded like someone kicked a desk."

I switched off my flashlight and Chewy did the same. We both looked towards the partially closed door, listening for anything out of the ordinary.

"Maybe it's Taggart?" Chewy said.

I moved slowly behind him towards the door. "Stay here."

My heartbeat, which had finally settled into a tolerable rhythm before hearing the sound, was racing again as I approached the outer room. I could feel my hands sweating inside my over-sized gloves.

I pulled open the door and stuck my head out of the room. I was suddenly blinded. A bright light was shining directly in my face, and it had the same effect as a freeze ray, rendering me unable to move.

"There you are. I thought I had missed you guys," I heard Brandon's voice come from the other side of the intense beam of light.

I relaxed enough to put my hand in front of my eyes. "Get that out of my face."

It was a few seconds after the light was redirected to the ground before I could focus again.

"I think you almost blinded me," I said.

Brandon moved the shaft of light back and forth across the ground. "Pretty cool, huh? It's got a 100-watt halogen bulb that puts out 4,100 lumens. I got it on eBay."

Chewy appeared beside me. "Brandon? What are you doing here?"

"Delta told me what you guys were planning and I wanted to help. Did you realize you left the window open you came in through? Talk about amateurish. Don't worry, I closed it."

There was a half-dozen things I wanted to say to him, all of which would make a sailor blush, but I was too upset with the real cause of this awkward development. Delta was in for a real talking to in her near future.

I didn't hear him approach, but Taggart appeared beside Brandon.

"Explain your presence," Taggart said.

"Delta told him," I answered for Brandon.

"I want to help," Brandon said.

"You can stand right where you are and not move," Taggart snapped.

"Are you having any luck with the computer system?" Chewy asked.

Even in the dim lighting, I could see Taggart shaking his head. "Negative. I might as well be helping you."

"Wait a minute, do you need to break into their system," Brandon said. "What are you after?"

"This quarter's enrollment records," Taggart answered cautiously.

"I can help. I don't want to brag, but I'm a pretty fair hacker."

Taggart stared at Brandon, then looked at me.

"What have we got to lose? Let him try," I said.

Taggart removed his gloves and handed them to Brandon. "Put these on and follow me. You two should probably get back to the files."

Chewy and I did as we were instructed. Fifteen minutes later, we were both finishing up snapping pictures of our last files when Taggart and Brandon appeared at the door. Taggart handed me a piece of paper.

"I need you to pull these files as well," he said.

"Who are they?"

"New female enrollees who fit the age profile. There's five of them."

Ten minutes later, with Taggart's assistance, we had pictures of the added files.

Taggart checked his watch. "The next drive by will be in fifteen minutes. Time to go."

We followed him into the bathroom, shut and locked the door, then moved to the window. I was right behind Taggart as he reached the wall when he abruptly dropped to the ground, so everyone else did the same.

"What is it?" I asked quietly.

"The campus patrol is early and right outside the window."

We both peeked over the bottom lip of the window and just as he said, the Ford Explorer was parked in the street directly in front of the window. But the worst part was that the driver, a campus security guard, was illuminated by the car's headlights standing with his hands on his hips, talking to Delta.

"What is she doing?" I heard Brandon whisper behind me.

None of us bothered to answer the question, instead watched Delta and the security guard continue to chat. Whatever she was saying, Delta was being extremely animated. After a few more minutes of the same thing, the guard pointed his finger at Delta, she nodded her head vigorously and then embraced him in a hug. The guard climbed back in his vehicle and Delta waved as it drove away. As soon as it turned the corner and disappeared, Delta stopped walking away in the opposite direction and signaled that the coast was clear.

Taggart opened the window, we all hurried out of the building and watched as he closed the window and set the screen back in place. Then we all darted across the street and joined Delta.

"What was all that about?" I asked.

"I saw him coming up the street using his floodlight, checking some of the buildings, and I was afraid he would spot the missing screen on the window. So, I distracted him by pretending that I had just had a fight with my boyfriend and was wandering around campus to unwind."

"He bought that?" Brandon asked.

"Sprinkle in some tears and most guys will buy anything. Did we get what we needed?"

"We did, in part thanks to Brandon," Taggart stated.

The smile on Brandon's face threatened to connect his ear canals.

"We're going to have a discussion when we get back about boundaries," I said to Delta using the most menacing voice I could muster. "But right now, I need sleep."

"Me too," said Chewy.

"Please email me those pictures as soon as you can. Let's get together tomorrow after class at my apartment?" Taggart asked.

We embraced each other firmly and I planted a kiss on his cheek. "I'll be there."

"Bring everyone. And make sure you stay together going back," he said as he moved towards an alley which was a short cut back to his apartment.

The rest of us walked in silence back to the dorm. If everyone was like me, there wasn't enough energy left to sustain anything coherent anyway.

After dropping Brandon off, Chewy, Delta, and I zombie-walked back to our room. I was about to insert my key in the lock when I noticed something written on our dry-erase board.

QPQ

"What's that supposed to mean?" I asked.

Delta and Chewy looked at the neatly written letters, but neither of them had a comment.

I let us in and had only taken a couple of steps when I noticed something out of place.

"Who put that there?" Chewy asked.

All of our eyes were on the doll dangling from the stationary ceiling fan. A noose made of clothesline rope was fashioned around its neck with the other end tied to one of the fan's blades. The back of the doll was facing the door, so I slowly made my way around so I could see its front. When I could finally see its face, I started shaking.

Plump, freckle covered cheeks.

Pudgy nose.

Blonde hair with twin pigtails and even bangs.

"That doll reminds me of that girl in your group. Angela, I think," Delta commented.

Of course it would, I thought to myself. It was a cabbage patch doll.

Twenty-One
Thursday, July 26th 3:45 PM

Although classes resumed today, it definitely wasn't business as usual.

The sun shone brightly bringing moderate temperatures, but the mood on campus matched my own—gloomy. The feeling wasn't because I'd only managed a couple hours of sleep and skipped my daily run. No, there was a sense of palpable melancholia in the air. Casual conversations, when there were any, were in hushed tones. I wouldn't go so far to say that the campus felt like a ghost town because there were still plenty of students moving about, but the numbers were noticeably down, and those who were still here weren't saying much.

Making my way to class, I noticed that the majority of media vans had disappeared from the front of the administration building. I suspected they had moved onto the next breaking news story. I'm sure the school administrators were hoping—or praying—that things would begin to return to normal now, but since the CDC vehicles were still here, that was probably wishful thinking.

After finding that doll hanging in our common room, I was more worried than ever that something might have happened to Angela and was trying to ignore the possible threat to our own safety. None of those concerns were going to stop me from making it to all my classes. However, it was undoubtedly going to be a challenge. There were times when my mind would spiral into endless theories about who could be behind what was happening. It didn't help that Taggart's theory about his sister being enrolled at Truman made me question every interaction I'd had since stepping on campus. With all those thoughts running through my head, I briefly wondered what the point of going to class was. Focusing on lectures was next to impossible. What helped was the knowledge that Taggart was out there doing everything he could to find the person responsible.

After my last class of the day, I headed towards the Commons in front of our dorm to meet Delta, Eve, Brandon, and Tony. Chewy had returned home that morning to check in with his mom and told us he would come back as soon as he could. I worried that having him around might be putting him in danger, but his presence was comforting, and I was selfishly pleased he could be here to help. Delta said the same thing.

Walking up to the Commons, I spotted Delta, Eve, and Brandon. Delta and Brandon were carrying on a conversation while Eve studied her phone. Delta laughed at something Brandon said and I thought about how at ease she looked. I had to admit my best friend acted differently around Brandon, much more than she did with any of her previous romantic interests. Around them, she always appeared to be exerting too much effort—trying to be more attentive, funnier, prettier, sophisticated, even smarter. However, with Brandon, she seemed at ease. And on the flip side, Brandon had been acting more subdued, less annoying, eager to help. Them as a couple told me something about myself. I would be a terrible matchmaker.

"Hey, where's Tony?" I asked when I walked up.

"He'll join us later. He texted me to say he had things to take care of first," Brandon answered.

"Did you give him Taggart's address?"

"He said he already had it."

Eve put away her phone. "Has anyone called you back about Angela?"

After finding the doll last night, I called everyone I could think of before class to see if Angela was safe. Her cell number went straight to voicemail. Her roommate said she hadn't seen her and couldn't tell if she had packed up to go home or not. I got the impression the two of them weren't close. I also called Talia Davis since she intended on visiting Angela after leaving our room yesterday, but Talia also wasn't answering her phone and I had to leave a message.

"Nobody's called me back, and I'm starting to get really worried."

"She probably went home," Delta said. "She almost said as much, remember?"

"Yeah, maybe," I said.

"Changing topics… who would leave a doll hanging in our room like that, anyway?" Eve said. "It's sick."

"True dat," Brandon said.

Eve's head snapped around to look at him. "Oh, shut up, Brandon."

Brandon looked genuinely shocked. "What did I say?"

"If I didn't know you were with Cassie and Delta last night, I'd blame you for hanging that doll."

"Hey, that's not fair."

"Right, says the person who wondered out loud if Jim crapped his pants when he hung himself?"

I was surprised to see Brandon's face turn red. He looked embarrassed when he glanced at Delta, then turned to stare at the ground. Delta's reaction, on the other hand, was unreadable.

"And how did they get in?" Eve continued. "That's what got me scared the most."

"Listen, we can't answer these questions here. Why don't we head over to Taggart's," I suggested.

Eve stomped off across the Commons in the direction of Taggart's apartment, which wasn't easy because she was wearing flip flops. Delta, Brandon, and I followed silently in her wake.

After a couple of minutes, I heard Brandon say softly, "I can be a jerk sometimes."

"We all have our moments," Delta responded.

When Brandon didn't say anything else, Delta decided to elaborate. "The important thing is you recognize that as a fault, and you work to improve yourself. That's assuming you want to, of course."

"I do," he replied quickly.

"Good. I can help with that if you want?"

"Do you charge by the hour?"

There was a slight pause before Delta replied. "Maybe instead of a smart-alec remark, you instead say, that would be great."

"I'm sorry. That would be great."

"Good. You can consider that my first consultation."

I smiled to myself.

We reached Taggart's apartment quicker than usual because of the blazing pace Eve maintained. Taggart must have been watching from the window because he was standing in the doorway when we drew near. He looked more ragged than normal with droopy eyes and a slight slouch in his stance. He gave Eve a perfunctory smile as she stepped past him, then wrapped his arms around me.

All I wanted at that moment was to remain in those strong arms as long as I possibly could, but Delta clearing her throat behind me brought that fantasy to an end.

Taggart relaxed his arms and the two of us moved out of the doorway and into the apartment. Delta and Brandon followed behind us and closed the door.

"I'm guessing you didn't get much rest last night," I said, giving his arm an extra hug.

"I haven't been to sleep."

"I thought as much." I cupped his face with my hands. "Listen to me. I know you're locked in on this, and I can't tell you how safe that makes me feel, but you're not going to be much use if you don't find time to rest."

"Now that you and the others are here, I was planning on taking a nap while you double-check my work."

I reached up and kissed his forehead. "Perfect. Did you look at those pictures of the doll I sent?"

"I did. Standard issue Cabbage Patch doll. That particular model is available on Amazon for $29.99. Free shipping, of course."

"What about the letters written on our door? QPQ?"

"I believe I know what that means."

"What is all this?" Eve interrupted. She was standing in front of Taggart's table, looking at multiple stacks of paper.

"Somebody's been busy," Delta commented.

"That is what we secured last night—at least in part. I knew we needed numerous eyes to review the material, so I went to the library this morning and had them all printed."

Eve's forehead furrowed as she studied the paper on the table. "Wait. This is my enrollment application."

"We have the files of everyone who was part of the freshman orientation group, as well as five other female students who meet the age criteria."

Eve spun around to look at Taggart. "Age criteria? I'm confused. What exactly are you looking for?"

I looked into Taggart's eyes and could tell he was thinking the same I was. The time had finally come to let the cat out of the bag. If we were going to ask for everyone's help, they needed to know what we were looking for.

"We believe Taggart's sister is the person responsible for the faked suicides. There's a chance she's enrolled here at Truman."

Eve appeared stunned. "His sister? I don't understand… why would she do that?"

"We think she holds him responsible for the death of their mother."

"Which brings me back to your question regarding the letters written on your door," Taggart interjected. "I postulate that it stands for Quid Pro Quo. Latin translation— something for something."

"So let me get this straight, Taggart has a crazy sister who's killing people because she's pissed he knocked off their mom?" Brandon said.

"That's the theory," Delta said.

"But why not just walk up behind him and stick a knife in his back?" Brandon asked, looking around the room at us, trying to understand. "He doesn't know what she looks like, right, so it would be easy. Why kill people in our group?"

"We don't know much about her, but if she's anything like her mother then this twisted sort of revenge is not a surprise," I explained.

"But how do you know all this? Cassie, you told me that he doesn't have any idea who his sister is or where she's at. Why do you suddenly think she's here now, murdering people?" Eve asked.

"Because I received a warning last week. It was a text message meant for Taggart. It stated that his sister was coming for him."

"Oh… that's not mysterious at all," Brandon commented sarcastically.

"Who was it from?" Eve asked.

"The number was blocked. Furthermore, the message was erased off my phone somehow, so we can't even show the police."

Brandon paced back and forth, shaking his head. "But you didn't fully answer my question. Why would anyone target us for something Taggart did? He's not part of the group."

"You weren't there when we talked about this before, but as hard as it is to believe, we are the one's he's hung out with the most here at Truman," I answered. "He comes to all of our meetings, so it would be easy to assume he's part of it."

"Oh, that's great. Three people are dead because—"

Delta quickly stepped in front of Brandon "That's enough, Brandon," she said forcefully.

Brandon locked eyes with Delta and you could almost see the exasperation bleed out of him. He lowered his head and stuck his hands in his pockets.

"I'm sorry, Taggart," he muttered.

At that moment my phone rang. I immediately answered it when I saw the caller was Talia Davis.

"Talia."

"Cassie, I'm so sorry it's taken me this long to call you back, but you can't imagine how crazy things have been here. Have you heard from Angela?"

"No, I haven't. I was hoping you had some news."

"I went by her room after I visited with you, but nobody was there. All of my calls to her cell phone go to voicemail."

"The same for me. I'm really worried that something has happened to her."

"I'm sure there's no reason to be concerned, and everything is fine. I'll get Angela's parents' home number and give them a try. She's probably there with them now."

"Please call me back as soon as you have any news."

"I will."

I looked up after disconnecting the call to find everyone staring at me.

"You probably heard, no news about Angela yet."

Nobody had anything to say to that.

A few seconds later, "Taggart, how old is your sister?" Brandon asked.

"Twenty-two, why?"

"Well, I don't want to be the conspiracy nut in the group, but Talia Davis is about that age. She's not a freshman, but it is her first quarter here at Truman. And she could have been the last person to see Angela."

"That is nuts," Eve said.

"Is it? Think about it, Jim was the first one murdered and that's when she took over the group. Coincidence, or did she create an opportunity for herself? She'd probably have access to a key that would let her into Cassie's suite, so she could have hung that doll there. Oh… oh… and remember what Tony said the other day, that he thought she was listening in at the door."

"I've already considered that possibility," Taggart surprised me by saying.

"And?" Brandon asked.

"I've not ruled it out. Unfortunately, I was unable to obtain her records last night."

Brandon made a show of cracking his knuckles. "Want me to try some more of my magic?"

Taggart pointed to his laptop at the end of the table. "That would be most helpful."

As Brandon took a seat, Taggart turned to us. "While Brandon is doing that, if you three can go through this paperwork and look for anything odd or suspicious. My examination proved fruitless, but I'm willing to admit to my own fallibility, combined with the fact I've gone without sleep for forty-eight hours, so double-checking my work seems prudent."

"We can do that. You get upstairs and get some sleep," I said.

Taggart nodded and moved towards the spiral staircase. For the first time since we arrived, I took a closer look around his apartment and noticed the multiple folding chairs.

"You bought more chairs?"

Taggart paused on the bottom step. "I knew I would be having guests, and appropriate seating was required."

"A sofa could be considered appropriate also," Delta said as she sat down near Brandon. "I'm just saying."

Taggart looked like he didn't know how to respond, so I shook my head at him and pointed upward. When he was gone, I joined Eve taking a seat at the table.

Forty-five minutes later, Brandon pushed back from the laptop and stretched his arms above his head.

"I don't think Talia is Taggart's sister," he said.

I looked up from the documents I was studying. "No?"

Brandon placed his hands behind his head and leaned back in his chair. "Nah. I found her school records but there was nothing strange there. So I searched her social media and ran a background check, but everything looks normal there to. She's not very active on social media, but what I found didn't look like serial killer material."

"From what I've looked at so far, I don't think any of these people are Taggart's sister," Eve said.

"You've got to keep an open mind, Eve. We said we would go through all of this and that's what we're going to do. But let's not wake Taggart 'til we're finished."

Brandon let his chair fall forward. "I can help ya'll now."

Delta pointed to two stacks of paper closest to Brandon. "You can take those."

Brandon slid the laptop to the side and pulled one of the stacks closer. A frown appeared on his face after he glanced at the top two pages, then he pulled the second stack over and did the same thing.

"These are Brent and Tony's records."

"So?"

"I thought we were looking for Taggart's sister. Why would I need to go through these?"

"Because Taggart wanted to look at everyone in the group. Maybe there's a different reason people in the group are being targeted other than hanging out with Taggart, and something in there might be a clue to why," I explained.

"Who has my stack?" Brandon asked, suddenly looking bothered.

"I do," Delta answered.

Now the expression on Brandon's face had turned into outright concern.

"Please don't read my essay."

Delta smiled. "Too late."

Brandon's face fell.

"What? There's nothing wrong with wanting to be the next Mark Zuckerberg."

"Oh, that's rich," Eve said. "You've already got the being a dick part down pat."

"Guys," I said a little louder than I needed to. "Let's get back to it, please."

After everyone was seated with a stack of paper in front of them, the room turned silent. Thirty minutes later, it was Delta's turn to stretch. "I'm hungry."

"I say we order pizza," Eve said. "I don't feel like hiking back to the food court."

"I like that idea," I said, pulling out my phone. "Anything you don't like on your pizza?"

Eve shook her head. "I'm okay with everything."

Using the app from the Italian Eatery we usually frequented, I punched in an order for two large pizzas.

"Brandon, what do you like?"

Our amateur hacker was engrossed with something he was looking at and acted like he didn't hear my question.

"Just get him a small Meat Lovers pizza," Eve suggested. "He's that type."

I added Eve's suggestion and completed the order. "Done. Should be here in thirty minutes."

"Uh… guys," Brandon said. "I think I have something."

We all looked in his direction. He was holding up a single piece of paper.

"What is it?" Delta asked.

"This is a copy of Tony's driver's license."

"What about it?" I asked.

"It's a fake."

"Fake?"

"That's what I said."

"Are you sure?" Delta asked.

"I used to sell fake IDs at my high school back home, even made a few myself, so I think I'm a decent judge. This is a pretty good one, but it's definitely a fake."

"Why would Tony need a fake ID?" I asked.

Brandon moved the laptop back in front of himself. "Because maybe Tony isn't who he says he is."

The three of us sat in anticipation as Brandon's fingers flew over the keyboard.

"The man has no social media. None. Zippo. Tell me that isn't weird."

"Maybe you should wake Taggart," Delta suggested.

"I'm already up," came Taggart's voice from the stairs. "I've heard."

Taggart came to stand by me as we all continued to watch Brandon's fevered assault on the laptop.

Minutes later, Brandon's eyes grew big as half-dollars. "Oh. My. God."

"What is it?" Eve asked what we were all thinking.

Brandon looked up from the screen, his eyes still popping out of their sockets.

"There's a court petition in Alabama filed two years ago, but it looks like it never went before a judge."

"A petition to do what?" Taggart asked.

"Two things. One was to change his name."

"And the other?"

Brandon glanced at the screen again. He was taking so long that I almost reached across the table and grabbed his neck.

"Let me put it this way. It turns out Tony used to be called – Tonya."

Twenty-Two
Thursday, July 26th 5:25 PM

I had no words, and apparently, neither did anyone else. This was a shocker. Tony used to be a girl. I had never met a transgender person before, or at least not that I was aware of. In New Haven, we had our fair share of gay people and for the most part they were accepted like anyone else, but this was different. I was okay with transgender people and supported their right to correct what they knew was a disconnect between their brain and body, but I wasn't sure how I felt about Tony's secrecy. Then again, given the high rates of hate crimes, why would someone disclose this to anyone other than their inner circle.

"Aren't we violating his privacy by doing this?" Eve asked.

"This is part of the public record," Brandon countered, pointing to the screen. "You just need to know how to look."

"So why didn't he go through with the petition?" Delta asked.

"Two-thirds of US universities have updated their policies, including codes of conduct, with many receiving a Title IX religious exemption from the U.S. Department of Education to openly discriminate against LGBTQ+ people. Truman is one of those, so they may have denied his enrollment if he went through with it," Taggart stated.

"That's awful," I said. That was something that wasn't in the brochures, just like the way they treated students with mental health issues. I was starting to realize that my research into Truman college was woefully lacking.

"That's why he's using a fake driver's license. A legal one would show him as female," Eve observed.

"Guys, aren't you missing the important part here?" Brandon said.

"I'm not following," Delta said.

"Tony is a girl—"

"He's not a girl, not anymore," I corrected.

"Fine, he WAS a girl, and his age lines up. That means he could be Taggart's sister and therefore the one doing the killing. It's the perfect disguise."

That took a moment to sink in, and the longer it did, the more sense it made.

"He is in a room by himself, so there's no one to track his movements," I said.

"And physically he looks capable enough to carry out the murders," Taggart said.

"I heard transsexuality runs in the family. Do you ever feel like you should have been a girl, Taggart?" Brandon asked.

"That term is considered offensive to many in the community. On a technical level, transexual is someone who has had medical intervention to match their body to their gender identity. Not all transgender people choose to do this.

"Transgender" is the umbrella term. Besides, your statement is not factual. Studies suggest that there are likely genetic causes, although the precise genes involved are not fully understood. Any notion that the phenomenon runs in families is false and saying so propagates misinformation."

"Relax, McGill. I was just joking."

"A joke is a brief oral narrative with a climactic humorous twist. Most of what comes out of your mouth falls short of that definition."

"Amen to that," Eve said.

Brandon opened his mouth to say something else but instead looked at Delta.

"Why don't you give the humor a rest for a while," she said, forcing a smile. "I think you're trying too hard."

To his credit, Brandon made a show of zippering his mouth closed.

"You aren't seriously thinking Tony is your sister, are you Taggart?" Eve asked.

"At the moment, I have no evidence to rule out that possibility."

"The two of you look nothing alike," Delta said.

"My sister and I have different fathers. Dissimilar features are not unusual. Additionally, she could have had plastic surgery."

"Brandon, isn't there anything else you can find online that can help us?" I asked.

He unzippered his mouth. "I've already looked. The guy, and his previous identity have next to zero online footprint. That by itself would make me suspicious."

"So, what do we do?" Delta asked.

The ringing of my phone postponed that decision as I answered it.

"Cassie?" Talia's voice in my ear said.

"Talia. Did you get hold of Angela's parents?"

"No. There is no answer at the phone number on her admission paperwork. I've tried numerous times and left several messages. I've also sent an email to the address on file. I'm not sure what else I can do?"

"Can't the school report her as missing and have the police check her home?"

"Cassie, do you know how many students decide to drop out of school and simply go home? We can't report them all as missing, and Angela is no different."

I was becoming more frustrated. "Fine. Can you at least give me her home address so I can check it out myself?"

After a short pause, "I'm not supposed to, but in this case, I will. Do you have something to write this down?"

As Talia read off the address to me, I typed it into my phone.

"This time, will you let me know what you find out?" Talia asked.

"I will. Thank you," I said before disconnecting the call.

"Still nothing on Angela," I told the rest of the group.

"I'm still not one hundred percent convinced Talia isn't involved somehow," Delta said.

"Hang on," I said as I composed a text to Chewy with Angela's home address and asked him to go by when he could to see if anybody was home.

"Let's not lose focus. We were talking about what to do about Tony," I said when finishing the text.

"I say we confront him," Eve stated.

"What? No," I replied.

"Why not?"

"Because he'll just deny everything."

"Or we'll catch him off guard and he'll accidentally admit something. Isn't that how police interrogations work?"

"Maybe on TV," Delta said.

"And the person who is committing these crimes is extremely organized and careful. Not somebody who would be easily tripped up in an interrogation," Taggart said.

"So, what then?"

"If you're going to suggest we try to catch him—or her—in the act, then I want to be the first person NOT to volunteer as bait," Brandon said.

Once again Brandon had managed to get under my skin. "Tony identifies as him, Brandon, so get that through your thick skull."

Brandon put up his hands. "Sorry. Don't rip my tongue out for being confused."

I glanced at Taggart to see if he would back me up, but he had a faraway look in his eyes.

"I need to get into Tony's room," Taggart said.

"You think he has evidence lying around in his room?" I asked.

"It's a start. If I can find something substantive to link him to any of the deaths, then we'll turn everything over to Detective Moss."

"Okay, when?"

A knock on the apartment door rattled everyone.

"It's just the pizza," I said, half-laughing at the way everyone looked. I went to the door and pulled it open.

"I'm not too late, am I?" Tony asked from the doorstep.

I hoped my expression didn't betray the shock I was feeling. Just in case, I decided to provide a reasonable explanation.

"Tony, I didn't realize you were coming."

He looked confused. "I told Brandon I had things to do and would come later. Didn't he tell you?"

"I guess not."

"Figures. Can I come in?"

"Sure," I said, stepping aside and letting him walk past me. After closing the door, I joined him greeting the others.

"Nice digs you have here, Taggart," Tony said after scrutinizing the room. "Could use an upgrade in the furniture department, though."

"It suits my needs," Taggart replied.

Studying Tony from the side, I found myself searching for feminine characteristics in his features. Were his cheeks more prominent, fuller? Was his forehead smoother than most men? Were his eyebrows more arched? What about his jawline, was it less square than a woman's? The closer I looked, the more I thought I recognized, but could that just be me seeing what I thought I should see?

"What's all that?" Tony asked, gesturing towards the paper spread across the table. Out of the corner of my eye, I saw Brandon close the laptop and turn over a piece of paper.

"That's what we've been working on," I answered.

"What is it?"

Thinking quickly, I said, "Taggart believes the person responsible for these deaths is someone from our old school with a grudge against him, so this is the files of everyone from New Haven who is attending Truman."

Tony looked at Taggart. "That's unbelievable. Any leads?"

"Actually, no. It was a bust. We were just about to head back to the dorm."

"Oh, then I am too late."

Another knock on the door made me groan internally. This time it had to be the pizza.

"I'll get it," I said as I went to the door. I opened it as narrowly as I could to slip outside and came face to face with a bewildered delivery boy.

"Listen, we changed our minds. I've already paid for the pizza, so can you take it with you and, I don't know, maybe donate it to someone."

I could tell that my instructions weren't registering with the teenager. "You don't want it?"

"No. Just give it to someone else."

"Who?"

"I don't know. Do you have any friends who live in this area?"

The delivery boy thought about that for a moment. "Jacob lives on the next street over."

"Great, give it to him," I said and slipped back inside.

Everyone looked at me expectantly when I returned. "Girl scouts selling cookies. I told them we weren't interested."

"That's too bad," Delta lamented. "I'm hungry."

"Yeah, who doesn't buy Girl Scout cookies?" Brandon said.

"So, let's get back to campus and we can get something to eat," I suggested.

"I'm sorry I got here late everybody," Tony said. "Would you want me to take this stuff back with me and look it over for you tonight? Just in case you missed something?"

"We had five pairs of eyes on it already. There's nothing there to find," Taggart said.

"Okay, if you say so," Tony said. "I'll walk back with everyone then."

Eve, Delta, and Brandon rose from their seats and followed Tony out the door while I hung back.

"Let's get into Tony's room sometime tomorrow. I'll skip class. I don't know his schedule, but we can watch his room until we see him leave."

"I'll be there at seven," he replied.

We embraced and before I let him go, planted a kiss on his cheek.

"I think we're getting close."

Twenty-Three
Friday, July 27th 8:10 AM

Barksdale dormitory only had two main entrances, so after Taggart arrived sharply at seven, I set up on the side that emptied into the Commons, and he took the exit on the opposite side of the building. None of the classes at Truman began earlier than seven-thirty, but we wanted to make sure we didn't miss seeing Tony leave, so we were ready early.

Just after seven forty-five, Taggart stuck his head out of the door and signaled to me.

"He just left," he said after I joined him in the lobby.

Early morning classes either started at seven-thirty or eight o'clock, but regardless of the start time, they all ended at nine o'clock. That meant we had at least an hour to search Tony's room. We needed to get inside and do it without being seen.

We hung out in the lobby, doing our best to look inconspicuous, until ten minutes past the hour to make sure everybody heading to their eight o'clock class had cleared the building. Moving up the stairs to the second floor, we stopped at Tony's room, which was the first one on the right as you exited the stairwell. As our luck would have it, the hallway was deserted. I leaned against the wall right past Tony's door to shield Taggart from anyone who might suddenly step into the foyer. He knelt in front of the door, his lock picking tools already in his hands.

When I heard the door open behind me, I swung around and quickly followed Taggart inside.

"You know, since we've known each other, I've broken into a funeral home, a university admissions office, and now a dorm room. I'm starting to think you might not be a good influence."

"You don't need to be here if this bothers you."

"Are you kidding? Where would Harry be without Hermione, helping him figure out the clues?"

"Who is Harry and Hermione?"

"Never mind. Let's get to it."

I had imagined that the single rooms in Barksdale were more luxurious than the suites we occupied, but looking around, I could see that they had the same drabness, with less space. Directly upon entering the room there was a door to the left that led to a claustrophobic bathroom. Opposite that was an accordion door that revealed a closet. Just beyond the closet was a small sink area. The entire room was approximately twenty feet deep and stepping towards the outer wall with a lone window, you could see a single bed on the left, the head of which butted against the bathroom wall, and on the right was a tiny, unimpressive, desk. Between the desk and the wall a small refrigerator hummed.

The room felt crowded with just me and Taggart standing there. We started looking around immediately.

They say you can tell a lot about a person by what they surround themselves with. I think that is true to some degree, but I find it doesn't always tell the whole story. Taggart is a prime example. All there is in his apartment are the bare essentials, a table, chair (now chairs), a mattress, a laptop, a stack of books, and various small items to help him prepare meals or maintain his personal hygiene. After seeing all of that, someone might assume that Taggart was a cold-hearted, one dimensional, zero-personality, loner. And on the surface—to most people—that is precisely who he is. But the real Taggart, the one I've come to know, is inquisitive, insightful, multi-layered, multi-faceted, continuously anxious, but a genuinely caring individual. He just doesn't put much worth on personal possessions. What he values most is personal relationships, and of those, there were precious few.

My initial impression of Tony's room told me he was a lot like Taggart, which I knew wasn't right. Nothing hanging on the walls, no trinkets scattered around, no TV, no personal items anywhere. Then I looked in his closet and bathroom. The amount of clothing he had jammed in that small space was impressive in both numbers and assortment. And the limited amount of shelf space in the bathroom was overflowing with health and beauty aids. This told me I was in the room of someone who was intelligent and focused, but also extremely conscious about their appearance. But I already knew that, which made me ask myself what was there about Tony I didn't see, like with Taggart's apartment?

What I didn't see was anything connecting him to the murders of Jim, Lisa, or Brent. No excess rope, no drugs, no revealing surveillance pictures.

"I don't see anything," I said softly.

Taggart straightened up on his knees after pulling something from under the bed. It appeared to be some sort of lockbox. On the front of the unit was a keypad that required a five-numeral PIN to open.

"What do you think is in there?" I asked.

"Unless I'm mistaken, this is a gun safe, so odds are there's a handgun inside."

I felt the back of my neck start to tingle. "A gun. Why would he have one of those?"

"I can think of several reasons." Taggart scanned the room once more. "It's possible he could be storing items somewhere else."

"Where?"

"A self-storage unit off-campus?"

"How are we going to find out if he has one of those?"

"We'll have to follow him and hope he leads us to it."

"Okay, so let's get out of here then."

Taggart had pushed the lockbox back under the bed and risen to his feet when the hallway door swung open. At first, Tony was focused on removing his key from the lock, but when he looked up and saw the two of us standing there, he went motionless.

The three of us remained frozen in place for several seconds, but then suddenly Tony whipped his backpack around and reached into it. Before Taggart or I could react, Tony had his arms out straight, pointing a silver-plated handgun at us.

"What the hell are the two of you doing in my room?" he shouted.

Instinctively my hands went up and I took a step backward. Taggart's hands were up as well.

"There is no need for that, Tony," Taggart said calmly, slowly placing himself between Tony and me.

"I'll be the judge of that. I repeat, what are you doing here?"

"We'll answer your questions, but not while there's a loaded weapon pointed at us."

"You're in no position to dictate rules to me."

"Or what, you'll shoot one of us? Is that really what you see happening here?" Taggart said.

"I'd be within my rights."

"Maybe so, but I doubt you'd welcome the resulting scrutiny afterward. Isn't that correct, Tonya?"

Peeking around Taggart, I watched Tony blink hard several times. His arms sagged a bit, but the gun remained pointing in our direction.

"You know?"

"We know, and we are not a threat to you. You can put the gun away."

Tony let his hand holding the gun drop to his side. A look of profound sadness had come over him. "Who else knows?"

"Eve, Delta, and Brandon," I answered, stepping out from behind Taggart.

Tony clamped his eyes shut. "Oh god, Brandon knows?"

"Yes. He is the one who discovered your past," Taggart answered.

Tony raised his face towards the ceiling; his eyes still closed. Seconds later, his eyes opened and he leveled his gaze at us.

"So, why did you break into my room?" Tony asked. He seemed resigned to the fact his secret was out in the open now.

"This may sound awkward, but we suspected you might be Taggart's sister," I said.

Tony's eyebrows shot up. "I'm sorry, you're going to have to run that by me again."

"Maybe we should take a seat first," Taggart suggested. "This may take a while to explain."

After Taggart and I sat down on the bed, Tony got down on his knees between us. He pulled the lockbox out from under the bed, opened it by entering a code, placed the gun inside, then locked it back and returned it under the bed.

After Tony took a seat in the desk chair, Taggart and I took turns explaining how we thought Taggart's sister was responsible for the deaths in our group. We went on to detail how we accidentally stumbled across his secret, and why his situation led us to believe he might be involved.

"Wow, I've been called a lot of things, but serial killer is a new one. I'm sure glad my economics instructor was sick today, or I would never have known the two of you were here. Since you're telling me all this, should I assume you've had a change of heart? I can show you my birth certificate if you want. I was born in California."

That was a question that had been on my mind since Taggart started spilling the beans. Why was Taggart so relaxed now?

"The way you reacted when you found us, told me what I needed to know. If you were involved, you would have tried to smooth things over with lies, then get us out of here as soon as possible. You didn't do that; in fact, you did the exact opposite of what I would expect. The gun was a surprise, of course."

"There are people in this world who are opposed to my situation, violently so. It's for protection."

"I understand," Taggart said.

"May I ask you a question?" I asked.

"Why not."

"Why didn't you go through with the petition and legally change your name and gender?"

Tony gave me a cold smile. "Both of my parents graduated from Truman. My grandfather graduated from

Truman. There has ever only been one college on my list. You can imagine how crushed I was when I discovered they didn't accept trans people."

"I can only imagine."

"I had already filed the petitions with the court when I found out. At first, I was going to go through with it anyway, choose a different university, and get on with my life. But the more I thought about it, the more I got angry. When people find out I'm trans, they tend to focus on the transition rather than who I am as a person, who I was always meant to be. I've never wanted to be a cause politicians fight over. Why should Truman deny me an education because of a check box on a piece of paper? So I decided not to go through with the legal process and bought an ID that represented who I am. My parents talked me into letting them provide the money for this single room, to alleviate their fears that someone would find out and raise a stink. It looks like that's a bust now."

"I won't tell anybody," I said.

"Nor I," said Taggart.

"And I'm sure the others won't say anything either," I quickly added.

Tony smiled. "Cassie, you really think Brandon will keep his big mouth shut?"

I thought about Delta's newfound influence over Brandon. "It's possible."

"Thank you both for saying that, but I'm not going to worry over it. Whatever happens, happens."

"We are really sorry we caused this," I said.

"Don't sweat it. Your intentions weren't malicious. But speaking of that, I might know something that could be relevant about your sister, that's if you still think she's here on campus?"

"Really? What's that?"

"Weeks ago, before one of our group meetings, I was talking to Lisa, comparing our rooming situation. She was jealous of my single room, even though she was in a suite room by herself. Considering everything, she had more space than I have here, even though she had to share some of it with her suitemates."

"I'm not sure how that helps?" Taggart said.

"I'm getting to it. Lisa told me she was initially signed up to be in a different suite and at the last minute got moved into that room. There was no explanation given, just an email days before she arrived changing the room assignment. She didn't complain about it though when she discovered she had the room to herself," Tony said.

Delta's late enrollment and the hoops we had to jump through to get her assigned to my room popped into my head. "I think I can explain that," I said. "Delta registered for Truman late, and they had to make some last-minute moves so we could room together."

"I remembered you telling us that when we first met," Tony responded, nodding. "But here's what made me think something was odd. Lisa was pretty sure you weren't her originally scheduled roommate. You're a Sociology major, right?"

"Yeah, why does that matter?"

"Lisa's original room assignment had listed on it the name and major of the person she was to be rooming with. Although she couldn't recall the girl's name, she did remember her major. She recalled it because it made her laugh when she read it. Recreation and Leisure Studies. She couldn't believe Truman would offer something like that."

Hearing what Tony was telling us triggered something in the back of mind that was trying to get my attention, but it was still too fuzzy. The whole thing was confusing.

"I'm still not following you. What has any of that got to do with Taggart's sister?"

"I think I know what he's getting at," Taggart said. "Cassie, do you remember who you were going to be paired with before Delta?"

I thought back to when I received my original roommate notification. "No. To be frank, I didn't look at it because Delta had just surprised me with her decision to switch schools, and I was determined we would be together."

"Okay. Then let's call the girl you were going to room with before Delta, girl X. We know that there was an unoccupied room, the one Lisa was eventually moved into. With Delta's late enrollment and your desire to be together, rational thinking would dictate that girl X should have been moved into that unoccupied room to clear the way for Delta. Logistically that would involve moving the least amount of people. But instead of that happening, Lisa is moved into the empty room, and we know that she wasn't girl X because she was originally to room with a girl majoring in Recreation and Leisure Studies. Why? And more importantly, where did girl X go? I postulate this; girl X was moved from Cassie's room into the room with a girl majoring in Leisure Studies, switching Lisa into the solo room. But again, we are left with the question of why? It is indeed suspicious."

"See, I told you. Odd." Tony said.

The something bothering me in the back of my mind was throwing a fit now, but no matter how hard I tried to coerce it into the light, it still remained elusive.

"I know how I can find out who my original roommate was supposed to be, girl X," I said as I pulled out my phone and dialed my mom's number. She picked up on the third ring.

"Cassie. Is something wrong? Have you changed your mind about coming home?" my mom spewed out. I could hear the worry in her voice, and it made my heart ache.

"No Mom, I haven't changed my mind, and there's nothing wrong. You need to stop worrying yourself."

"That's not happening. How is school going? Your father tells me your getting good grades."

"I am. I'd like to chat, but I'm kind of in a hurry and I need a quick favor."

"Oh, okay. What is it?"

"In my room on my desk next to where my laptop used to sit, there's a pile of papers from Truman. There's one particular piece of paper I need you to read something off for me."

"Oh, okay. Hang on. I'm already upstairs."

I heard the sounds of my mom moving through the house. "How's Taggart?"

Other than being terrorized by his murderous sister? "Oh… he's adjusting…"

"That's wonderful. Okay, I'm standing in front of your desk. What paper am I looking for?"

"It's a notification from Truman about dorm room assignments. It should be near the top of the stack."

I could hear papers rustling in the background.

"I'm not seeing it, darling."

"It's there, I'm sure—"

"Oh, here it is. I have it. It was stuck behind—"

"Whose name does it say I was going to be roommates with?"

"Does that matter now?"

"Mom, just read me the name."

"Cassie, there's no need to be snippy. Let's see…ummmm."

"Kinda in a hurry here, Mom."

"Here it is."

I held my breath.

Twenty-Four
Friday, July 27th 9:22 AM

Walking towards the student center with Taggart and Tony, I felt numb. Not upset. Not frightened. Not even apprehensive. Just nothing. I think my mind was still trying to figure out how I should feel, and the jury was still out. Taggart kept giving me these little side-looks, so I knew he was concerned, or maybe confused by my lack of reaction. I think if there was a window in the side of my head like a computer monitor, all you'd see was a spinning cursor. Still processing.

Eve had been initially assigned to be my roommate. No big deal, right? But luckily, I spoke to a super nice person in University Housing who'd heard about what had happened to us in New Haven and understood the comfort we'd get rooming together. Delta was placed in my room, but apparently something odd happened. Instead of the school moving Eve into the available solo-occupant room, she got assigned to the other room in our suite with JJ, displacing Lisa. How did that happen? Why did it happen? Maybe there was a reasonable explanation? Was it just coincidence? Or could something more sinister be going on?

Regardless of how I felt, we had to find out the answer to that question. That meant I needed to do something that a week ago I wouldn't have thought conceivable.

Call Brandon for help.

After we arrived at the Hideaway and secured a table in the back, I dialed the number Tony provided.

"Go for Carter," Brandon's voice came over my cell phones handsfree speaker.

"Brandon, it's Cassie," I said, talking over the top of my phone, which lay on the table between the three of us.

"Wow, this is a surprise. What can I do you for, Underwood?"

"I'm here with Taggart and Tony, and we need your computer skills again."

There was a long pause before Brandon replied. "You're with Taggart… and Tony?"

Looking over at Tony, I saw him display a lopsided grin.

"You can relax, Brandon. Tony's not who we thought he was."

"Do you mean he's not—"

"Related to Taggart in any way." I scanned the room to make sure no one was listening.

"That's good, I guess."

"How soon can you meet us at the Hideaway?"

"I'm not sure. I haven't had breakfast yet."

"Brandon, we'll buy you breakfast," Tony spoke up. "This is important."

"Oh… okay. Give me fifteen minutes."

Twenty minutes later, there was still no Brandon, but I did receive a text from Chewy.

WENT BY THE ADDRESS YOU SENT ME. NOBODY HOME. PEEKED IN WINDOWS BUT DIDN'T SEE ANYTHING UNUSUAL. THERE IS ONE CAR IN THE DRIVEWAY. MAILBOX LOOKS LIKE IT HAS SEVERAL DAYS WORTH OF MAIL IN IT AND LAWN NEEDS MOWING. NEIGHBORS CLUELESS ABOUT WHEREABOUTS. WHAT DO I DO NOW?

I replied to Chewy, telling him to leave the house as is and head back to Truman when he could. Ten minutes later, Brandon finally appeared in the Hideaway doorway. He was wearing a pair of faded jeans and a white t-shirt with CUSTOMER SUPPORT'S MOST WANTED: ID10T emblazoned across the chest.

"You're late," I said as he approached.

"I got hung up by some guy from the school's outreach center wanting to check on my mental health."

I thought about the man who'd visited Delta and me shortly after Jim's death. "Was his name Gerald Batiste?"

"Could be, I didn't pay that much attention. He really had a hard-on to ask me questions, but I told him people were waiting on me. He seemed kind of upset when I split."

"Did you bring your laptop?" Taggart asked.

Brandon tapped the shoulder strap to his backpack. "Right here."

"Great, this is what we need –"

Brandon held up his hand to form a stop symbol. "You remember I told you I hadn't had my breakfast yet, right?"

I sighed deeply.

"What do you want?" Tony asked. "I'll go get it while you get started."

Brandon rattled off a long list of breakfast foods, including a tall cup of orange juice. While he was giving his order, I couldn't help but notice that he wouldn't look directly at Tony, nor had he since he arrived.

"Got it," Tony said when Brandon was finished. "Anybody else want anything?"

"Coffee, black," I said.

"Same," Taggart said.

"Be right back," Tony said and then was gone. Brandon swung his backpack off his shoulder and began setting up his laptop on the table. When he was finished, he cracked his knuckles.

"Okay, what am I after?"

Together, Taggart and I explained the situation with Eve and the odd room placement.

"So basically, you want me to find out if anybody has been finagling room assignments behind the scenes?"

"Exactly."

"Piece of cake," Brandon said as he launched into his assignment. As he worked, his face adopted a stern expression. I had to give Brandon that much, he might act like an irritating flake socially, but when it came to his efforts with the computer, he was all business.

Ten minutes later, Tony returned with a tray full of food and drinks. When all the food was spread out on the table, Brandon grabbed a breakfast burrito and shoved it into his mouth. After several bites, he resumed his work on the laptop.

Ten minutes following his last bite of food, Brandon pushed his chair away from the table.

"I think I ate too fast," he said, rubbing his stomach.

"If you belch, I'm going to ram that cup down your throat," I said.

Brandon put up his hands. "Relax, how crass do you think I am?"

I let that question pass. "Did you find anything?" I asked instead.

"I did, and it turns out you have reason to be sweating it. Your original roommate was supposed to be a girl named Cheryl Tombs, whoever that is. But before the initial room notifications were sent out, the housing system was hacked, and Eve's name was swapped for Cheryl's. You can tell that it was manipulated because a normal room transfer follows a specific set of system transactions, and this didn't happen here. So you and Eve were all set to be assigned together, but when you added Delta into your room, Eve was moved into an empty room. But that didn't last very long because somebody hacked the system again and swapped Lisa and Eve, putting Lisa in the other suite and Eve in with JJ. Somebody really wanted Eve to be in that suite with you girls."

"I don't suppose you can tell who it was who did the hacking?" I asked.

Brandon shook his head. "No. It looks like whoever did it was using a public server, like an internet café."

"What better way to monitor my activities than to insert herself in your affairs," Taggart stated.

A thought popped into my head. Actually, it was several thoughts, but I decided to act on the one that seemed most relevant. I pulled out my phone, found the name in my contacts, and dialed.

"Hello," a girl's voice answered.

"Tammy, this is Cassie Underwood, Eve's friend."

"Oh, hi. What's up?"

"Just a quick question, the other night when Eve spent the evening with you, was she there all night?"

"Sure. Why do you ask?"

"Are you positive? It's important."

A brief pause proceeded the response. "Well, I'm almost positive."

"What do you mean by almost positive?"

"Well, she slept on the couch in the common room. I tried to get her to take my old roommate's bed, but she said she'd be more comfortable on the couch. She was there when I woke up the next morning, but I couldn't swear she didn't slip out sometime during the night. Why is it so important?"

"The girls in our suite have been pulling pranks on one another, and I just wanted to see if Eve could have pulled off this one."

"Oh. Well, I guess it's possible."

"Thanks, Tammy," I said and hung up. "Eve could have hung that doll in our room when we were breaking into the admissions building. Brandon, I need you to dig some more. Find out everything you can about Eve."

"I'm on it."

I searched for another contact number on my phone.

"Who are you calling now?" Tony asked.

I held up my index finger as the number I dialed began to ring.

"Hello," the familiar voice answered on the third ring.

"JJ, it's Cassie."

"Cassie! It's so great to hear your voice. I sure miss you guys."

"We miss you also. How are you adapting to being a civilian again?"

"My parents have me researching other schools already. How are things there?"

"That's the reason I'm calling. I was wondering if I could ask you some questions."

"Sure. About what?"

"Eve."

"Eve? I don't understand."

"Just humor me, Okay? What kind of roommate was she?"

"Roommate? The best. When she was there, she was quiet. Easy to get along with. We never fought. She always let me watch whatever I wanted on TV. She was pretty much drama-free."

"You said when she was there?"

"Yeah, she disappeared a lot. I'm not sure where she went, and she never said."

"Did she study much?"

"Uhhhhh… not really. She was always on her laptop, but I'm not sure if that was studying. It's kind of ironic. She was always pestering me to study, but I never saw her reading a book from one of her classes."

"How about phone calls? Did she get any?"

"No, now that you ask, I guess not. Oh, wait. There was one call I walked in on. Whoever it was on the other end of the call, she was royally pissed at them. That was the only time I heard her cuss. She hung up pretty quick after I came in though. She was more quiet than usual after that call."

"She didn't mention any names during the call?"

"No, like I said, it was pretty brief."

"Did you ever, uh, snoop through any of her stuff?

"Cassie!"

"Listen, we all do it. It's human nature. You're left alone in the room, and you can't help look through the pictures or other memorabilia your roommate brought with them from home. I've done it to Delta."

"I suppose, but Eve didn't have anything personal lying about. She was kind of a neat freak."

"Okay. Is there anything else you can think of that was out of the ordinary?"

"You mean other than her telling us about her suicide attempt? What's going on, Cassie? Why all the questions about Eve? Does it have anything to do with the fake suicides?"

"I'm not sure yet, and I can't say much else right now. Please don't tell her I called if you speak to her, okay?"

"Okay, but you got me worried now."

"Don't be. I'll call you again soon. Thanks, JJ."

Putting away my phone, I saw Brandon still hard at work on his laptop. Taggart and Tony were looking at me.

"JJ overheard a brief phone call between Eve and somebody else where Eve was distraught. Not sure what it was about."

"I found something else," Brandon suddenly spat out. "I did a search using Eve's parents name, Janey, and I found adoption papers. A baby girl named Jane Doe was adopted by Steve and Carlotta Janey in May of 1998 and became Eve Janey."

Taggart's eyes locked with mine.

"According to the age on these adoption papers, Eve lied about her age when she enrolled at Truman also. She's three years older than the rest of us."

"Taggart," I said.

"I know," he replied.

"Does that mean something?" Tony asked, looking confused.

"One of few things we know about Taggart's sister was that she was three years older than him," I explained. "But the last name on her birth certificate was Tinge. Why would it say Doe on the adoption papers?"

"One possible explanation is that my mother abandoned her. It would explain the subsequent adoption."

"All of her social media, which isn't much, is from the last year or so. Nothing before that. But what I see here is pretty normal stuff. What isn't normal is the size of her bank account. I'm looking at her financial records and the chick has a lot of dough. I'm talking oodles."

"Taggart, even if she is your sister—" Tony started to say.

"She is," Taggart stated emphatically.

"Fine, she is. But do you still think she's the one responsible for these deaths? There's no way she could manhandle Jim and Brent's bodies."

"Agreed. She would need help."

"She was in the foster care system," Brandon continued spilling facts he was finding. "From early 1998, when she was only two years old until she was adopted the following year."

"So that means your mother didn't raise Bella," I observed.

"But it doesn't rule out my mother being influential in her life somehow."

"This Steve Janey, Eve's adoptive father, is a big deal. He's running for the US Senate. Did we know that?" Brandon said.

Taggart suddenly stood up.

"Where are you going?" I asked.

"Back to my apartment. I need to think."

"Do you want me to come with you?"

Even though it was still fairly early in the morning, Taggart suddenly looked tired. "I prefer to be alone right now if that's okay?"

I realized that Taggart needed time to process. "Sure. I get it."

"I'll call you later," Taggart said and took off.

An awkward silence descended upon the table after Taggart left. Brandon closed the lid on his laptop but remained motionless. Tony shifted uncomfortably in his seat.

"Can't say I blame Taggart. Kind of a lot to take in, having your murderous big sister covertly rooming in the same suite as your girlfriend," Tony observed.

"Imagine how I feel," I said.

"No thanks," Tony replied, grinning, which made me laugh.

"It's good that we can laugh about it," I said. "When I first found out, I was kind of in a daze. Not sure if you noticed."

"You did look a bit shell-shocked," Tony said.

"Like you did when you found us in your room," I said.

My reminder of that encounter inadvertently caused the conversation to dry up. Brandon turned off his portable mouse and slid his laptop into his backpack, doing his best to ignore us.

"Brandon, thank you for doing all that for us," I said. "I don't know where we'd be if you weren't here to help."

"I like doing that kind of stuff, so its good that it helped somebody," he replied, gathering up the trash from his meal and still not looking at us.

I looked at Tony and tilted my head in Brandon's direction. Tony changed seats, so he was sitting in the chair next to Brandon.

"Brandon, listen, you found out something about me that I really didn't want anyone to know, so –"

Brandon stopped what he was doing. "I ran across that stuff by accident. I wasn't looking for it."

"I know. You were just trying to help out, like you were today. But if people find out –"

For the first time Brandon looked directly at Tony. "Why would they find out?"

That surprised Tony. "I… well… you might –"

"I wouldn't tell anyone," Brandon said firmly.

Tony looked at me, imploring me to help somehow.

"I think what Tony is trying to say is that the two of you haven't always been cordial to one another and he's afraid you might use that information against him someday."

Brandon glanced at me, then looked back at Tony. "I might be a dick sometimes, but I'm not a complete asshole. Some things you don't mess around with. Your life is your life. All I see when I look at you is a dude named Tony. End of story."

It didn't slip my attention that Brandon used Tony's first name.

Tony was struggling to maintain his composure. "I… uh… thank you. Coming from you, that means a lot."

Brandon shrugged his shoulders. "Still doesn't mean I like you."

Tony smiled. "Same here."

Twenty-Five
Friday, July 27th 4:51 PM

The endless waiting was driving me out of my mind.

After returning to my room from the Hideaway, I knew there was no way I could go to the rest of my classes, so I decided to kill time until Taggart decided what our next move would be. At first, I tried going over chapters for class, but after re-reading the same page four times, I gave up on that. Then I tried playing Sudoku on my phone, and that was even worse. I debated calling Taggart to check on him, maybe nudging him towards some sort of action to relieve my feeling of ineptitude, but I nixed that idea. The last thing he needed was an impatient girlfriend bothering him while he contemplated how to approach a sister he's never met, who's been killing people he doesn't care about. That last part was kind of brutal, but not too far from the truth.

A knock on our door came as a relief, until I saw who it was.

Chewy… and Tunes… stood there smiling at me.

Tunes was still a couple inches shorter than Chewy, but he had filled out his frame. His straight black hair still sported the same bowl cut, and the split in his left eyebrow from an old scar was less noticeable now. His over-the-ear headphones he used to combat his attention deficit hyperactivity disorder, a form of ADHD that caused him to be distracted by sound, had been upgraded to a pair of air pods.

I shook off my initial shock and embraced Tunes.

"This is a surprise," I said, giving Chewy a knowing glance. "What are you doing here?"

"Chewy told me what was going on, so I came right up," he said as we separated. His eyes quickly scanned the inside of my room. "I'd been meaning to visit anyway."

"Delta is at class," I said, answering the unasked question. "Come on in."

"What's the latest?" Chewy asked as he plopped down on my bed.

I was tempted to tell them everything we had discovered since he'd been gone, but I held my tongue. Why? Because Delta would be getting out of class soon and she would never let me hear the end of it if I told the boys before her.

"You'll find out soon enough. How is your mother doing with her cancer treatments?"

Chewy was starting to provide a recap when I heard the hallway door open. I halted Chewy in mid-sentence to listen. Instead of my door opening inward, the sound of the other room's door opening and closing came through the wall.

"Eve is back," I said softly.

"Why are we whispering?" Tunes asked.

"We're not," I said a little louder.

"Whatever the level just above whispering is, that's what you're doing. How come?" Chewy said.

"I can't tell you until Delta gets back."

"Why?"

"She'll be pissed that I told you first."

"Okay, so tell us, and then we'll pretend we're hearing it for the first time when she gets here."

That made me frown. "Really? You want to be that kind of guy?"

Now Chewy looked embarrassed. "No, not really. But having to wait is torture."

"Welcome to my afternoon."

The sound of the outside door opening caught our attention. This time the door to our room opened immediately after that, and in stepped Delta wearing a cream-color halter top and shorts. Her colorful backpack draped across her back. The 70's hippy chick style was strong with this one.

"Greetings minions," she said, then froze when she noticed Tunes sitting next to Chewy.

"Hey Delta," Tunes said, accompanied by a limp-wristed half-wave.

Delta shot me a look and all I could do was offer her a crooked smile. I felt for my best friend. Even though Tunes was still a junior in high school and Delta was a college freshman, and he was still living in New Haven, and she was a couple hundred miles away, they made a good couple. She had reconciled herself to the challenges and moved on, but it was obvious that Tunes hadn't. There couldn't be a worse time for emotional turmoil, and I didn't have the bandwidth to be a relationship counselor right now.

Delta tossed her backpack into her upper bunk and hugged Tunes when he stood.

As I pushed the door shut Delta's eyebrows creased together when she saw the serious look on my face. "What's going on?"

I took a deep breath.

"Eve is Taggart's sister," I said softly, looking back and forth between all of them.

"You're shittin' me," Delta blurted out. Chewy locked his fingers together on top of his head, making a face like he was blowing up a balloon.

"Shhhhh… careful. Eve's next door."

"Holy crapola. Are you sure she's Taggart's sister?" Delta asked.

"One hundred percent."

"You were pretty sure Tony was his sister yesterday," Delta pointed out.

"Wait. What? Tony?" Chewy said, looking confused.

I remembered that Chewy wasn't there yesterday when we found out about Tony. "Long story, but it was a mistake. We're sure this time. Brandon confirmed it."

"This is mind-blowing. She was right here under our noses the whole time," Delta said.

"I have to say that she's not what I was expecting," said Chewy.

"What were you expecting?"

"I don't know, maybe someone like the female cyborg from Terminator three."

"Not quite."

"What do we do now?"

"I don't know. I'm waiting for Taggart to come up with a plan."

"How's he taking it?"

I shrugged my shoulders. "He's being more quiet than usual. He wanted to be by himself while he thought—"

The sound of a door opening, followed by a soft knocking at our door, made me freeze.

"Come in," I said.

The door swung open, and Eve stuck her head inside. Her hair was tucked underneath a pale blue hat. Lines formed on her forehead when she saw the three of us gathered together in the corner of the room.

"Oh, hello," Eve said when she saw Tunes.

"This is Tunes, another of our friends from New Haven," I said. "Tunes, this is Eve, our suite-mate."

To Tunes credit his expression didn't giveaway what I had just told him about Eve. "Hi," he said.

"I wanted to let you know I'm going to the library for a while. And don't worry, I'll steer clear of any strangers, and I'm sure there'll be plenty of people there."

"Okay. Call if it gets late and we'll come escort you back," I said.

"That's sweet. Okay, bye."

When the door was closed and I heard the hallway door close as well, I jumped up from the desk.

"I have to follow her."

"You have to what?" Delta asked, staring up at me.

"Follow her. JJ told me that Eve would sometimes disappear for long periods, so we should follow her and see where she goes."

"And if she's just going to the library?"

"Then fine. No harm, no foul. But if she isn't, I need to know."

"I'll go with you," Chewy said, standing as well.

"Good." I reached into my closet and pulled out a windbreaker to slip on. "Delta, you stay here with Tunes."

Delta made a face like I had just asked her to jump out the window. "What? Why don't we all go?"

"Someone needs to stay, in case we lose her and she comes back. You and Tunes can use this time to catch up."

I could tell Delta wanted to respond, but anything she might say would only hurt Tunes' feelings so instead she simply nodded.

"Let's go," I said to Chewy, throwing open the door. Out in the hallway, I looked in both directions, but Eve was nowhere in sight.

"Shit, we waited too long."

I tried to decide which direction to go. If Eve were going to the library, then she would take the rear exit. But what if she was heading somewhere else? I thought it was a safe assumption that she would purposefully give us a destination in the opposite direction from where she really intended to go. Considering that's what I would do, I turned left and headed towards the front exit. Walking briskly, Chewy and I made our way down the stairs and out of the doorway.

I exhaled in relief when I spotted Eve twenty yards ahead of us, walking purposefully along Campaign Avenue. Chewy took a step to go after her and I pulled him back.

"Let's give her some more distance first," I said.

Chewy and I hung back, patiently watching Eve getting farther and farther away. When the distance had reached fifty yards, I said, "That's enough," and started walking.

Instead of taking the sidewalk that bordered the street, we chose to stay closer to the buildings just in case we needed to duck out of sight. Eve turned right on Hastings Street, so Chewy and I jogged to the corner so that we wouldn't lose sight of her. After she turned left again three blocks later, I started to suspect where she might be heading. My suspicion was confirmed five minutes later when the outline of the Hard Bean Café came into view.

Picking up the speed to close the distance between us, we were only a block away when she entered the cafe.

"Let's go over there," I said to Chewy, pointing to a small bookshop directly across from the coffee shop. We crossed the street casually and entered the book shop. Right as you entered, the display window showcased the top sellers and the latest releases. The window also faced the Hard Bean Café and provided a perfect view of its sitting area.

"Can I help you find anything," a voice came from behind us. It was a girl, probably a student working as a part-timer, standing behind a cash register near the back of the shop.

"No, thanks," I replied. "We're good."

I grabbed a hardback book from a nearby shelf and flipped open the cover, allowing my eyes to look over the top of the book and focus on the café across the street.

I located Eve right away. She was seated at a small table in the dine-in section, facing in my direction, talking to some guy. From where Chewy and I stood, all I could make out of the stranger was the back of his head and shoulders. He had brown hair and wore a solid black polo shirt.

He also seemed to be on the receiving end of Eve's scorn because, by the animated way in which she was speaking to him, it suggested she wasn't happy. The conversation paused when a server appeared at the table. Eve shook her head, but the stranger must have ordered because the server wrote something down on her notepad. When the waitress left, Eve's verbal assault continued.

I pulled out my phone and dialed Taggart's landline.

"Hello?"

"Taggart. Me and Chewy trailed Eve and she's talking to some guy I don't recognize at the Hard Bean Café. We're in the bookstore across the street and she seems pissed."

"You shouldn't be doing that."

"Why not?"

"It could be dangerous."

"We had to do something, besides, Chewy's with me. So, are you coming or what?"

"I'll be right there," he said and hung up.

Chewy and I continued to watch the heated discussion. This was a side of Eve I hadn't seen before, and I was glad of it. The stranger, on the other hand, was remaining calm, giving no signs that he was a willing participant in the drama. The server returned with drinks, then left again.

"Who do you think that is?" Chewy asked.

"No clue. Maybe her accomplice."

"Are you sure I can't help you with something," the girl at the register called out again.

"Still good," I replied, giving her a half-wave.

When I looked back, I saw that Eve was now on her feet, looking as if she was about to leave. The stranger was still seated. Eve appeared to be listening to something the stranger was saying, then slowly re-took her seat. A good deal of the intensity she had displayed before seemed to be gone now.

Taggart walked into the bookstore minutes later and followed our gaze across the street.

"Any idea who that is?" I asked.

"None."

Suddenly Eve was standing again, pointing a finger at the stranger, then she abruptly departed.

"Chewy, please continue to follow Eve," Taggart instructed.

"What are you going to do?"

"Cassie and I will follow her companion."

Chewy headed for the door. "I'm on it."

"Chewy," I said, which caused him to pause. "Be careful."

"Yes, mom," he said, offering me a smile before disappearing.

Looking back across the street I saw the stranger, standing now, lay money on the table then head towards the rear exit. Stepping outside, he made his way to the parking lot and stopped next to a black Escalade.

"Come on," Taggart said, grabbing my hand. "My car's just up the street."

I clumsily placed the book I had been using as a disguise back on the shelf right before Taggart pulled me out of the store. Running down the sidewalk, away from the café, I worried that we wouldn't make it to Taggart's car in time to catch the stranger driving from the coffee shop. But in no time, we were in Taggart's Chevy Impala and pulling away from the curb.

Just as we pulled even with the Hard Bean, I spotted the Escalade turning left at the stop sign ahead of us.

"There," I said, pointing.

"I got it," he replied.

Gunning the engine, we sped forward, pausing briefly at the stop sign, then accelerated again through the turn. There were no cars between us and the Escalade, which was now half a dozen car lengths in front of us. Taggart did an excellent job of matching its speed and maintaining the distance between him and us. A couple of turns later, we found ourselves on the I-20 onramp.

"It appears we are heading into Atlanta," Taggart remarked.

Twenty minutes later, we were exiting I-20 for the I-285 north loop. Traffic was moderately heavy but thankfully the Escalade was easy to track. Things became more complicated once we exited I-285 towards the inner city, and the traffic got a whole lot heavier.

"Do you know where we are?" I asked, searching for a sign or landmark I could recognize.

"Buckhead."

We followed the Escalade for a couple more miles until it pulled off the road into the entrance for covered parking. Driving past slowly, we watched as the driver inserted a key card into an unmanned station, causing the barrier gate to rise and allow the escalade to go inside.

Taggart sped into a nearby short-term parking lot and parked.

"Wait here," he said as he jumped out of the car. I watched him run towards the building adjacent to the parking lot we saw the Escalade pull into. Ten minutes later, he came jogging back.

"Do you have Brandon's number?" he said as he slid into his seat.

"I do."

"Please call him for me."

I made the call and put it on speaker.

"Go for Carter."

"Brandon, this is Taggart."

"McGill. I didn't think you had a cell phone."

"Cassie let me use hers. I need your assistance once again."

"Let me guess, you've been surfing porn sites, and you have all these pop-up ads you need help getting rid of?"

"Hardly. Take down the name of this company."

"Hang on a sec. Okay, shoot."

"Gentry Security. They have an office in Buckhead. I need to know everything you can find out about them, specifically how they might be connected with Eve."

"Ahhh, the mystery deepens. Okay, but it'll be a few minutes, though. I'm running a virus check on my laptop."

"Is something wrong?" Taggart asked.

"No, just need to get rid of a few pop-up ads."

My phone beeped, indicating another call was coming in. "We got to go, Brandon, I have another call," I announced.

"Is that you, Cassie? Shit!"

I ended that call and answered the new one.

"Hello?"

"Cassie, it's Chewy."

"Chewy, I'm here with Taggart. Did you follow Eve back to the dorm?"

"I followed her, but she didn't go back to the dorm."

"She didn't? Where did she go?'

"I'm going to give you the address, and you can see for yourself."

Twenty-Six
Friday, July 27th 6:31 PM

The sun was dropping below the horizon when we spotted Chewy standing in the road, waving his arms. Taggart steered his car into the parking space Chewy pointed us towards and killed the engine.

"Why are we parking here?" I asked as I climbed out of the car. "Isn't the address you gave us down that street back there?"

The location where Chewy had directed us to was approximately a ten-minute walk from The Hard Bean Café and even further away from the Truman campus. It was a part of the city surrounding the university that they purposefully left off the tour when prospective students came to visit. The district's just off campus had benefited from a major renovation recently and was a significant selling point for the school. Then there was what everyone called the demilitarized zone – a section a little farther out from the school where construction was commonplace as the city continued to expand their face-lift efforts. People overlooked the mess and inconvenience because of the promise of things to come. Then there was the area right past the demilitarized zone where we were now—the dead zone. This area was made up of mostly rundown neighborhoods filled with small decrepit homes with broken down cars in the front yard and lawns that were covered with more trash than grass.

"The house is at the end of a cul-de-sac, and if you parked on that street, Eve would see you when she left. We're out of sight up here," Chewy explained.

"Good thinking," Taggart said, surveying the area.

Chewy pointed to a road a little further past where we parked. "We can go down that street. It runs parallel to the one Eve is on and it ends in a dead-end as well. I've been down there. One of the houses is under construction and nobody is home, so we can scope things out from there."

"Excellent, let's go," Taggart said.

We let Chewy lead the way. Walking briskly, we soon reached the street he referenced and turned right.

The road looked to be half a football field in length with three homes situated around a cul-de-sac. Lights illuminated the porches on two of those houses, but the third one to the far right was utterly dark. We made our way to the darkened house and came to a stop next to a pallet of roof shingles.

Although the house that Chewy pointed to was still a ways off, and the light was fading fast, I could still see it pretty clear. It was a small grey house. Probably a two-bedroom. The house was up on cinder blocks, leaving a three-foot crawlspace underneath it. Several bushes, each in need of a severe trimming, ran down the side of the house. The lot the house was on was small, leaving little room for a backyard. A huge drainage ditch ran along the back of the property, fenced off by a chain-link fence, which also continued past the land where we were standing.

A single light was visible through the main window at the front of the house and as I stared at it a sense of dread came over me. This was the type of house I imagined serial killers would use to hold their victims before performing their horrible acts. A shudder ran down my spine.

"I think she's in there alone," Chewy said. "No cars in front and I saw her use a key to get in."

"Cassie, I need to borrow your phone again," Taggart said.

I pulled my phone out of my back pocket and handed it to him. "You know, sooner or later, you need to get one for yourself."

Ignoring me, Taggart instead dialed a number on my phone and put it on speaker.

"Go for Carter."

"What did you find out about Gentry Security?"

"Well, hello to you too, McGill. I'm doing great, thanks for asking."

"Gentry Security."

"I got squat. Well, next to squat. Their name is well earned because I was unable to penetrate their firewalls. I'm talking top-notch stuff. The only thing I did find was a phone call from Eve to them yesterday, and I got that by looking at her phone records."

"Just the one?"

"Affirmative."

"She could have used the public phone in the Barksdale basement," I suggested.

Taggart nodded.

"But get this," Brandon continued. "Gentry Security has been in the news this past year, and not in a good way. They've been linked to some shady dealings like extortion and blackmail. There haven't been any charges filed yet."

"That's helpful, but I need something else."

"Shocker."

"I need to know who owns or rents this address."

After Taggart relayed the information, Brandon asked, "Is that all?"

"There's one more thing," Taggart said, then walked away far enough that I couldn't hear what he was saying.

I stood there wondering what it was that Taggart could be saying to Brandon when suddenly Chewy was shaking my arm.

"She's leaving," he whispered.

Instinctively, Chewy and I bent down behind the stack of roof shingles, even though it was dark enough now that I doubt she'd be able to see us where we were standing. I watched Eve lock the door behind her, and then start walking away. When we were sure she was out of sight, we relaxed. Taggart rejoined us, handing me my phone back.

"Chewy, follow her," Taggart said.

"No way, I'm coming with you," Chewy retorted.

"Wait a minute, where are we going?" I asked, momentarily confused.

"Where do you think?" Chewy answered. "He's going to break into that house."

"Oh." I looked at Taggart and his bland expression told me Chewy was right. "Not again."

"You can't be surprised, can you?" Chewy added.

I threw up my arms. "Excuse me. I can't help it if my default response to everything isn't to commit a felony."

"All of the answers we're searching for could be in that house," Taggart said.

"Which is why I want to go with you," Chewy pleaded.

"I know, and I get it. It's just that —" I stopped what I was going to say because I didn't know what to say. In my head, I knew this was the right thing to do. It made sense, and honestly, there were no other options available to us. It was just that breaking the law, even for the right reason, was unsettling to me. I suppose having a conscience was a good thing, but in this case, it was in the way.

"Never mind. If we're going to do this, let's do this."

The three of us trudged across the open land between the houses and eventually stepped into the other cul-de-sac. I looked up the street to make sure Eve wasn't still lurking somewhere, but there was no one in sight. Chewy and I followed Taggart up the steps, my eyes scanning the street to make sure nobody was watching us. When Taggart pulled his lock pick tools from his back pocket Chewy and I turned around to face the road, standing shoulder to shoulder to block Taggart's activity from view.

"Do you need light?" I asked over my shoulder.

"I'm good. This is more about touch than sight."

Seconds later, I heard the door click open, prompting Chewy and me to swing around and follow Taggart into the house.

I almost ran into Taggart just inside the door. He had come to a complete stop and was staring at something on the wall. Following his gaze, I found what drew his attention.

A blinking light on a security system keypad.

"Shit," Chewy said softly, obviously looking at the same thing.

None of us had thought to question whether there was a security system. In a neighborhood like this, and a house in the condition this one was, who could blame us. Taggart didn't have time to properly case the place either. Picking locks was one thing, but I was sure that disabling security systems was beyond Taggart's capabilities. When it went off, all we could do is run like hell and hope for the best.

But it didn't go off. It blinked two more times while we stood frozen in place, then went out.

"It's not armed," Taggart said, his shoulders sagging a bit. "It was just the door sensor."

"My mom does that all the time too. We pay for this fancy security system, and she always forgets to turn it on when we go somewhere," Chewy said.

"Let's be grateful for small favors," I said.

"Can the two of you engage the flashlights on your phones, please?" Taggart asked.

I did as he requested, shooting a beam of light across the room, then turned the phone over to him.

Panning the light around, it looked like we were standing in the living room area. There was a small leather sofa against the wall and an LCD television hung on the opposite wall. Nothing else, though. The walls were bare, no magazines or other reading materials lying around, nothing to suggest who might live there.

Stepping further into the house, we entered what I imagined was supposed to be a dining area, but the only furniture in the room was a rolltop desk and chair. But it was what hung on the wall behind the desk that drew my attention. Watching Taggart use the light from my phone, combined with Chewy's, it lit up the entire wall. The three of us stood side by side, taking the sight in.

What we saw on that wall was every newspaper story, every magazine article, every online story, every picture, every sketch, in essence anything having to do even remotely with Taggart McGill. There were things on that wall that I had never seen. There were handwritten notes with information about Taggart's grandparents pinned up there.

But that was not everything on display. There were pictures and things about me as well. The page from our high school yearbook with my class picture was there. Other images from my Instagram account were there as well. A shiver ran through my body when I spotted a copy of my sister's obituary.

My phone rang in Taggart's hand. The wall was once again plunged into darkness as Taggart answered the call by choosing the speakerphone.

"Brandon?"

"Yeah. I got that information on the house for you."

"Go ahead."

"It was owned by a lady named Alma Epperson, but passed away last year and left it to her son who lives in Michigan. The house, however, is managed by a real estate agency here in Wolfs Head and is currently rented to—get this—Eve Janey."

"Anything else?"

"No, only that she's been there, or at least the lease was signed back in March."

"Thank you."

"Oh, that other thing is done as well."

"Very good."

"Do you need anything else, or can I go eat now?"

"Enjoy your dinner," Taggart said, then hung up and pointed the phone's flashlight back at the wall.

"Can we call the police now?" I asked, motioning towards the wall.

"Not yet. This proves nothing. We need to find something that links her to the deaths. Excess rope, narcotics, anything else that could tie her to the crime scenes."

"And what if there is none? What if she's that good and there is no evidence like that? Or what if Gentry Security did all the dirty work and we're not able to get any dirt on them? What do we do then?"

"I refuse to believe in that scenario. We will find something."

Without warning, the room bloomed with light, momentarily blinding me. As my eyes adjusted, I became aware that the overhead fixture had been turned on. I turned toward the door where the switch was located and froze. I could feel my beating heart forcing its way into my throat.

Eve stood in the door, her hand still on the light switch.

"Your lives are in danger."

Twenty-Seven
Friday, July 27th 6:31 PM

"You think we're scared of you?" Chewy said, making what I thought was a weak attempt at bravado.

Eve removed her hand from the light switch and overlapped her arms across her chest. She looked amused. "You're not in danger from me, Chewy."

"We're not?" I said, struggling to keep my emotions under control.

The playful expression on Eve's face disappeared when she turned her attention to me, replacing it with a direct sincerity. She removed the baseball cap she was wearing and let her hair fall loose. She tossed the hat onto the sofa.

"No, you are not. I swear it."

"You'll need to explain this then," Taggart spoke up for the first time, motioning towards the wall behind us covered with paper and pictures.

When Eve's eyes shifted to Taggart, I saw something in them change. The intensity was no longer there and her whole face had softened.

"There is a lot I need to explain."

"You knew we would break in here," Taggart said. "That's why the alarm wasn't set."

Eve nodded.

"How did you know?" Taggart asked.

"I became suspicious when I walked in on Cassie this afternoon. The three of them looked like they had been caught taking an early peek at their Christmas gifts. But I knew for sure when I spotted Chewy following me here. You gotta work on your tailing skills, fella."

Chewy took a sudden interest in the top of his shoes.

When Taggart didn't say anything else, I glanced over at him. He was still looking at Eve, but there was something different in his eyes now as well. It was a look that up until then, I had only seen him direct at me.

"You're my sister."

A tiny smile appeared at the corners of Eve's mouth. "You're my brother."

"And you didn't murder those people?" I asked.

"Heavens no," Eve half-laughed.

"Then—"

Eve raised her hand. "Why don't we sit down. Can I get anyone something to drink?"

All three of us declined the offer and shuffled over to the sofa to sit. Eve rolled the desk chair over near the sofa and sat as well.

"You have a definite advantage here," Taggart stated, glancing at the wall behind the roll-top desk. "You know a good deal about me. I, on the other hand, know next to nothing about you, and what I thought I knew is obviously incorrect. I would be grateful if you could fill in the gaps for us?"

Eve crossed her legs. "I can do that. The best place to start is the beginning. My wonderful mother, sorry, our mother, abandoned me when I was very young. She left me at this crappy little diner in Alabama in the middle of the night. The woman who found me, her name was Trina, kept me as her own for several years until she got ill and passed away. Cancer. Trina called me Crystal. After she was gone, I went into the foster care system and stayed with several families before eventually being adopted by the Janey's. Eve is the middle name that the Janey's gave me."

"So, growing up, you had no idea of who your real mother and father were?" Taggart asked.

"None. I eventually figured out who my mother was, but I still have no clue about my father."

"I may know something about him," Taggart said, which caused Eve's eyes to get big.

"You're kidding. How?"

"I was recently provided a copy of your birth certificate by an investigative reporter. Your real name is Bella Tinge."

Eve pursed her lips. "Bella…huh? I think I like that."

"Your father was listed as Sylvester Tinge," Taggart continued. "I did some research on him. He was only married to our mother for a short while and was considerably older than she was. He was also extremely rich. He left a large sum of money to her in his will, which she never actually collected because the whole matter became tied up in probate court. It seems Sylvester died under mysterious circumstances."

"No big surprise there, given what we know about her," Eve said.

"I should also point out that given Sylvester's advanced age and our mother's propensity for twisting the truth, the chances that he's not your biological father are quite significant. I fear you may never truly have that answer."

"I've made peace with not knowing who my father was a long time ago."

"How did you track down your mother?" I asked.

"When I was found at the diner, there was an envelope left with me in my carrier. Written on the face of the envelope were instructions. The instructions said the envelope was to be given to me… unopened… on my eighteenth birthday."

"What did it say?" Chewy asked, his leg bouncing anxiously.

Eve rose from her chair and walked over to the desk. She unpinned a piece of paper from the wall directly behind the desk and returned to her chair. She handed Taggart the paper.

"Read for yourself," she said.

Chewy and I both leaned over so we could read the note in Taggart's lap. It was written in ink, faded, but painstakingly scripted.

Neither of us is ready for this right now...but one day – when you're old enough - I'll come for you. I'll be using the name WORTHY - because by then - I will be.

Taggart and I looked up from the note at the same time.

"To be truthful, I didn't read this until a couple of years after my eighteenth birthday. At eighteen I was in a bad place and couldn't have cared less who or where my real parents were. They abandoned me like a dirty diaper, so why would I ever want to go looking for them."

"The story you told us about the suicide attempt. That was true?"

Eve nodded. "Every word. That all happened when I was seventeen. I was still recovering and in therapy when I turned eighteen. I only got up the courage to read the note six months before the news of what went on in New Haven broke."

"It appears our mother chose her alias for a specific purpose. You read about Miss Worthy in the paper and put two and two together?" Taggart asked.

"Not at first. I heard the stories. Who didn't, it was all over the news. I recognized the name but chalked it up to coincidence. It wasn't until I read a follow-up story revealing the fact that Miss Worthy also had a daughter nobody could locate, then it clicked. The dates and timing… along with the name… it all made sense. We'd have to take a DNA test to make it one hundred percent official, but I was reasonably sure you had to be my brother."

"Why all this secrecy then?" I asked. "When you found out, why not just come to New Haven and introduce yourself?"

For the first time, Eve appeared embarrassed. "Two reasons, neither of which I'm proud of. The first was because of my adoptive-father. As you know, he's running for office, which means our entire family is under scrutiny. Telling him I was going to hang out with my maybe-brother, who was recently caught up in a scandal involving a crazy female serial-killer, who also might be my real mother, wasn't going to play too well."

"I imagine," Taggart stated.

"And the other reason?" I asked.

Eve dipped her head. "I wasn't sure I wanted Taggart to know who I was."

I glanced at Taggart, but there was no reaction on his face.

"What?"

Eve raised her head and held her hands open in front of her. "You've got to see it from my perspective. The way

Taggart was portrayed in the media wasn't flattering, to say the least. He looked like a first-class jerk. So, can you blame me for being cautious? Look, Cassie, didn't I read in an article that before you got to know Taggart, you couldn't stand him either?"

"That is true, Cassie," Chewy said. "We all kind of felt the same way."

What they were saying was the truth. It was unnerving to realize how easy it was to forget what it was like back then, especially when back then wasn't that long ago.

"I'm an acquired taste," Taggart said with a smirk on his face, breaking the tension.

"That's an understatement," Eve replied, smiling. "So, to appease my father and assure I could back away quietly if things didn't turn out how I hoped, I arranged the circumstances so I could get to know you indirectly and anonymously."

"You had someone hack the housing system to put yourself in the suite with Cassie."

"Not someone, I did it. Brandon is a pretty good hacker, but I'm better if I do say so myself. That's something we both probably inherited from our mom, a heightened IQ."

"And modesty," Chewy quipped, which drew a look from Eve and Taggart.

"And what about this place?" I asked, looking around the room.

"I needed a place to escape and carry on with my research, away from prying eyes. I would have stayed here instead of the dorm, but I needed to be close to you, Cassie—and by extension—Taggart. The expense wasn't an issue because my adoptive father's way of dealing with problems is to throw money at it."

The way that Eve always referred to her father as her adoptive-father struck me as odd. I wondered what the dynamic between the two of them was like. But there was a more urgent matter on my mind right now.

"So here's the million-dollar question," I said. "Who would send Taggart that text warning him his sister was coming for him? That's the whole reason we thought you were behind the deaths."

Eve's eyebrows knotted together. "I have absolutely no idea."

"Someone in your family, perhaps?" I asked.

Eve shook her head. "I've not told them what I found out about my mother or anything about Taggart. As far as they know, I'm just going to college."

"Then, who?"

"I don't know. I've been racking my brain ever since you told us about that."

"That's something else. Why didn't you come clean when Taggart first told the group he thought his sister was the one responsible?" Chewy asked.

"First off, I knew it wasn't true, and secondly, at the time, I doubted they were even murders. No offence Taggart, but I was convinced they killed themselves and you and Cassie were creating this big conspiracy because of that misleading text. I was certain nothing was ever going to come from any of it, so I decided to keep quiet. I think a part of me was also embarrassed about what I was doing."

"We exposed Tony's secret because you kept silent," I said.

"I know, and I feel bad about that."

"You said at the time you doubted they were murders. You feel differently now?" Taggart asked.

"I do, and as terrible as it is to imagine, I might even know who's behind it all."

"Who?" Taggart asked. My own curiosity had jumped into hyper-drive.

Eve bit her lower lip before answering. "My adoptive-father."

I'm not sure what I expected Eve to say, but it certainly wasn't that. "The soon-to-be senator?"

Eve nodded, her lower lip still firmly clamped between her teeth.

"An explanation would be appreciated," Taggart said.

Eve released her lip and sat forward in her seat. "A couple of weeks ago, before all this started, I thought I was being followed around campus. There was this guy, older than a student and at first I thought maybe he was an instructor. But I kept seeing him everywhere I went, and I was certain it was more than a coincidence. He disappeared and after a while, I didn't think about it again. That is until I saw the same guy a couple of days after Jim's death. This time however, I outmaneuvered him. I confronted the man and learned he worked for a security firm hired by my father to keep tabs on me."

"Gentry Security?" Taggart asked.

"Yeah, how did you know that?"

"We observed your meeting earlier at the Hard Bean and followed your table guest back to his office. You seemed upset."

"That's because after I cornered that guy and found out who he worked for, I told them in no uncertain terms to back off and leave me alone. But then Cassie said she was being followed and two days ago someone was again shadowing me. It was a different guy this time. He was better than the last one, but he was definitely tailing me. He vanished before

I could confront him, so I set up a meeting with the head man at Gentry, the one you saw, and let him know how I felt. Of course, he denied sending anyone out here, but what else was he going to say?"

"This is all very interesting, Eve, or should we call you Crystal or Bella now?" Taggart said.

Eve considered her answer for a moment. "It might take some getting used to, but I think I'd like to be called Bella now. It's time to become the real me. "

Taggart smiled. "Bella it is. I'm still not seeing how being followed relates to the murders."

"I believe my adoptive-father intends to have me murdered, and he's doing it under the guise of a suicide cluster. Jim, Lisa, and Brent were killed to lay the groundwork for my own eventual suicide, and with my history, it would be totally plausible. That's why I think your lives might be in danger. Any one of you could end up being another victim in this. I'm being set up to become part of a mental health epidemic."

"That's an interesting theory. I have two questions. The first is, why was Jim Books' body left in my apartment?"

"I don't know."

"Okay. The second, and this one is actually the more relevant, why? Why would your father—"

"Adoptive-father," Eve corrected.

"Why would your adoptive-father want to kill you?"

Bella's whole body language changed. She started wringing her hands, shifting her head and shoulders as if she were reacting to unwanted touch, rapidly tapping her right foot.

"I… um… I knew this was coming… but—"

I could see how visibly upset Bella was becoming. I wanted to do something to help, but I wasn't sure what. I was certain that although Taggart probably wanted to, he definitely couldn't.

"Bella, you're among friends and family. Take a deep breath and relax. Just take your time and tell us when you're ready," I urged.

The smile Bella showed us was twisted, tortured. "Chewy. Would it be okay if I asked you to step outside for a minute?"

"Sure, no problem, Bella," Chewy answered. There was obvious concern on his face when he closed the door behind him.

Bella drew in a deep breath and blew it out slowly, her eyes closed. Then she did it again. After the third time, her shoulders relaxed, her hands lay open in her lap, but her foot continued to tap slightly.

"I've only told this to one other person. It's been so long since I've talked about this out loud that I… well… it's hard," Bella said softly. Her eyes remained closed.

"Take your time," I coaxed.

Bella nodded.

"My adoptive-father… he… he sexually abused me."

A firestorm of emotions, each in conflict with the other, erupted inside of me. On the one hand, there was the rage. Pure, white-hot, unrepressed, fury. I clenched both of my fists at my sides and my toes curled in my shoes. But another emotion coursed through me at the same time. A deep, crushing, sadness. While my anger compelled me to leap from the sofa and shatter every piece of furniture I could get my hands on, the sorrow only wanted to wrap Bella in my arms. Those feelings were all battling for a foothold within me, none of them successful, leaving me confused and helpless.

Though Bella's eyes remained closed, I fought like hell to keep my expression neutral.

"It started when I was ten and continued right up until my suicide attempt. He said it was our little secret. That we had a special relationship. He told me that no one else would understand and could never know about it. I'm sure you've heard the stories or seen the lifetime movies, and for the most part, they're all true. Looking back on it now, I can almost see myself as a cliché. On the outside, to the world, I was the perfect daughter, bringing home straight A's and never causing problems. I was this bright red, shiny apple, with a worm eating away at my core."

Bella paused to wipe away the tears that were flowing from her closed eyes. I wiped mine away as well.

"My mother. Well, she's not one to look at things too closely. She ignores anything that upsets the status quo or pushes it to the side. I always felt that her love was conditional upon life being perfect. She doesn't do well with… messy. She's all for whatever makes her husband happy, and I made him happy."

Bella paused for a moment.

"After my suicide attempt, my adoptive-father finally left me alone. They put me into therapy, and I dropped out of school for a year. Overall, considering everything, I think I've recovered pretty well. I still struggle with my self-esteem from time to time, but I understand the cause and I have the tools to keep growing."

"Is it okay if I take your hand?" I asked softly.

When Bella nodded her head, I reached out and squeezed her hand.

"I'm afraid to open my eyes. I don't want to see how you're looking at me right now."

"What I see is a brave young woman who has endured more than anyone should have to and still managed to develop into this amazing person," Taggart said. "I am proud to call you my big sister."

Bella's eyes shot open and she launched herself into Taggart's arms. As the two of them embraced, rocking back and forth, I couldn't help but recall memories of my own little sister. I turned my head to make sure they didn't see my bottom lip quivering.

"Do you mind if I ask some questions?" Taggart asked when they finally broke apart.

"Certainly," Bella answered, sniffling.

"You never told the authorities about your adoptive-father's actions?"

Bella shook her head. "I didn't even tell my therapist until I was nineteen."

"But you said you did tell someone else." I pointed out.

Bella nodded. "Theresa Battle."

"The girl you made the suicide pact with?" Taggart asked.

"Yes."

"Why didn't you tell anyone else?"

"Shame. Fear. The fear of not being believed. Fear of punishment. Fear of the knowledge that I was partly responsible. Fear that if I told my mother she would be okay with it. Pick one. I buried it. As long as he left me alone, I was okay with just getting on with my life."

The emotion in her voice as she responded made me pause. "Bella, I know you've said that you've done well with your recovery, but I would suggest that when this is all over you consider more therapy. I just think that until you deal with the secrets, the manipulation, you can't be fully healed."

Bella smiled at me. "You're pretty perceptive, Cassie, and you're right. I've still got work to do."

"Why, after all this time, do you think your adoptive-father would want to harm you now?" Taggart asked.

"I'm a loose end. He's in the middle of this senate race. He knows that at any moment I can have a change of heart and expose him, ending everything."

"But why would he think that? You've remained silent all this time, why—"

"I have a younger sister."

That caused me to fall silent.

"They adopted a second child nine years ago. She turns ten this year," Bella added.

The ramification of that fact sank in.

Twenty-Eight
Saturday, July 28th 3:33 PM

Bella (formerly Eve), Chewy, Taggart, and I arrived back at our room in Barksdale only to come across someone knocking on the door.

"Who's that?" Chewy asked.

"Jon?" I said, recognizing the pitiful mustache on Delta's old boyfriend before anything else. He was wearing a throwback Beastie Boys t-shirt and baggy shorts that hung a couple inches below his knees. I thought about Tunes inside with Delta, and Brandon already on his way here now.

Things were definitely going to get interesting.

Jon turned to meet us just as the door swung open. Delta looked at Jon, then at us, confused.

"We just walked up," I explained. "He was already here."

"What do you want, Jon?" Delta asked, looking more uncomfortable than I seen her look in sometime.

Jon grinned awkwardly. "I was wondering if we could talk?"

"I don't mean to be rude," Bella said as she navigated her way past Jon and Delta. "But I really have to pee."

After Bella disappeared into her room, Delta turned back to Jon.

"I don't think we have anything to talk about."

I debated following Bella's lead and pushing past the two of them to get to our own room, but my instincts were telling me I needed to stick around.

"Don't be like that, Delta. We had a fun time together, didn't we? I just want a chance to prove that we still make a good couple, even if I'm no longer a student."

"I don't know. Now's not really a good time to—"

"Is that the Brandon guy you told me about?" I heard Tunes' voice from inside the room.

I glanced at Chewy, who was looking downward and covering his eyes with his hand. Taggart just looked impatient.

"No, it's not. Go back inside," Delta commanded.

"Who's that?" Jon asked, tilting his head to try to get a look into the room.

"A friend from New Haven."

"So, come on, Delta. What harm could a few minutes of talking do?"

I could see Delta's resolve fading against Jon's persistence. She looked at me, as if to ask permission. I knew if I gave her some sign, like a frown or crinkled nose, she would send Jon packing. But I didn't want that on my conscience. This was a decision she needed to make, so I did the only thing I could think of. I shrugged my shoulders.

"Do I get a vote?" Taggart asked.

"No," both me and Delta said simultaneously.

Delta sighed and let her arms drop. "Okay, Jon, but only for a little while."

Jon smiled. "You got it."

We all followed Delta back into the common room where Tunes was standing right outside the door to our bedroom. I slipped into a chair at the closest desk and Delta sat down on the couch, pinching her arms between her knees. Chewy and Taggart had kept walking like they were going to my bedroom, but when they noticed I had taken a seat, they both stopped.

"You guys can hang out in my room," I told them. "Tunes, you too."

Tunes didn't look too happy about being shoo'd away but relented none the less.

Chewy followed Tunes through the door, but Taggart hung back and leaned against the wall.

When Jon noticed Taggart and I intended to stay, he suddenly looked uncomfortable.

"Ummmm… I was hoping this could just be the two of us," Jon said.

"I'm fine with them being here," Delta commented. "We don't keep any secrets from one another."

"Delta, now that I think about it, I told the others to meet us here at four o'clock, so it might be a good idea if you make this quick," I said. I had called Brandon and Tony on our walk back and told them to meet us in our room. We had some serious news to relay.

"The others?" Delta asked.

"Tony and *Brandon*," I replied, trying not to make it too obvious.

Now it was Delta's turn to look uncomfortable.

"I can come back later, then," Jon said.

Delta glanced at the clock on the wall. "No. We have some time. Just say what you came to say."

"Oh… okay… this isn't awkward at all," Jon said, taking a seat next to Delta. "Whatever. So, how have you been?"

"Tense."

"Yeah, I bet. I understand things have been pretty nuts around here," Jon said.

"That's an understatement if I ever heard one," Delta replied. "JJ, one of our suitemates, she had to withdraw from school. Her parents forced her to."

"Wow. Maybe I dropped out just in time," Jon said.

"I don't know about that. Are you still working at your dad's hardware store?"

"For now, until I can figure out what I really want to do." After a brief pause, "Weren't the ones who killed themselves part of your orientation group?"

Delta shook her head. "Not my group, Cassie's."

I had been only half-listening to their conversation, mostly to ensure that if things turned nasty, I could help keep it civil. I remembered how ugly it became when I broke up with my long-term boyfriend, and I didn't want that to happen to Delta. But when I noticed Taggart unexpectedly take an interest, I knew something was amiss.

Jon turned towards me. "I bet that's weird, huh, Cassie? I know I would be freaked."

"Uh… I guess so," I said.

"Is your group still holding meetings?"

Taggart pushed himself off the wall where he had been leaning. "Why are you asking about the suicides?"

Jon looked at Taggart, making a poor attempt to appear confused. He looked like someone who had just been caught with his hand in the cookie jar.

"I'm just making conversation," Jon explained.

"Not exactly the sort of dialogue suited for repairing a broken relationship. Am I wrong about that, Cassie?"

Taggart had a point, but I wasn't sure where he was headed with it. "No, you're right."

"I'm sorry I'm not a brilliant conversationalist like all of ya'll."

"Taggart, what's your problem?" Delta chirped.

The door to Bella's room opened, and she stepped into the common area with the rest of us.

"The authorities haven't released the fact that the deaths involved students from the same orientation group to the news yet. How did you know that fact, Jon?" Taggart asked.

"Whoa… what did I walk in on?" Bella said.

Jon threw up his hands. "I don't remember, Taggart. I heard it around somewhere. People talk, you know, at least us humans do. I'm not sure about you."

"Why are you here? My interpretation of your relationship when you were seeing one another registered as lukewarm at best. So I repeat, why are you really back?"

"Your interpretation? What a joke. That's like asking the scarecrow when it's time to harvest the corn."

"He's right, Jon," Delta said, rising to her feet. "It surprised me how upset you were when we stopped seeing one another because I thought we were barely casual. I felt like you would miss the free meals more than me. So, answer Taggart's question. Why are you here?"

Jon started for the door. "I don't need this," he said.

Taggart blocked his path.

"He's here for some other purpose," Taggart said, staring daggers at Jon.

"What's going on, Jon?" Delta asked forcefully.

Jon turned away from Taggart and looked at the rest of us. We were all standing now and surrounding him. Chewy had even stuck his head out from my bedroom to see what the commotion was about.

Jon seemed to deflate in front of us. "Okay, okay. I guess this is what I get for doing a good deed."

"What do you mean?" I asked.

Jon pointed to Delta. "Her father asked me to feed him information on the down low about all of you guys."

Delta scrunched up her face. "What?"

"Yeah. He was really worried about how you would take to college-life, and specifically the type of influences your roommates would have on you."

"And you did this out of the kindness of your heart?" Taggart asked.

Jon looked at the ground. "There was a financial element to it as well."

"That's why you were so upset when we broke up… your paycheck was drying up," Delta said.

"So, why did you come back today?" I asked.

"My car payment is overdue and since I dropped out of school, my dad said he wouldn't cover it anymore. I thought if I could get some new info, Delta's dad would help me out."

"Your father would really do something like that?" Bella asked.

Delta laughed. "No way. Whoever you were feeding information to, it wasn't my father."

Jon's face went blank. "But he said he was. He acted really concerned, too."

"What sort of information did you provide this person?" Taggart asked.

"Comings and goings, as best as I could remember, habits and hobbies, likes and dislikes. Anything and everything, really."

"What did he look like?" Taggart continued the interrogation.

"Tall, kinda older, looked like a dad. I'm not good at describing stuff."

"It could be someone from Gentry Security," Bella pointed out.

"Who's that?" Delta asked.

"Will fill you in when the others get here," I answered.

Taggart asked Jon another question. "When was the last time you spoke to him?"

"The guy called just after Delta broke it off with me. He's how I knew the suicides were all from the same group. He said he was more worried than ever and needed me to find out if Delta was involved with that group. When I told him we were no longer seeing each other, he hung up on me."

"Do you have that number?"

Jon pulled out his phone and showed Taggart the call history, pointing out the number in question.

"It's most likely a burner phone, but we can have Brandon check it out," Taggart remarked.

"I've tried calling it, but nobody picks up," Jon offered.

Delta stepped over to the door to the hallway and pulled it open. "It's time for you to go now, Jon."

Jon walked to the door but stopped short of leaving.

"I'm sorry, Delta. I really thought he was your dad," he said.

"Jon, even if he was my dad, what you did was wrong. You not knowing that makes me sick to my stomach that I ever went out with you."

Jon opened his mouth to say something else but thought better of it and walked out the door instead. Delta slammed it behind him.

Twenty-Nine
Saturday, July 28th 4:10 PM

I pulled Delta away from the others as soon as I got the opportunity.

"How did it go with Tunes?" I asked using a hush tone.

"Fine, actually. I told him I was seeing somebody else, which he already knew from Chewy, but he drove up here anyway because he wanted to make sure the new guy was treating me right. I think Tunes might be more mature than I am."

"He's more mature than a lot of people. Just don't rub it in his face while he's here."

Delta frowned. "I would never do that. I do still have feelings for him you know."

"Good. Keep an eye on Brandon, though. I doubt he's as mature as Tunes and having an ex-boyfriend around might get his hair up."

"Noted."

It wasn't ten minutes later that Tony and Brandon appeared. In an effort to avoid any potential conflicts I took charge by introducing Tunes to both of them as another one of our friends from New Haven who was here to help. I naturally didn't mention the prior relationship between him and Delta.

Taggart then brought everyone up to speed with what we had learned.

"Let's see if I got everything straight?" Brandon said after Taggart had finished. "First, you thought Talia Davis was behind the murders. Next, it was Tony, then Eve, and now you think it's Eve's father, the senator? Does this feel like a bizarre game of spin the bottle to anyone else?"

"We're calling her Bella now, remember?" I reminded him.

"Oh, right."

"You're the only one who thought Talia was a suspect," Bella pointed out. "Plus, my **ADOPTIVE** father is only running for senator, not actually one yet. If you're going to recap the facts, you can at least get them right."

Brandon made a face mimicking Bella, which drew a sharp elbow to the ribs from Delta.

The eight of us—Brandon, Delta, Tony, Chewy, Tunes, Bella, Taggart, and me—were crammed into the study room in our suite. Taggart had purposefully omitted the part about Bella's past abuse when laying out everything we knew.

"And this is all because he wants to kill her for a reason you won't tell us about, and plans to make it look like she got caught up in some suicide cluster? Does this sound like some dime-store paperback mystery bullshit to anyone else?" Brandon said.

"Like you would read anything other than a comic book," Bella quipped.

"Touche. Still, why won't you tell us why he wants you dead?" Brandon continued, looking sideways at Bella.

"I'm sure they have their reasons for not telling us," Tunes blurted out, his eyes locking with Brandon's.

Bella's eyes were fixed on the floor, and her right foot was tapping.

"Bella has information that would be damaging to Mr. Janey's senate campaign, and that's all anyone needs to know. The details of that information are not important," Taggart stated emphatically.

"Before Chewy and Tunes drove out here to Truman—" I said, trying to change the subject. "—he rechecked Angela's parents' house, and they are still not home, which to me sounds like they are away on vacation and Angela is probably with them. The car in their driveway is registered to Angela, but it doesn't have a Truman parking sticker on it, so we don't think she had it here on campus."

"Yeah, but we don't know for sure she went on vacation with them. She could be truly missing," Tony said. It had warmed my heart to see that nobody had been treating him any differently since he arrived a few minutes ago.

"That's true," Taggart said. "So, we'll continue to look for ways to verify Angela's location, but our focus needs to be on the immediate threat."

"You think Gentry Security is responsible for the killings?" Chewy asked.

"It's a distinct possibility, but it could also be an independent third party engaged by Mr. Janey. It's best if we don't overly narrow our focus."

"But no one has explained why Jim's body was left in your apartment, Taggart. How does that fit into their plan?" Delta asked.

Taggart frowned. "I struggle to understand that as well. My only explanation is somehow the responsible party knew about Jim's plagiarism of my work and tried to use his presence in my apartment as a way to reinforce the artificial suicide ruse."

"Maybe they figured out that Eve was Bella?" Chewy said. "I mean that she was Taggart's sister Bella, so they planted the body there to incriminate him somehow?"

"Seems like there would be easier ways of accomplishing the same thing," Tony pointed out.

"I agree. Something is missing, a piece of information we do not have yet that might better explain it," Taggart said.

"So, what do we do now?" I asked.

"We continue to work in pairs or threesomes."

"Ewwww, kinky," Brandon said with a smile, drawing yet another nudge from Delta.

"Brandon, Delta, and Tony, I would like you to continue trying to locate Angela. See if there are any financial transactions that might give us a clue as to her parents' whereabouts. Cassie and Bella, I need you to pay a visit to detective Moss and get a read on where he is in his investigation. Attempt to nudge him in the right direction at the same time. Then we need someone to seek out campus security and inquire about gaining access to their closed-circuit camera footage from the student center on the date Bella was last followed. Maybe we can get a look at our mysterious shadow."

"I can do that," Delta stated emphatically. "I kind of formed a rapport with that one security guard outside of the records building that night so maybe I can sweet talk him into letting me see that footage because I think my abusive ex-boyfriend is following me, but not sure enough to file an official complaint."

Delta looked at me and cocked her head to the side. "Yeah, I know that's not very feminist of me, but extraordinary circumstances call for pulling out all of the stops.”

“But you’re supposed to help me and Travis,” Brandon half-moaned.

“We can all go do this first.”

“What do you want me and Tunes to do?” Chewy asked.

“The three of us will pay another visit to Gentry Security.”

“What do you think that will achieve?” Tony asked. “You know they're not going to tell you anything.”

“Often, you can learn a lot by asking the right questions and just listening.”

“Taggart is pretty much a human lie detector,” Delta said.

“That's not entirely correct,” Taggart responded.

“You didn't do so well with her,” Brandon said, jerking his thumb at Bella. “Or Tony, for that matter.”

Taggart appeared unflustered. “Neither of them lied to me, nor did I put them in a position where they needed to mislead me. I assure you that will not be the case when I speak to the people at Gentry.”

A soft knock on the door Taggart was leaning next to made everyone go silent.

“Are we expecting someone else?” Bella asked.

The blank look on everyone's faces was her answer. When the knock came again, Taggart pulled open the door.

“I turned in my key when I left,” JJ said, standing in the hall wearing black jeans with holes at the knees and an oversized t-shirt that was tied into a knot at the waist.

Bella sprang to her feet and embraced her old roommate.

“Now that's what I call a Hallmark moment,” Brandon quipped.

This time Delta slapped Brandon in the back of his head with her open palm. I couldn't help but smile at the two of them. Tunes was smiling as well.

"What are you doing here?" Bella asked, holding JJ at arm's length. "Are you back in school?"

JJ shook her head. "No. Cassie called last night and filled me in on what was going on. When I heard my girl was in trouble, I had to come and see if I could help in some way."

I looked at Taggart, who in turn, redirected his attention to Delta. "Can you take JJ with you?"

Delta smiled. "Sure, no problem."

"Great. We all know what to do then," I said.

Tony sprung up from his chair. "Let's go then."

"Lead the way," JJ replied. She squeezed Bella's hand following Tony out the door.

Before Delta pulled the door shut behind them, she flashed Tunes a warm smile.

Bella headed towards her bedroom. "I'm going to change before we go."

Taggart walked over to where I was sitting and put his hand on my knee. "Chewy, Tunes, and I will go now as well. Please use your considerable influence to get the detective to see things our way. We need his help."

I smiled at him. "I have considerable influence?"

I didn't get a smile in return, but there was amusement in his eyes. "I might be somewhat biased."

I slid forward on the desk and stuck out my face. "You'd better be more than that."

Taggart bent over and gave me the kiss I had been trolling for.

"I'd say get a room, but it's right there," Chewy said, moving to the door. "Let's go, Taggart, I want to get me and Tunes home before dark."

Taggart grinned as he pulled away, and then the three of them were gone.

I jumped down off the desk, slid my phone into my back pocket, and slipped on my cross-trainers. I was tying the last lace when Bella reappeared. She had changed into a pair of denim shorts and a casual crop top that perfectly complemented the shorts. She'd rounded it off with some stylish slip-ons.

"You do know we're going to see the police, not cruise for guys at the park, right?"

"What? We need the detective to see things our way, don't we? This can't hurt."

"I guess not. Want to take your car or mine?"

"Let's take mine," Bella replied. "I had to park way out in the back last time I drove, so maybe I can score a better spot when we get back. It's Saturday."

As the two of us walked to Bella's car, which was quite a stretch aways, she filled me in on what her life was like after she graduated from high school. She told me that even though she was near the top of her class and readily accepted into the University of Colorado, she was surprised to find that she struggled with focus and a sense of purpose in college. Without the goal-oriented structure of high school, she felt adrift. She ended up dropping out after one semester, and that was when she finally decided to read her mother's note. It was that note and the subsequent discovery that she possibly had a brother, that resulted in her renewed purpose. She made it her mission to learn everything she could about Taggart, and when she read about his enrollment in Truman, a plan began to form.

"Knowing what I know now, of course I would do it all differently," Bella said as we approached her car. Her grey Toyota was backed into a spot that butted up against the fence separating the lot from a large, wooded area. A good portion of the parking lot had emptied for the weekend, but there were still several vehicles on the back row, including a white Ford van in the spot next to Bella's. I felt sorry for the owner of the van because its front driver's side was suspended off the ground by a floor jack. There didn't look to be anybody attending to it though.

"But I know Taggart doesn't blame you for doing what you did," I reassured her, waiting next to the passenger door while she dug in her purse for her keys while walking to the other side.

"I really hope you're right."

Without warning, a man appeared from the other side of the van, giving me a start until I recognized who it was.

"Mr. Batiste?" I said, relaxing. "Are you having problems with your van?"

Mr. Batiste didn't seem to hear my question; his attention was focused on Bella instead. He looked different from the last time we met. He looked as if he hadn't shaved in days and his clothes were wrinkled.

I glanced at Bella, and I immediately knew something was wrong. She looked like she was staring at a ghost.

"Mr. Battle? What are you doing here?" Bella asked.

At first, I wondered if Bella had mispronounced his name, but then the name she used seemed significant somehow.

"Battle? I don't understand," I said.

The man reached his hand behind his back and when it returned, it was holding a handgun. It was pointed directly at me.

"Of course you don't," Mr. Battle said. "But, you will soon enough."

Thirty
Saturday, July 28th 4:35 PM

"Not one word," Battle said calmly. "Not a whimper, not a moan, not one sound. If either of you draws attention to us in any way, I'll put a bullet in each of your skulls and walk away. Nod if you understand."

I did as I was instructed, too petrified to do anything else. I couldn't even pull my eyes away from the gun, the barrel of which was now moving back and forth between Bella and me.

"That's good," Battle said. With his free hand he reached out and twisted the end of the floor jack, causing the van to drop to the ground. He then dug into the front pocket of his slacks and pulled out a key fob. He depressed a button on the device and the side door of the van began humming before it ultimately slid open.

"Climb inside," Battle ordered.

I watched as Bella climbed inside the van, then after Battle motioned for me to do the same, I walked around the front of the Toyota. The closer I got to Battle, and the gun, the more my body shook. When I was past him, I almost ran to the van door.

The inside of the van was unusually dim, but I quickly noticed it was because the windows had been painted over. From what light there was from the open door, I could tell there were no seats inside, just a bare metal floor, and there was a partition erected between the rear of the van and the front—effectively sealing off the two sections. Bella had already sat down next to the left wheel well, so I climbed in next to her. I could feel her trembling as much as I was.

Battle tucked the fob back into his pocket and pulled a clear plastic bag from his rear pocket, keeping his gun trained on us the entire time. He shook the bag once to widen the opening at the top.

"Turn your phones off and put them in the bag."

We did as we were instructed and dropped our phones into the bag.

"So far so good," Battle commented. "These doors will not open from the inside, so don't bother to fiddle with them. We're going to take a little drive now, but the same rules apply. Draw any sort of attention to this vehicle, or yourselves, and not only will the two of you punch your funeral ticket, but some innocent bystanders might die as well. You wouldn't want that on your conscience, would you?"

"If this goes the way you plan, my conscience is the last thing I'm worried about," I said.

Battle smirked. "Just keep your traps shut."

The man pressed a button on the outside of the van door and it slowly closed, enveloping the two of us with complete darkness.

"I'm so sorry I got you into this Cassie," Bella whispered.

"Why do I know that name, Battle?"

I heard something heavy clanging on the front floorboard, probably the jack, then the slamming of the passenger door followed seconds later by the opening and closing of the driver's door. The van's engine roared to life.

"He's Theresa Battle's father."

The realization hit me, and the pieces started falling into place. The pit of my stomach tumbled as well.

"The girl you —"

"The same. I haven't seen him since before Theresa died."

I felt the van start to move and struggled to stay upright as it navigated several quick turns.

"I couldn't go to Theresa's funeral because I was still in the hospital, and I'm not sure I would have had the courage to go even if I wasn't. Why did you call him Batiste?"

"He came by our suite when Delta and I were there alone. He said his name was Gerald Batiste and he worked for the school's outreach program. He told us he and others from the school were out checking on everyone."

"He was probably scouting you as potential victims. I bet he was the one who was following me that last time. The manager from Gentry wasn't lying when he said he hadn't sent anyone else out here."

"It was probably him following me after I ran that day, too. And he fooled Jon into believing he was Delta's father to get information about us. You think he's working for your father?"

"No. The two of them can't stand one another. My mother told me Mr. Battle said some pretty hateful things about our family and me after the funeral, but we never heard anything else from him after that."

"Until now."

"Until now."

We rode together in silence for several minutes, feeling the motion of the road beneath us and listening to the sounds of the city we could sometimes hear. I detected a scent inside the van, but I couldn't quite place it. It smelled a little like motor oil.

"Shit," I heard Bella mutter, then the rattle of car keys.

"What is it?"

"I forgot I had this," she said right before a beam of light shot out from her hand. A tiny penlight attached to her key ring was providing the light.

Whatever hope I briefly felt as Bella began directing the tiny spotlight around the inside of the van swiftly evaporated. Battle hadn't been kidding about the doors. The mechanisms to trigger them to open had been removed and sheet metal welded in its place. There was no way to open the windows either, or nothing was lying about that we could use as a weapon.

Bella set the penlight on the ground, allowing the two of us to see one another in the glow.

"What do you think he's going to do with us?" Bella asked.

"I'm trying not to think about that," I replied. "We need to think of a way to get that gun away from him."

"That's not going to be easy."

"Why do you say that?"

"Because he's a cop. Or at least he used to be."

I didn't think it was possible to feel any more helpless, but now I knew that it was.

"Shit."

I felt the van slow down, come to a stop, then reverse direction, backing up. When it stopped again, the engine cut out and there was the sound of the driver's door opening and closing.

"Kill your light," I instructed Bella, which she did. She had just finished ramming her keys back into her pocket when the sliding door retracted.

The sunlight that poured in through the door forced me to squint, but I could still make out Battle standing there, gun in hand.

"This is stop number one. Let's go."

I climbed out first and after I got my bearings, the surroundings felt familiar to me. It was nighttime when I was here before, but I recognized the area enough to realize where we were.

"This is my house," Bella exclaimed as she exited the van.

"Inside," was Battle's response.

He had backed the van down along the right side of the house. It was now parked next to the rear porch. Battle used his gun to gesture towards the back door, which already stood open. I followed Bella toward the house, managing only a glance towards the street. Nobody from the neighborhood was visible, which was probably a good thing because then I wouldn't be tempted to draw their attention by screaming. As we walked inside, terror washed over me as I wondered if I'd ever walk out again.

Inside the house, we stepped past a mudroom on the right and a small kitchen area on the left, pausing as Battle closed and locked the back door. He then gestured for us to continue on. We stopped in front of the roll-top desk I remembered from the night before. I tried to recall if there was anything in the room we could use as a weapon, but I was drawing blanks.

"The two of you should grab a seat on the couch, we're going to be here for a while," Battle barked.

After we were seated, Battle pulled a pair of handcuffs from his back pocket. He clicked one end to the sofa's metal frame and the other around my wrist. When he grew nearer, I could smell stale cigarettes. Then he did the same to Bella.

"You've been in my house before?" Bella said.

"Many times. I've been in your dorm room also." He used the tip of his gun to point at the Truman logo on his polo shirt. "It's amazing how anonymous you become when your my age and wearing one of these shirts. It's like you kids purposefully avoid looking at us. By the way, I should thank the two of you for making this so easy. I thought I'd have to grab each of you individually and make multiple trips. Imagine my surprise when I saw the two of you walking to your car together."

"What are you planning on doing with us?" I asked.

Battle shook his head while he grabbed the desk chair and pulled it closer. "Nope. Nope. Let's not rush things. We have a couple of hours to waste, so why don't we catch up first? How about it, Eve?"

Bella remained silent next to me. Her right leg had begun bouncing up and down.

Battle straddled the chair, letting the gun dangle over the seatback. "Cat got your tongue? Oh well, can't say that I blame you. I'd probably do the same thing if the situation were reversed. The thing is, you don't really need to talk because I pretty much know everything you've been up to since you and Theresa —"

Battle made an expression like he was holding back a jolt of pain, almost as if somebody had sucker-punched him. He quickly recovered with a lop-sided smile.

"But you probably haven't heard what I've been doing these past five years. Let's see. I lost my job with the department. That wasn't too long ago. Twenty-seven years down the drain. In case you weren't aware, that's a long time in cop years. It was probably for the best however; I needed more time for my side project anyway. What else? Oh, you remember my wife Cynthia, Mrs. Battle, right? Well, she left me. She complained that I couldn't get over the loss of our daughter. Can you imagine that? Punishing me because I loved our daughter? The thing is she was the one who had the problem. I wanted to have another child right away, but she wasn't having it. Said she needed time to grieve. Like I wasn't grieving? I just knew that another baby would fix everything."

"Especially if it was a girl, right?" Bella said. The way that she said it caused me to look at her. What I saw surprised me. There was an intense fire behind her eyes and her bouncing leg had become still.

Mr. Battle's entire demeanor changed. He seemed to shrink in his chair, becoming more closed off. His expression changed from that of a friendly conversationalist to an angry interrogator.

"Theresa told me," Bella continued.

"I don't know what you're talking about." The tone in Battles' voice was lower now.

"We were so much alike, the two of us, weren't we? Same tastes in clothing, music, books. We were so similar in every…unimaginable…disgusting…way."

"I'm not sure what Theresa told you, but –"

"I was a wreck after what we did, what I did. There is no good way to describe how I felt, it's just not possible. The closest I can come is a color. The color black. I felt like the color. Empty. Unthinkable guilt. But for the longest time I held onto one thing. A thought. It helped me get me through the worst of it. Minute by minute, hour by hour, day by day. It buoyed me in that never-ending sea of despair doing its best to drown me. Do you want to know what that thought was?"

Mr. Battle remained silent.

"That she was finally away from you."

Battle raised the gun and pointed it at Bella's head, but she didn't flinch.

"But even that small silver lining was tarnished. I realized after I got the help I needed that we could have both easily escaped the prisons we were trapped in. Theresa killed herself to escape you, and the worse thing is she didn't have to."

"SHE DIDN'T KILL HERSELF. YOU MURDERED HER." Battle roared, his face red. The gun quivered in his hand, and I honestly thought it would go off any moment.

After a short time, Battle seemed to get control of himself again and he lowered the weapon. "Which is why you're going to finish what you started."

Thirty-One
Saturday, July 28th 4:52 PM

"That's what this is all about? Retribution?" I cried out.

Battle rocked back in his chair, shocked. "The way you say it makes it sound so blasé. She has to pay for what she did. She took my daughter away from me."

"I didn't take your daughter away. I robbed you of your plaything."

Battle leaped to his feet, pointed the gun at Bella, and cocked the hammer. "I loved my daughter."

"Of course you did," I blurted out, trying to draw his attention.

"That wasn't love," Bella growled back. "That's sickness."

I wanted to be annoyed at Bella for stoking a flame that might blow up in our faces any moment, but I couldn't. I understood where her pain was coming from and how hard it must be to control her emotions. Still, I had to think of a way to get Bella to back off or distract Battle because if I didn't, she was going to push him too far.

"So why make the deaths look like suicides?" I said urgently. "Why were those necessary?"

Battle and Bella continued to glare at one another.

"Those were a lot of risks to take," I added.

That did it. Battle blinked rapidly before easing the hammer back in place and lowering the gun. He sat back down and looked at me.

"They weren't necessary, but they weren't that risky either. I thought it might be fun to watch Eve suffer before her turn came. You know, seeing all her friends end up like Theresa."

"I get it. But why stage one of the bodies in my boyfriend's apartment?"

Battle had the nerve to actually smile. "That's kind of a funny story. It wasn't my intent to kill Jim Book that night. I was there for Taggart."

Bella and I shared a look. "I don't understand," I said.

Battle pointed to the display on the wall behind the rolltop desk. "Look at that. The girl obviously has the jones for Taggart McGill. And he lives alone. He was the obvious choice for my first victim. And she would have been devastated by his death."

"I'm still confused."

"There I was in Taggart's apartment, all set up to do the deed once he came home, and who do you think breaks in?"

"Jim broke into Taggart's apartment?"

Battle nodded. "The guy was quite talkative for a burglar and a plagiarist, but then again, Chlordiazepoxide will do that sometimes if you mix it with alcohol. He must have had a couple beers to work up his courage before making his move. Anyway, he said he was looking for some more material to turn in as his own. Anyway, I couldn't let him go after seeing me, and I knew he dated Bella for a while, so he became plan B."

I wanted to think about how close I had come to losing Taggart, but I knew I couldn't let my focus be diverted. I had to keep Battle talking.

"What about the girl who slit her wrists?" I asked.

"Oh… that wasn't me. An unfortunate coincidence, I guess."

I debated pointing out how his actions had probably caused an innocent girl, who had nothing to do with any of this, to take her life, but then I remembered that Jim, Lisa, Brent were all innocent as well.

"Is Angela alive?" Bella asked.

Battle looked confused. "Angela? Is that the girl who looked like a cabbage patch doll?"

"A little," Bella answered, being generous.

"Unfortunately, yes, she's still alive somewhere. She was next on my list. I had everything arranged, but when I went to get her, she was gone. Poof. Your squirrely roommate, JJ, I think, was supposed to be after that, but she cut out too. It was so frustrating. I got the idea to use the doll as a substitute, a way to ratchet up your anxiety. I thought the idea was quite inspired. What did you think, did it work?"

"It was effective," I answered honestly, probably because I was so relieved that Angela was alive somewhere.

"Good. Anyway, with kids going home and your friends pairing up everywhere they went, I decided it was time to bring this to an end."

"The end being?"

"Eve in another suicide pact, of course. This time you get to be the co-star."

My heart, which had been racing ever since Battle pulled a gun in the school parking lot, jumped to warp speed. I felt myself breathing faster and didn't want to hyperventilate, so I began taking slow deep breaths. I had faced imminent death before and still remember the paralyzing fear I experienced then. Unfortunately, repetition failed to make me any more prepared. I was terrified.

"Mr. Battle, I understand you feel like you have to do this, but Cassie has nothing to do with us. Take me if you must, but please leave Cassie alone."

"Oh, Eve, if only you felt that same way the first time you wanted to take your life. But no, instead you infected my Theresa with your toxic thoughts and put a noose around her neck. This time your death wish will come true, and right next to you will be another person who doesn't belong there."

I realized that if Bella and I were to have any kind of chance, we needed to keep our wits and think ahead. Taggart and the others had no clue where we were or who we were with, so whatever happened would be up to us. I set aside the dread in the pit of my stomach and tried to focus on getting information.

"You're going to hang us… here?" I managed to say.

"I was, at first, but I have something else planned for you. But we'll need to wait a little longer… until it gets dark. Think about that while I go take a leak."

Battle stepped away from his chair, wedged his gun into a spot in his back, then strolled into the hallway leading to the bathroom. He left the door open while he was doing his business, but I couldn't see him from where I was sitting.

Bella leaned over towards me as far as she could. "I have a taser in the top drawer of the desk," she whispered.

I thought about that for a moment, then said, "When he comes back, I'm going to ask to go to the bathroom. When I come back, try to distract him somehow."

Bella nodded her understanding. The anger in her eyes was gone now, replaced by a combination of terror, sorrow, and determination.

Battle was pulling up his zipper when he walked back into the room.

"I need to use the restroom also," I said, using the neediest voice I could muster.

Battle put his hands on his hips. "You're not going to give me any trouble, are you?"

"I just gotta pee."

Grinning, Battle took a small key from his front pocket and unlocked my binding. I got up and marched straight to the bathroom.

"Leave it open," Battle demanded when I began closing the door. "Don't worry. I won't look, much."

I resisted the temptation to argue with him and unzipped my shorts instead. Battle turned sideways, pretending to examine imaginary dirt under his fingernails, so I went ahead. When I pulled my shorts back up, I began to mentally prepare for what was coming. I had no idea what sort of surprise Bella had planned, so I needed to be prepared to react and be flexible. The key would be not to try and do too much. I knew there was no chance I could overpower Battle, an experienced police officer, especially with Bella still restrained, so I needed to concentrate on just getting the taser, no matter what else happened in the other room.

Taking a deep breath, I walked past Battle through the door into the open room. The rolltop desk was directly in front of me, about ten feet away. The sofa where Bella was sitting was to the right of me, maybe fifteen feet away on the same wall. When I glanced in her direction, I thought I saw something in her hand.

Battle must have seen what I did at the same time because he suddenly burst past me. Bella had removed one of her slip-ons from her foot and was cocking her arm to throw it at the window overlooking the front lawn. As the man launched himself at Bella, I wasted no time in moving to the desk and sliding open the top drawer.

There was no taser.

The only thing in the drawer was a bunch of paperclips. Thinking quickly, I managed to grab a couple of the clips, but when I pulled my hand back a third clip must have clung to my sweaty skin and it tumbled to the floor, landing an inch away from the desk footing.

As Battle wrestled the slip-on shoe from a screeching Bella's grasp, I turned to jump back to where I'd been. Then I had a last-minute thought.

I rushed Battle instead.

I was almost on him, my fists raised above my head when the gun was suddenly in his hand, pointing at my chest. Everyone froze.

Battle took two steps backward. "Sit," he instructed.

I plopped down in my same spot on the sofa, slipping the paperclips underneath me as I did.

Battle cuffed me again and then retook his seat, shaking his head as he did.

"That was stupid. Truly inept. But to be honest, I'd have been disappointed if you didn't try something. I confiscated that taser weeks ago. I expected more from a couple of college girls, though."

"This whole suicide pact thing you're planning, it won't work. Nobody will believe it. Our friends are out there right now working with the police to prove these are murders, and they'll catch you sooner or later," I said.

"You may be right—about the first part. They might not buy the suicide scenario, but on the other hand, your friends will give them one hell of a lead to chase. Gentry Security, I believe it is. Yeah, I saw them trailing you on campus Eve, and I also followed Taggart on his ride out to their office. The firm works for Eve's father, right? They'll be an excellent suspect. You see, nobody knows about me. I was never here. I'll be just fine, but thanks for worrying about me. Now sit back and enjoy the time you have left. We still have a couple of hours to kill."

Everything he was saying was true, which depressed me until I realized it would only be valid if he succeeded with his plans for Bella and me. I just had to make sure that didn't happen.

I thought about the paperclips beneath me.

Thirty-Two
Saturday, July 28th 8:33 PM

"Not much longer now," Battle said as he stretched his arms above his head.

We had been sitting there for hours. Battle had never left the room, and he met our pleas to use the bathroom with laughter. If he wouldn't leave the room, I could never use the paper clips, and that was looking less and less likely. The sun was setting, and we were running out of options.

A knock on the front door startled everyone.

In a flash, Battle was up, peeking out of the blinds he had lowered to cover the front window. When he pulled back, he seemed to think for a moment, and then he came back to the sofa. He squatted between Bella and me.

"It's a couple of your friends," he whispered, looking at me. "If you don't want to see their brains splattered over these walls, you need to send them away. Do you understand me?"

I nodded.

Battle looked back and forth between Bella and me. "A false move by either of you, and it all ends now."

I struggled to think of a way I could signal for help without getting whoever was at the door killed. Any misstep, any odd reaction, and it was over for all of us.

Battle uncuffed us both and took Bella by the wrist. When he had pulled her out of sight, I took the paperclips from beneath me, slipped them into my pocket, then went to the door.

Chewy's awesome smile greeted me when I pulled open the door. Tunes was standing beside him.

"Hey, there you are," he said. "We were all wondering where you and Bella were. Taggart sent us to see if you were here by chance."

I smiled back at him. "Here we are. This was on the way back from the police station, so we decided to chill here for a while. I guess we lost track of time."

"We tried to call you, but just got your voice mail."

"Yeah, my battery's dead, and I don't have my charger."

"Bella's too?" Tunes asked.

I paused to think of a believable explanation. "Oh, she forgot her phone back in her dorm room."

Chewy bobbed his head and looked past me into the living room. I think he was waiting for me to invite him in.

"Well, I guess we're going to head back now," I said.

"Can we catch a ride with you?"

Another hiccup. "Bella's car is having some work done and the owner of the shop gave her a loaner to use. It's that van parked on the side of the house, but the thing is there's this big ole transmission in the back. Sorry, there's no room."

"No problem," Chewy replied, smiling.

"If you want, you two can squeeze in with Bella and I'll walk back?"

"Nah, it's a nice night for a walk anyway," Chewy said, still smiling. "We'll see you back at the dorm."

As my two friends walked away, I felt all hope disappearing with them.

"Chewy," I called out. When he turned around, I paused for a moment, then said, "Tell Taggart he should stop assuming the worst."

Chewy gave me a thumbs up, then the two of them continued walking away. I wondered if that would be the last time I would see them. I probably saved both their lives, and at the same time, just condemned my own.

"That was good," I heard Battle say behind me as I closed the door. He shoved Bella so that she stumbled up next to me.

"If you say so," I half-muttered.

"What's with the name change? Why did they refer to Eve as Bella?"

I glanced at Bella, but she gave no indication she intended to answer.

"Whatever, I don't care what you call yourself." Turning his attention back to me, "It was a bit of a gamble, offering to walk back yourself."

My heart felt heavy. "Not really. He would have never let me do it. They're both too nice."

"If you say so," Battle said, stepping to the side and holding his arm out towards the rear of the house. "We need to get going. It'll be plenty dark once we get there."

Bella and I walked robotically to the rear door. I still had the paperclips in my pocket, but Battle wasn't making a move to reclaim his handcuffs from the sofa. Whatever he had planned for us must not involve them, which couldn't be good. Did I risk getting the clips for nothing?

Before he ushered us into the van, he gave us the same speech about drawing attention.

"I know it will be tempting. What have you got to lose, right? Think about this though. The longer this goes on, the more chances there are that something could go wrong, and you'll get an opportunity to escape. Slim chances, but still. And like I said before, whoever you might attract to help you will end up in a grave right alongside you. I promise you that. Now you did a good job not getting that young boy killed before, so just keep doing that same thing."

Next thing I knew we were back in the van and the door was closing.

"Any ideas?" Bella asked as the van made its way through the streets.

"Not yet. He's doing this at night, so I'm guessing it'll be outside somewhere and that makes me think he'll try to hang us. He won't bind our hands because he wants it to look like a suicide, so we might get a chance to rush him when he's busy with the rope."

"But won't he drug us, like he did with the others?"

"Don't let him. Whatever he tries to give you, spit it out."

"He'll threaten to shoot us."

"That's a risk we'll have to take. I'm betting he's so intent on carrying out this fantasy, he won't want to ruin it."

"I hope you're right."

"Me too. Just be ready. When you see me make a move, jump him, and fight like hell."

"I will. I'm really sorry you're here, Cassie."

"You can apologize to me tomorrow."

We rode in silence for what felt like an eternity but was maybe closer to fifteen minutes. When the van came to a stop and I heard the driver's door open and close, my heart began racing again.

The van door slid open and a brilliant light blinded me. I heard something metallic clang on the floor of the van, followed by a loud hissing, then the van door slammed shut again. Within seconds I felt lightheaded, and I knew what was happening. I tried to hold my breath as long as I could, but ultimately, I gave in and after my first deep breath, I felt myself slipping away.

***

"Rise and shine, ladies."

My eyelids fluttered open. Battle was standing in front of me, a flashlight in one hand with its beam pointed at the ground, his gun in the other. As my senses returned, I could make out a body of water behind him and trees along a shoreline. We were in the wilderness somewhere. A lake maybe. There was moonlight sparkling on the lake's smooth surface. Turning my head from side to side, I recognized that we were on a pier that extended as much as twenty feet out into the water.

"Welcome to Truman Quarry," Battle said. "I read that it holds six billion gallons, and it is the college's sole source of water. Isn't that amazing?"

Bella was stirring beside me, sitting in a lawn chair like I apparently was. A heavy chain was wrapped around her feet, the other end attached to a pair of cinder blocks positioned at the edge of the pier. As she realized where she was and what was happening, a look of pure terror appeared in her eyes.

A second set of cinder blocks was bound to my feet with a chain.

The plastic bag holding our cell phones appeared in Battle's hands. He pulled my phone out and turned it on.

"Time for the classic suicide note."

I was surprised when he entered my four-digit pin.

He must have noticed my shock because he said, "I've been watching, and recording, all of you for some time now. Do you know how many times a day you enter your pin? It was easy to figure out your numbers."

Battle typed away on my phone for several minutes. While he did, I leaned forward to get a better view of the chain around my feet. My heart leaped when I saw the lock holding the two ends of the chain in place. The easiest lock in the world to pick, the one I had the best luck with when Taggart was teaching me how to pick locks, was a Master Lock #3. That just so happened to be the same model that was at my feet.

"That's one," Battle exclaimed as he set my phone on the pier. He retrieved Bella's from the bag and started on hers.

My best time for picking that particular type of lock when I was practicing with Taggart was thirty-five seconds, but that was in ideal conditions, using tools specifically made for that purpose, not at the bottom of a quarry in pitch darkness, using a paper clip. Even if I did manage to get free, then I had to locate Bella somehow and free her. And if miracles did exist and we both got free, Battle would still be on the pier waiting to see our last bubbles.

One massive problem at a time, I told myself.

"And that's two," Battle said, placing Bella's phone on the pier next to mine. "Quite a pair of heartfelt suicide notes if I don't say so myself. Nobody comes up here much, but the police will undoubtedly track your cell phones when you've been reported missing after a while, so you shouldn't worry about being left down there. Now let's get this over with."

Battle moved behind Bella's chair.

My mind furiously searched for a way to delay the inevitable. "Can I ask you a question first, Mr. Battle?"

"You've had all afternoon to ask your questions. You're just stalling now."

"It's an important question, though."

Battle moved back in front of us.

"Important, huh? Go ahead, ask your question."

I tilted my head and looked up to the sky. "Do you believe in God?"

Battle's expression went blank. "I was raised in the church."

"Then to your mind, Theresa is in heaven right now."

The ex-policeman began rubbing the back of his neck. "That's right."

"So, if you go ahead with this and take our lives, when your end eventually comes, you'll never see your daughter again because you'll be headed for a different destination."

Battle didn't respond, just continued staring at the two of us. Suddenly he moved back behind the chairs.

"May I say a prayer first?" Bella sobbed.

Battle hesitated, then took a step back. "Go ahead."

Bella closed her eyes and bowed her head. As the silent seconds stretched into minutes, I could see Battle growing impatient.

"That's enough," he finally said and grabbed the back of Bella's chair.

Just then, headlights appeared behind us and with it the roar of a car racing in our direction.

Battle glanced back at the oncoming car, then tilted Bella's chair forward, which caused her to tumble into the water. He kicked the cinder blocks into the water, the chain rattling as it followed, then he turned towards me.

"CASSIE," I heard Taggart's far off voice cry out.

"SAVE BELLA," I screamed as I stood up and met Battle. He grabbed me by my shoulders, and I wrapped my arms around his waist, trying to keep him from throwing me off the dock. My bound feet prevented me from maintaining my balance, and Battle was much too strong, so all it took was a mighty shove to propel me towards the dark water. But Battle's gun came with me. I had managed to pull it free from his belt before he sent me flying.

The icy temperature of the water stunned me as I plunged into it, nearly causing me to expel the deep breath I had taken. I let go of the gun, my instincts telling me to use my hands to tread water, but I knew the cinder block would soon pull me under, and I needed to be ready.

As I expected, when the weight yanked at my ankles, panic set in. I fought to stay afloat as best as I could, but the weight was too much, and it dragged me beneath the surface. I was sinking fast and the further I descended, the more my alarm rose, but I knew my best chance for survival was to wait until I was motionless. It seemed like it took an eternity, but I finally no longer felt the pull of the cinderblocks at my feet, and I knew I had reached the bottom of the quarry.

Pulling the paper clip from my pocket, I bent over and used my other hand to feel for the lock. The darkness and murky water made it impossible to see, requiring me to rely solely on touch. I located the lock, and then guided my hand with the paperclip to it. How long had I been down already? Would I have enough time to pick it?

I bent the paper clip to the shape I needed, then set to work. I was upside down, and my lungs were protesting, but I concentrated on the task. The lock wasn't budging. I tried to recall and focus on the technique, forcing myself to stay calm, but I sensed I was failing. Desperation started to rise in me. Why wasn't this working? Now my lungs were really burning. Oh god, I'm going to die in this cold dark place.

Suddenly the lock snapped open. I freed my legs from the chains and started kicking for the surface, which now felt miles away. My lungs felt like they were about to implode. I kicked as hard as I could and tried to pull myself through the water, but my arms felt like rubber. My brain was urging my body to fight, but everything seemed to be slowing down.

Out of nowhere, an arm grabbed me around my chest, and I sensed a feeling of acceleration. I finally broke the surface and urgently sucked in the frosty night air, causing me to cough spastically when I inhaled droplets of water at the same time.

When I could focus, I recognized Tony next to me with Brandon treading water a couple of yards away. Looking towards the dock Chewy and Tunes were standing there looking back in my direction, but there was no one else. Battle was nowhere to be seen. I scanned the surface of the quarry looking for Taggart and Bella, but there was nothing. A cold dread replaced the chilly quarry water on my skin.

Suddenly I heard someone break the surface not five feet away from me but when I spun around all I could see was Taggart. A dark bolt of terror shot through me when I thought he was alone, but when he swung around, I could see he had his arm around Bella's chest. The fear seized me yet again when I realized she wasn't moving.

We all watched as Taggart supported her head as he backstroked toward the shore. She was down longer than I was, and I had barely made it. Did Taggart not reach her in time? Was there still hope? Did anyone know CPR, because I had only seen it performed on TV?

Then Bella coughed.

Thirty-Three
Monday, July 30th 8:33 PM

"So, Chewy never told you what I said to him—that you shouldn't always assume the worst?" I asked, looking at Taggart behind the steering wheel.

"I never got the chance," Chewy said from his spot in the third-row seat next to Tony and JJ. "By the time I got back to the dorm, they were already rushing out the door on their way to you."

Taggart took his right hand off the steering wheel and laid it on my leg. "As soon as Battle turned on your phone to send that fake suicide note your position appeared on the tracking app Brandon was monitoring. It was fortuitous that the quarry was as close as it was."

"But how did you know we were in trouble?" Bella asked.

"When you were overdue from making inquiries with Detective Moss, I contacted him and he informed me you had not been by. I then had Brandon check his tracker and discovered Cassie's phone was turned off. That's when I knew something was wrong."

The nine of us—me, Taggart, Bella, Delta, Brandon, Tony, JJ, Tunes, and Chewy—were all in the university van heading down I-10. Yesterday had been an endless stream of police interviews, intermixed with our parents arriving at Truman en masse to hover over us as they tried to come to terms with what had happened. We finally received a phone call from Angela after she saw the news. She was vacationing with her parents in Key West and not at all sorry she missed the excitement.

My parents were especially upset when they arrived. At first, they were unusually distant towards Taggart, which should have bothered me more than it did. I was nearly murdered twice within a year, and it was mostly because of my relationship with him. So, I guess I couldn't blame my family for being upset. But after I talked with them, and they met Bella, they seemed to relax.

As for Bella, her parents were the sole no-shows at school yesterday, due to her insistence that no one contact them and tell them what happened. She was adamant, and being of age, they had no choice but to respect her wishes. Her silence was the main reason for today's trip. Following our ordeal, all most of us wanted was to rest, but when she informed us of her intentions, we realized it was crucial for us to attend too.

None of us had a vehicle large enough to hold us all for the trip, and instead of taking multiple cars, I took a chance and asked Talia Davis if we could borrow one of Truman's vans. She was hesitant, but when she heard the reason we needed it, she was totally supportive. She even made sure it had a full tank of gas.

"Damn, I thought that was a pretty good clue," I said, turning my attention to the passing scenery.

"I would have understood your meaning," Taggart stated, not bothering to take his eyes off the road. I might have doubted his sincerity if I didn't know he wouldn't tell a lie. Even so, it made me wonder.

"But we didn't need your clue because of the tracking software I put on your phone," Brandon said from the middle seat.

I pivoted in my seat to look back at him. "And I'm still not sure how I feel about that."

Bella patted Brandon's leg. "Well, I, for one, am glad you put it there."

"Well, full disclosure. It was Taggart's idea, and he was the one who gave me access."

I turned my gaze to Taggart, who was still looking straight ahead. "I'm torn about that as well."

"How can you say that?" JJ said. "It saved both of your lives."

"You saved our lives only because Battle took so long writing our suicide notes and Bella said the longest prayer in the history of prayers. If it weren't for that, you would have gotten there too late. A mile further away, or if the cell coverage sucked, or—"

"Cassie," I heard Taggart say softly. I turned back to see him looking at me. I recognized that I'd become agitated and had raised my voice. The tenderness in Taggart's eyes promptly calmed me.

"I'm sorry," I said to everyone. "Still a little sensitive about the whole thing."

"There's no need to apologize, Cassie," Delta said.

"Absolutely not," Bella added.

"I can only wish I was handling things half as well as you are, Bella."

Bella smiled warmly. "It helps when you have a mission."

I returned her smile, then sat back and reflected on what she said. She was right. Having something to do had helped keep the flashes of panic at bay when I found myself at the bottom of that quarry struggling with that lock. I could already tell it would be some time before I went swimming for pleasure again.

"You know, there's something that is still bothering me," Delta spoke up.

"What's that?" Chewy responded.

"The text. You know, the one that made Taggart think Bella was coming after him. Who sent it?"

"They were obviously wrong," Bella scoffed.

The realization shook me. "That's true, but whoever sent it knew you were at Truman."

"Your family knew you were at Truman," Delta said. "Maybe your father or someone from that security firm?"

"They didn't know about Taggart. No one did. It couldn't have come from them," Bella said.

"Who then?" Delta asked again. "Any ideas, Taggart?"

"I am at a loss to explain it," Taggart responded.

We rode along in silence as everyone struggled to solve the mysterious puzzle.

"Are we going to be there on time, Taggart?" Bella asked. "We can't be late."

"We'll arrive with time to spare," Taggart responded.

We drove on for the next thirty minutes, content to return to our relative silence. When the van pulled off I-10 and we spotted signs for the Donald L. Tucker Civic Center, everyone became more attentive. Taggart found a parking lot several blocks away, and we all left the van on foot. As we drew closer to the arena, the crowd swelled around us. When I spotted the outline of the Civic Center two blocks ahead of us, I grabbed Bella's arm and pulled her aside. The others gathered around us.

"Last chance to change your mind, Bella," I said. "Are you sure you still want to do this?"

"I'm positive," she said confidently. "Thank you all for being here with me."

"We're a support group, aren't we?" Tony said.

"I wouldn't miss this for the world," Brandon spoke up. "This is going to be epic."

"Okay then. Everybody remembers what to do?" I asked.

All of the heads in our circle nodded their acknowledgment. I checked the time on my phone.

"We all meet on the front steps in ten minutes."

The group dispersed, everyone heading off in different directions. Taggart, Bella, and I continued walking toward the Center, dodging in and out of the growing number of rally goers. Signs and posters stating JANEY FOR US SENATE, as well as other clever political slogans, seemed to be everywhere.

When we reached the steps in front of the Civic Center, Taggart and I stood next to Bella, waiting. A few minutes later the person I was expecting strolled up, still wearing conservative pants and polo shirt.

"What's this all about, Cassie," Jaime Henson from The Grind asked. "This isn't what we agreed to."

"You'll get your interview, Ms. Henson," Taggart interjected. "Me and my sister both will give you an exclusive, but we thought you'd want to be here for this first."

JJ returned with a man in a suit with a press pass around his neck.

"What's going on?" the man inquired.

"You'll find out with everyone else in a couple of minutes," I replied.

A minute later, a woman who also was wearing a press pass walked up. "Hey Ron, Jaime. Do you know what this is about?"

Both reporters shrugged their shoulders.

Seconds later, another pair of reporters joined the growing group. In no time, almost two dozen people had gathered in front of us, most of them reporters, but several of them were curious rally attendees.

The alarm on my phone went off just as Tony and Brandon came running up, followed closely by a reporter and a man carrying a video camera.

"It's time, Bella," I said, letting her see the best encouraging smile I could muster. Taggart and I stepped to the side as Bella climbed the steps. She turned and looked down at the crowd before her.

"Ladies and gentlemen, thank you for coming on such short notice, and in this informal manner. My name is Bella Janey, Steve Janey's adopted daughter. Early this morning I met with a reporter from a popular podcast called The Grind to give an interview, and that interview was posted online a few minutes ago. I'm here now to provide all of you, the mainstream media, the same information I gave him. The reason I chose this time and location will become apparent in a few minutes.

A couple of days ago, there was an attempt on my life. The person who tried to kill me was caught, but that's not what I want to talk about today. I want to tell you about a secret, a secret that I've been keeping for a very long time. In holding onto that secret, I've inadvertently contributed to the deaths of others, some of them very dear to me. I'll have to live with that for the rest of my life, but I also know that I'm not the bad guy. There's only one person who can own that label, and that is why I'm here before you today."

I was so proud of her at that moment. Her father may not have been the one who tried to kill her, but the secret she was carrying was having the same effect. Even though the man left her alone after her suicide attempt, he never said he was sorry, and after Bella talked with her little sister again, she was more convinced than ever that this was the right thing to do.

I glanced over at Taggart and could tell he was proud of Bella as well. The two of them had found one another after enduring hardships that were caused—directly or indirectly—by their mother. Their blossoming relationship gave me hope for a stable future for both of them. Bella was doing something that was a long time coming. Bravery comes in all forms and measures, from the smallest insignificant act to the grand heroic gesture. But there's one thing they all have in common—the lack of an expiration date.

Bella took a deep breath. "When I was ten years old—"

Epilogue
Wednesday, August 1st 7:33 PM

"Shit," I mumbled to myself when I spotted Taggart coming around the bend in the road. I immediately glanced back in the other direction, hoping to see Chewy's car coming down the street, but there was nothing there. It was just my luck that Taggart would be a little early and Chewy was running late. My surprise was going to be ruined, so I just had to make the best of it.

I rose from the steps leading to Taggarts apartment and smiled as he approached. I snuck another peek down the road before we embraced.

"What are you doing here?" Taggart asked when we broke apart, a confused look on his face. He reached into his back pocket and pulled out the cell phone my parents had just bought him, and insisted he take. "Did I miss a text?"

"No," I said, scrambling to come up with an excuse for being there. "I just wanted to see you. How was your lunch earlier?"

"The student center was congested today," Taggart said.

That didn't really shock me. Things had quickly returned to semi-normal on campus once word got out the recent deaths were due to a since captured serial-murderer and not a rash of suicides. I wasn't sure what to think about that.

"I bet. Did you see Bella?"

Taggart's head shook. "She said she wasn't hungry, just tired. She was going to bed early."

I wasn't surprised to hear that, considering the firestorm of activity that kicked off after her announcement outside her father's political rally. A constant stream of reporters and news people hounded her every step now. Even though the statute of limitations for her father's abuse had expired last year, the department of justice still had some questions for them both. All of that forced Taggart to become her de facto bodyguard, a task which he happily embraced. It filled me with joy to see him take to that role, even if it wasn't me he was protecting.

"I was surprised she decided to return to school."

"As was I," Taggart said. Then, after thinking for a second, he added, "I didn't ask her to."

I smiled. "I didn't say you did. Bella's a big girl, and I'm learning she's a lot tougher than she looks."

"She's not the only one."

I felt my face flush. I opened my mouth to say something silly, but the sound of a car pulling into a parking space nearby distracted me.

"Why are Chewy and Tunes here?" Taggart asked using a voice laced with suspicion.

Ignoring Taggarts question I jogged over to Chewy's late-model SUV and met him as he was climbing out from behind the wheel.

"How did she handle the drive?" I asked.

Tunes pulled a face. "She threw up on Chewy's backseat."

I opened the rear door and a blur of tri-colored hair sprung past me before I could do anything. The medium-sized dog made a beeline for a patch of grass between the street and sidewalk and lowered her backside to relieve itself.

"I don't think she's a fan of car rides," Chewy added.

"What's this?" Taggart said, appearing beside me.

"Well… this is your surprise," I answered. "Say hello to Cayenne."

Chewy was quick to attach a leash to Cayenne's collar, and she offered no resistance while continuing to empty what must have been a full bladder. When she finally finished, Cayenne sat back on her hind legs and regarded the rest of us. I marveled at how docile the animal was behaving, given how young she was. I had previously only seen pictures of her on my phone and she was much more impressive in person. She weighed somewhere close to forty pounds with beautiful red fur accented by a white chest and paws. More white fur covered her snout with a strip running up between her eyes and then fanning out on top of her head.

"I don't like that you're always here alone, so I got you someone to keep you company when I'm not around. She's four months old and crate trained."

A sliver of doubt creeped into my head when I noticed that Taggart wasn't saying anything. I went over and began petting Cayenne's head, to which she seemed to tolerate.

"Where did she come from?" Taggart asked plainly. His expression was unreadable.

"You remember the vet I worked for in New Haven… Dr. Weathers? Well, I've had him on the lookout for a dog for a while and he contacted me when he became aware of

Cayenne. He says she definitely has some Australian Shepard in her, but he didn't fully know her background."

All that information came out way faster than I wanted, because I was anxious and growing more nervous by the second. In my head this was a really good idea, but now I was worried that Taggart might decide otherwise. The way he was acting made me feel that might be the case.

"The previous owners had just returned her to the shelter."

I could see a subtle change come over Taggart after hearing that last part. For the first time he really seemed to look at the canine.

"Why did they return her?" Taggart asked.

"They told the people at the shelter that she wouldn't play or have anything to do with them. She wasn't violent or anything like that. She would just lay off by herself most of the time. The owners admitted that they adopted her because of how pretty she was, but they weren't going to shell out all that money on dog food and treats for an unloving dog."

Taggart moved forward and sat cross-legged in front of the panting dog. Cayenne's ears stood up.

"Dr. Weathers said it was probably like the thing you see in children sometimes."

"Attachment disorder," Taggart stated. "Why the name Cayenne?"

"The previous owners were originally from Louisiana, and they gave her the name Cayenne because she was supposed to be their sporty spice. Their Nola bug. Dr. Weathers says she's very intelligent, like you, and loves the outdoors. They call her Caya for short."

"Caya," Taggart repeated.

The Shephard suddenly closed its mouth and tilted its head to one side. The two of them sat staring at one another.

"Having trouble finding your place in the world too, huh Caya?"

The dog abruptly lunged forward and began licking Taggart's face. My heart almost exploded.

"Not anymore," Chewy remarked. "We need to unload her crate and food so Tunes and I can start back."

"Don't you want to stick around for—" the ringing of my phone interrupted my train of thought. The caller ID said it was my mom.

"Hey Mom," I said when I answered it.

"I'm sorry, Miss Underwood," a male voice I didn't recognize replied. "This obviously isn't your mother, but I needed to ensure you took the call."

A moment of confusion preceded a tremor of shock running up my spine.

"Who is this and why are you calling me on my mother's phone?"

Taggart must have recognized the tension in my voice and the change in my posture because he sprung to his feet and became very alert.

"I'm not calling from your mother's phone. I've utilized a simple hack to mask the identity of the caller. Can I assume Taggart is with you? At least his laptop is. I've been using it to track his location."

I glanced over at Taggart's backpack where he left it by the steps to his apartment.

"You didn't answer my question. Who is this?"

"This would be exceedingly more efficient if you put me on speakerphone so I can answer you both simultaneously."

I depressed the button on my phone to activate the speaker, then held it between Taggart and me.

"You're on speaker, so tell me who this is or I'm going to hang up."

"Good evening to you both. Let me start off by offering an apology. It seems I misinterpreted the situation and provided you with errant information in my previous communication. For that, I apologize."

"This is the individual who sent the text warning us about my sister's intentions?" Taggart said.

"Indeed. And not wanting to sound like a broken record, but my intelligence was flawed, and I drew an erroneous conclusion. But to be fair, when one finds crumbs on a forest path, it is usually safe to assume a loaf of bread is involved."

"Who is this? And how are you connected to the affairs of my family?"

"How I know about you is easy. Your mother, the woman you knew as Miss Worthy, was my offspring."

The expression on Taggart's face froze.

"The pregnancy that yielded the child wasn't planned, nor was I aware that she… and by extension, you… existed until just recently. But, by all accounts, you and Bella are my grandchildren."

"You expect me to just accept this as truth?"

"Accept it… or don't accept it… that is up to you. If you'd like to develop this association, I can provide details on how I found you, but that is a bit more technical and requires a much more in-depth conversation, one that I don't care to discuss over the phone. For now, suffice it to say that I head up an internationally recognized think-tank, one with near-limitless resources, which I made use of."

Taggart snatched the phone out of my hand. "For what purpose? Why are you calling?"

"It's simple, my boy," the voice answered, almost cheerfully. "I want to offer you a job."

Acknowledgments

I always struggle with this part.

So many people have been instrumental in my development as an author, believed in me when I doubted myself, so I worry that I'll forget to mention them here and forever slight their contribution. If I unintentionally do that… please accept my apology.

I want to start off with the folks who took the time to read my drafts… regardless of what book I was working on… and supply insight into how I could improve as a writer. Critique Partners, Beta Readers, Friends, the list goes on. It has been through their efforts over the years that have molded me into what you see today. Thank you, all! In alphabetical order - Angela Brown, Patricia Burroughs, Lindsay Carlson, Alexia Chamberlyn, Crystal Collier, Julie Dao, Patti Downing, Melissa Embry, Elise Falson, Chris Fries, Sierra Godfrey, Christy Hinz, Donna Hole, Liz Larson, Lori Lopez, Laura Maisano, Linda Masterson, Alex Perry, and Nancy Williams.

In one way or another, each of the following individuals have kept me moving in the right direction and boosted my self-confidence when I needed it most. A most heart-felt thanks to Shelly Lea, Brianne van Reenen, Lisa Regan, Dianne Salerni, Barbara Poelle, Sarah Negovetich, and Tina P. Schwartz.

Special recognition is reserved for everyone who contributed directly to JERK. Helen Castrucci, Katie Holder, Mandy Oliver, Mandy Simon, and Tina Czappa. They helped me shape this book into something that I'm extremely proud of. Thank you for the guidance!

Last, but most assuredly not least, is my family. My children—Cody, Jaime, Casey— and especially my best friend and wife, Kim. She has always been much more than my number one cheerleader. She is my sounding board and brainstorm partner. Thank you all for believing in me and allowing me to pursue this dream. It means the world to me. Love you!

Oh... wait... there's one more! You, my faithful reader. I can't forget about you. Thank you for sticking with Taggart and Cassie for yet another exhilarating tale. Stick around... there's more to come.

Much love!

A Letter From DL

I want to say thank you for choosing to spend some of your hard-earned income on JERK. If you want to keep up with what I have planned for the future, as well as some keen exclusive material, consider signing up for my newsletter at the link below. I also use my newsletter to recruit ARC (Advance Reader Copy) readers for future releases, so if that's something you'd be interested in, you're one click away. Your email address will never be shared, and you can unsubscribe at any time.

http://dlhammons.com/

Also, if you enjoyed this book then I'd really appreciate it if you'd leave a review or recommend it to a fellow booklover. Reviews and word-of-mouth recommendations are CRUCIAL for authors, especially Indie Authors, and the best way to introduce new readers to one of my books for the first time. No joke. These things make a difference. It doesn't have to be much. Even something like This book ROCKS is enough.

I'd also like to hear from you. You can usually find me hanging out at one of the social media places below, as well as my website listed above. Tell me what your reading experience was like, or just say HI. I don't bite (unless you're covered in caramel – then all bets are off).

Facebook
Goodreads
Instagram
TikTok

TOOL

The Next Taggart McGill Mystery

COMING

SPRING 2025

www.ingramcontent.com/pod-product-compliance
Lightning Source LLC
Chambersburg PA
CBHW070612300726
48975CB00006B/1800